D0992439

Endless
Honeymoon

Fictions of Don Webb

Endless Honeymoon

Don Webb

St. Martin's Minotaur ≈ New York

www.minotaurbooks.com

Designed by Lorelle Graffeo

Edited by Gordon Van Gelder

ISBN 0-312-26582-4

First Edition: February 2001

10   9   8   7   6   5   4   3   2   1

This book came into being as a wedding present to my muse, teacher, and soulmate—the yellow rose girl herself, Guiniviere. For the rest of you who may read it, know that you are not as blessed as I.

Acknowledgments

This long vacation would not have been possible without my instructors during the school year: Alain Robbe-Grillet, Robert Pinget, Brad Denton, Stewart Home, Gordon Van Gelder, David Lynch, Paul Waters, Richard Lupoff, and Howard Waldrop.

Endless
Honeymoon

1 Loki's Daughter

The ending of things always surrounds us, only the brave and the wicked take courage from this. The rest of us merely deny it.

The clock read two minutes to five.

The Ice Palace was cool and dry, and little, seemingly an oasis for the tired traveler off the highway. There was a line of customers on the hot summer day, which should have been a gladdening thing to the owner, Mrs. MacPhearson. Indeed, if it would have been, had she been the sort of creature that takes any joy in those few small moments that fall into the bitterest of human lives. . . .

She was dealing with two children.

"A big cone and a medium cone," the small black boy said.

"Well, yes, darling. Now let me see if you have money for your ice cream before I make it."

The boy laid out the mass of pennies, nickels, quarters, and dimes while Mrs. MacPhearson managed a smile that didn't fool the eleven-year-old lad. He did have just enough, and she almost hid her displeasure. She swept the money off the counter into her hand and just put it in a pocket of her apron. She filled up the two soft custard cones and gave them to the boy and his sister.

A man and woman stepped up to the counter.

"We're closed," said Mrs. MacPhearson.

The small radio alarm clock had begun to play KDJW, the Voice of the Hill Country, and DJ Don Walker was explaining what a hot day it was.

"You can't be closed. We were in line," said the man.

He was young and tall, almost handsome except for a slight overintensity in his steel gray eyes. He wore a T-shirt with the less-than-clever motto, THINKING: TRY IT TODAY. The woman with him was a raven-haired, alabaster-skinned beauty, the only strangeness to her proportion an overly high forehead. She was in a safari outfit from Banana Republic or some other high-priced outfitter of daring urban dwellers.

"I close every day at five. I can't make exceptions. If I started to, I would be late every day. I would miss choir practice."

"Could we just have something cold to drink, then. My wife and I are very parched. We spent the day in Celsius State Park. We are on our honeymoon." He added the last like a magic phrase, an *Open Sesame* that would surely work on any old woman with a wedding ring.

"This ain't much of a place to take someone on their honeymoon," Mrs. MacPhearson opined. "Anyway, rules is rules. The convenience store in town has cool drinks, or you could take a sip from the hose outside."

The man had had enough, "I'm not about to drink . . ." he began, but his wife intervened. "Come on, honey. She's right. She probably wants to get home early because of the trouble."

"What trouble?" both the man and Mrs. MacPhearson asked simultaneously (and instantly regretted speaking).

"I heard on the radio"—The woman pointed at the radio, which was now playing the country classic, "If My Nose Were Full of Nickels I'd Blow It All on You"—"that there's a killer stalking fast food places in the Texas Hill Country. He preys on good folks, who have spent their lives building up a good business, because he's lazy an' shiftless. He sneaks into their business or home, and—bang—that's all she wrote."

"I haven't heard of this," said Mrs. MacPhearson.

"Well," said the woman, "you probably don't keep your radio on during business hours."

"No, that would be frivolous."

The woman continued, "You keep listening tonight. I bet you'll hear it."

"Thank you for telling me, ma'am," said Mrs. MacPhearson, "You know, I could bend the rules this once and get you nice young people a drink."

"I don't think so," said the woman. "I mean, I appreciate your kind offer, but now as I stand here I sort of get a chill about even being in a fast food place. I think we will head into town. Come along, James."

The man left with her. They got into a small blue car, and soon Mrs. MacPhearson heard the car peel off in a great hurry.

Mrs. MacPhearson wondered if this was a little prank to scare old women or if there really was a danger. The more she thought about it, the more she thought that it was a prank. They were just mad they didn't get their ice cream cone. Spoiled yuppies. Her husband never took her on a honeymoon. No, they had to start business right away. Their wedding night had been spent here in the Ice Palace, copulating on the tables. "For luck," he had said. That was six months before he ran off with that girl with the short skirt who liked dipped cones. For the thousandth time, Mrs. MacPhearson dreamed of that girl choking to death on a cone, not considering how damn difficult it would be to choke on soft serve.

She toyed with the idea of calling the sheriff to tell him the whole incident. She wished she had been able to see the car's license plates.

As Mr. and Mrs. Willis Spencer sped toward their motel

room, they engaged in the only arguments they ever had—criticisms of performance.

Willis (mocking Virginia's tone): "He kills the *good* people. Isn't that a little thick?"

Virginia replied, "You weren't any better. That was the blandest opening I ever heard. Aren't you getting a little tired of the honeymoon line?"

"But it's true, hon. I feel like we are on a honeymoon."

"That's the kind of thing that could give the FBI a pattern, you know. I think we need to do a few of these with only one of us appearing to the victim."

"That wouldn't be very fun," he said.

She was taking her black wig off her short blond hair, a cut so short and butch she was always being mistaken for a dyke—a fact she had used many times to her advantage.

She said, "Let's go over tomorrow night's script really well, so it really works for us. I don't think we can do another one until next month. For one thing, I'm not going to have the time. Kids will be coming in to rent as soon as August rolls around."

"We'll go over the script as soon as I go over you," said Willis.

"Promise?" she said, and he knew she was the hottest woman in the world.

"Promise," he said.

"I've got one worry. What if she goes to the town fireworks display?"

"She isn't the type. We already ran her through the Program, but even if she does, we can just wait at her house until she gets back."

"You know what I wish. I wish that black kid had been a penny short, so that she would have denied the cones to him. God, that would have really got me hot."

"Denying a honeymooning couple a drink because it's straight up closing time? Jesus, that ought to be enough for anybody," he said.

"I like it better when we can see them act that way, rather than stage these little dramas for them."

He was pulling up to the motel.

"Well, last month, she did make that old lady pay for a glass of water to take her heart medicine with. You might want to play that in your mind for a while."

"Did you know the old lady was her cousin? I checked up on her."

"You're not shitting me? She made her flesh and blood buy a drink to take medicine with? Oh, god. I can't wait to hear the gun go off."

"Not a flesh-and-blood cousin. A cousin of her husband. The profile said that likely there was some deep marital trouble in their lives that made her turn out the way she did."

They were walking to their room.

Willis said, "The poor people of this town. I wonder how much venom she has dripped on tourists coming out of the park. She is a little weed with deep roots."

Virginia said, "It's really not her fault. It was just a bad pattern that got deeply established."

"You and I both had shit in our lives," said Willis. "We overcame it."

"With the help of technology." said Virginia in a tone guiding their conversation toward liturgy.

"Thank god for that," they both said as they crossed into the motel room's dark interior.

They had left the AC blowing at its highest setting; the maid had turned it to LOW. They looked at each other for a moment while they considered if this was a worthwhile offense.

"Well, saving energy is a good thing," said Willis.

"And it probably wasn't her decision," said Virginia.

"Well, I don't know if that counts. I mean, there is the Nuremberg Principle."

"Yeah, maybe," she admitted. "But I don't think that applies

to people with English as a second language. We couldn't explain it to them."

"I can be pretty persuasive."

"Yeah?" she said, all hot again. "Why don't you persuade
me of something, daddy?"

"Daddy has to get his belt to persuade you," said Willis.

"No, I don't want the belt. I want to do it with the gun in
the bed with us."

"It could go off," he said.

"Well, something is going to."

2 The Irony of Explosions

"You know," Willis said to her as they crouched low in the small public library, "I like fire. I really like fireworks."

"That's what profiles of people like us say," Virginia said. "Well, at least guys—likes fire, strongly religious, and bed wetters." She saw something in his face. She said with surprise, "You were a bed wetter, weren't you? I can tell. Oh, sweetie, why didn't you tell me?"

"It's not a great pickup line," he said. "But I wet my bed into the third grade. I had a bladder problem. My folks thought I was just lazy or something. They got me an alarm that would go off when I wet the bed. They would yell at me, and told me that the other kids would really make fun of me when they knew what a baby I was. But in third grade, they took me to a urologist. A little reaming out of the bladder and I wasn't a baby anymore."

"My poor baby, I bet that's why you can't stand alarm clocks. You always wake up just before the alarm and turn it off. It's one of the things I most like about being married to you. I tell you what, let's sneak out of here and find out when the fireworks start. Then we can do her early and watch the fireworks."

"No. We may need to leave right after we do her."

"Do you suppose we could make it look like we were at the fireworks show all along?"

"Nothing really good comes to mind," said Willis. He was getting excited only now. Usually he was excited early on, because he usually had a special role to play. His favorite part had been last April when he had played an old man.

The public library of Doublesign, Texas, stood across the street from the widow MacPhearson's. It had been easy to break in while most of the town gathered for the annual fireworks show. The Spencers were crouching in Applied Science looking at the widow MacPhearson. She kept the Ice Palace closed on the Fourth, a day that logically would be one of the best draws for the store. She sat at home reading old Reader's Digests and talking to a picture of her absconded husband.

The plan was to wait until dark, which comes at about nine so near summer solstice, and then cut her phone lines. She seldom used the phone after dark. The Spencers had parked a couple of streets away. It was about six.

Virginia said, "I'm really beginning to worry about the scope of our activities. If we keep striking so close to home, we could make a pattern for an investigator. Most of our kills are within six hours of our house."

"What we could do," said Willis, "is strike in a six-hour circle from Dallas or Houston or San Antonio. We could work very hard to make a very predictable pattern, so that they would be centering on a victim of choice."

"That would be cool. Could we do a simulation on their methods?" she asked.

"Well, no. They just put purple dots on the map."

"How many agents do you think that they have assigned to us?"

"Hundreds," he said. In his heart, he said, "None, for god's sake, let it be none."

He looked at her, her face glowing green from the light of the library's tinted window, her eyes luminous as she foresaw a perfect media death, and knew that if happiness were ever to fully come to him, it would be from Virginia. So, he repeated himself, "Hundreds. I bet we have more agents after us now than are after the Railroad Killer."

"We're so much smarter than he is. I just wish he didn't have victims in Texas," she said.

He thought for a moment of Ramirez's brutal crimes, which had earned the killer a spread in *People* magazine this month. With weapons of choice like sledgehammers and garden shears, he was more suitable as one of their victims than as a competitor.

They sneaked out of the library for dinner at the Kuntry Kitchen, near where they had parked their car. They made small talk with the waitress, mentioning that they were heading back to Dallas after dinner. They had an unexpected payoff when the waitress commented on Virginia's black hair. They asked where the nearest gas station was.

They drove to the gas station, filled up their car, and asked the attendant which highway to take to Dallas. They parked the car in the alley behind the library, in a small niche that couldn't easily be seen, unless someone drove down the alley. The parking spot belonged to the chief librarian.

They returned to their surveillance of the widow Mac-Phearson's. She had (disappointingly) pulled down her shades— that was unexpected: she usually waited until just before she was ready for bed, which was at ten. It might not be as fun if they had to wake her up.

As their information had indicated, the house to the north of the widow's was empty; that family was on vacation. The woman in the house to the south was—as the postman had so genteelly phrased it—"so deaf that she can't hear herself fart." Behind the widow's lived a flag-displaying WWII veteran who always attended the fireworks show, and, of course, in front of the widow's was a vacant library.

She could, if she wanted to, scream real loud.

That was nice.

At nine they left the library. They put on their gloves, got their tools out of a special satchel. The town was weirdly quiet. There wasn't anyone on the street, but they could hear the crowd at the park some blocks away. Willis simply walked up to the gate to the backyard and let himself in. He cut Mrs. MacPhearson's phone line, then turned off the power to the house.

Virginia followed.

The widow slept upstairs.

Virginia removed a screen and gently opened the window to the unused guest bedroom. Very often people like the widow are careful to lock their windows, but Doublesign was notoriously free of crime. As the two prepared to enter, they could hear the national anthem, and a couple of red fireworks went off.

Willis stood at mock attention for the singing of the national anthem.

Then the fireworks show started in earnest.

The first shells were titanium salutes. The loud explosives got the crowd's attention and seemed to echo from inside the still house. The Spencers quickly went in the window. They ran quietly to the base of the stairs.

From the base of the stairs, Willis called up to the widow. "Mrs. MacPhearson, I am hungry for some good soft ice cream. I was so sad that you closed today, so I came down just to get some ice cream. You see, I have a rule that I must have ice cream every day, and you know that rules can't be broken."

A very high, very shaky voice called back.

"Go away. I have a gun. Get off my property. I am calling the police.

Willis answered, "Mrs. MacPhearson, we know you don't

have a gun, a friend of ours told us, and we know you don't have a phone. All you have is ice cream. Please don't tell us we can't have ice cream, we are on our honeymoon. You can't let down honeymooners. We are coming up now."

The fireworks were popping outside like automatic weapons in a war-torn zone.

They ran up the stairs, in case the widow might have the bright idea of moving some furniture in front of her door. Never underestimate the strength of someone in mortal danger.

They burst into her room.

She was facing the window, seated in her straight-back antique chair. She had opened the blinds. Willis signaled Virginia that if the widow moved, they would have to be quick. The street below was empty.

"Do you know what your problem is, Mrs. MacPhearson?" began Willis. "Your problem is one of motivation. You don't run the Ice Palace to make money like any normal person would. No, you run it every day to screw people over. Have you ever thought about how damn mean that is? An ice cream parlor is supposed to be a place of happiness. Everyone goes there for a smile, not just a frozen confection. It should be the good breast, not the denying mother. If you had had a good breast, do you know what you would have got? Do you know, Mrs. MacPhearson? You would have had years of marital bliss. Your husband ran off, didn't he? Because you are really the Ice Queen. You, Mrs. MacPhearson, are Hel."

Hel, Loki's daughter, did not respond.

"Now you have to pay the piper. There are no second chances. That's the rule, and you know the great truth: Rules cannot be broken. So, be prepared for your last icy treat."

He signaled Virginia.

Virginia sprang over to the widow's chair and spun it around. The widow fell from the chair, and as she pitched forward to Willis, he aimed the gun and fired. A great orange sucker dart landed—smack—in the middle of the widow's forehead. But Willis didn't break into the usual laughter at this point in the game.

Someone else had shot the widow.

But that other shooter hadn't used a sucker dart. He or she hadn't shot as part of a harmless game.

The killer had used a .22 at very close range.

The sucker dart landed about half an inch from the wound and had fallen off because of the slippery blood.

Virginia didn't see the wound and thought that the widow had passed out, so she was trying to pick up the body.

"For god's sakes, don't touch her!" yelled Willis, then he changed his tone, whispering, "She's dead. Somebody killed her."

Virginia had discovered this fact on her own and froze in a midmovement crouch. She threw the body down.

"Goddammit! Some son of a bitch did it for real. Son of a bitch! We have spent so much goddamn time on this. Goddammit!" she said.

"Shut up!" he said. "Think, the murderer has to be here. In this house, right now, with us. We've got to run!"

This message got through. They ran. At the park, the finale rack was being fired off, so the sky was lit with all kinds of colors as 120 fireworks shells burst every few seconds. The colored lights somehow made the air seem thick, as though they were running underwater. Years later, Virginia would dream this scene again and again. Her black wig fell in the street, but they were too scared to stop. They ran around the library, straight to their car.

It wouldn't start at first, and when it did, Willis gave it too much gas and clipped the side of the library, leaving a mark of metallic blue paint.

Ten minutes later, they were stopped for speeding on I-20, and the officer gave them both Breathalyzer tests and recorded their agitated state.

But even before they were out of the house, the widow's closet door opened and a small dark figure stepped out. He crossed to the widow's body and picked up the sucker dart. He snapped it in two with his gloved hand.

"Son of a bitch," he said. "What are the odds?"

Then he laughed, a little too long and loud.

3 A Suspect Epistle

The letter had been written on July 9, Tesla's birthday. The return address was Box 4200, Comesee, Texas 78666, which the Bureau computer had already identified as nonexistent. Special Agent William Mondragon suspected that it was a prank from some of his colleagues. He had been assigned one of the worst cases in the Bureau: the so-called ShitKiller. Everyone made fun of the case. It had been passed around from agent to agent for ten years, as a prelude to removing the agent. Only in the deepest depths of his mind had he begun to suspect that the case was given to him because he was a pain in the ass rather than a genius.

It couldn't be solved.

Most people thought it was unsolvable because there was no case. It had a bad rep. It made people go crazy. Abel Salazar, the last agent stuck with the case, had developed a strange theory of international secret societies that spanned centuries, perhaps even having connection with eldritch beings beyond the globe. If you want to be released quick from the Bureau, just include the word *eldritch* in your report. The Bureau has a strict no-eldritch policy. Salazar would have been fired, but he went missing.

On the surface, Agent William Mondragon thought he'd been given the ShitKiller case because of his ability to put together odd bits of data. He was sure of himself—so sure that not only had he solved cases that belonged to more senior men, he bragged about it to anyone who could or would listen to him. He took the ShitKiller as a challenge.

Of course, the first challenge was to prove there was a ShitKiller.

In 1970 the Bureau began using some sophisticated pattern recognition software, originally made for the insurance industry. The software had been designed to look for connections between causes of death. For example, it could spot the incidence of the same sort of cancer in a geographic region, or the likelihood of certain age groups dying by violence.

The Bureau had dumped tons of unsolved murder cases into the program. The software began noticing an interesting anomaly.

There is a type of human garbage, a sort of psychic vampire, that seems to live off the misery of others. We have all encountered these people, usually on the other side of a desk, where they hold some talisman of power, such as the ability to give us a driver's license. Not too surprisingly, these people often meet violent ends. The miscreant robbing the liquor store interacts with the unpopular clerk and improves the world with a quick shot.

But the program revealed that many unsolved murders had some remarks by the investigators that the victims were "unpleasant," "irritating," or even "generally despised." These weren't murders in the course of a robbery. These murders happened in the homes or businesses of the victims. The method was similar in many cases: a .22 shot at very close range, very professionally. No prints, the gun showing up a month or two later, having been left on the street in a bad part of the victim's town. The victims almost always had no dependents. No children at home, no wives or husbands, no aged parents in nursing homes.

The crimes were seldom investigated locally.

After all, no one gave a shit about the victims. No one seemed to be hurt other than the victims. The crimes were not brutal, and there didn't seem to be anything linking the victims to one another.

There could be one perp, a group of perps, copycat killings, or just coincidence.

Or it could be any mixture of the above.

The ShitKiller scenario didn't even explain how many victims there were. Sixty or so murders made up the "classic cases," but there were hundreds more that fit the parameters— going back to the Second World War.

It was hard even to identify the cases as they came in. Local sheriffs weren't interested in calling the Feds when it came to a simple shooting of an unpopular butcher, a mean-spirited bank loan officer, an ill-tempered high school counselor.

A few of the cases got some attention.

An overzealous traffic cop in Ohio, an important (but frustrating) member of the railroad commission in Texas, a land-stealing mayor in Florida. These people had jobs that demanded justice.

One of the first agents had guessed that perhaps ten of the classic cases were the actions of a lone gunman. The ten cases were clustered in the Washington-Boston corridor. He went crazy looking for the gunman by acting out various evil roles in Washington, hoping to attract the ShitKiller's attention. A psychotic fit led him to believe that he was the person he portrayed. He became an evil landlord and refused to believe that he had ever had contact with the Bureau.

The fifth agent decided that there were perhaps as many as ten thousand cases that fit the MO. She arrived at that figure by removing the criterion of the victim not being well-liked. She didn't think anyone was well-liked, nor should they be. As she investigated murder after murder, looking for reasons *why* the victim "deserved" killing, her misanthropy grew. She began to hate everybody. Then one day she took an assault rifle with her to lunch and started wasting people on the Mall. She took down six before Secret Service agents offed her with a head shot.

William Mondragon was the seventh agent to be assigned the ShitKiller case.

The letter before him bore no prints. The computer paper was common, the envelope standard. The address on the front was written in mechanical pencil in very well formed but slightly elongated letters.

It read,

Dear Special Agent Salazar,

Although as far as you know we have never met, I have taken a good deal of interest in one of your current cases, the so-called ShitKiller case. Whereas I think you people should earn your salary by figuring things out, I do have a duty to my fellow man to help you along. The most recent SKilling was in Doublesign, Texas—a sleepy little town about an hour north of Fort Worth, until recently ruled over by an autocratic sheriff named Mason Aldones. Aldones's disappearance is a possible SKilling, but a definite kill is Mrs. Velma MacPhearson, the owner/operator of the local frozen custard restaurant, the Ice Palace. Velma had lorded it over her clients for years, taking especial heart in making children cry and older people screw up their orders. Well-hated in Doublesign—and even well hated in my hometown of Comesee, Mrs. MacPhearson was a perfect victim for the SK. She struck on the night of the Fourth of July, with a male accomplice. When she fled the scene of the crime she dropped her wig. I have both the wig and her .22, and would gladly turn them over to the FBI for a small fee of $100.00. If you would like to collect the money simply run an ad in the Doublesign *Significator*. "Desperately seeking

Cinderella" with a newspaper box. I will send the goods there, and I will trust you to leave the $100.00 in an envelope behind the public library.

By the way, you should look at the back of the public library. The SK's car left a big blue streak there as she drove away from her hideous deed. You can just tape the envelope to the building over the paint streak.

I have committed no crime. I live in a house by the side of the road and I am friend to man.

There was no signature. It would be easy to dismiss this as a typical crank letter, however, it differed in two respects. First, there had never been any coverage of the ShitKiller in the media. It was something known only inside the Bureau. Second, most such letters either ask for money (and certainly in amounts greater than one hundred dollars) up front. If this wasn't a hoax aimed at him, the letter writer knew something.

It bothered Mondragon that the letter was addressed to Salazar. The Bureau hired very few Hispanics, and he had felt a great affinity with Abel. He flirted with the idea that Abel had sent the letter, trying to see who was on the case now, seeing how he measured up by finding out who replaced him. William's dad had worked his whole life in a big grocery warehouse, and when he quit, the boss had to hire two Anglos to take his place. His dad was proud of that until the day he died. The only other thing that loomed as large for Dad was William's working for the FBI. Dad had tried very hard to make William employable. He wouldn't let Spanish be spoken at home because of all the trouble he had had in school. He picked his son's Anglo first name as well.

William had picked up Spanish in high school. His inability to speak Spanish as a kid had cost him a lot of Chicano friends growing up, but his perfect English, hard work, and Spanish surname had opened any number of employment opportunities. Slowly he came to believe in himself as much as his dad believed in him. He didn't just want to be a good agent, he wanted to be a Bureau legend. He would be the "solitary bird" the poet Jimenez spoke of—of no particular color sitting higher than any other bird.

William Mondragon called the travel secretary and got a ticket to Dallas.

As he drove north to Doublesign, his mind munched on the idea that the ShitKiller was a woman. None of the profiles had ever suggested a woman, but a few of what he thought of as the best cases did—those in the late fifties, early sixties. Many of the corpses were found in areas that had been meticulously cleaned up. Investigators had grouped these cases under the name of the "housewife killings," but most had assumed that these were done by a man dressing up or acting as a woman. Female serial killers were rare, and catching one that had been active for three decades would make his name for all time. He could actually see the *Newsweek* spread about him as he drove through Comesee, Texas—a village a few miles before Doublesign. The village was too small to have a post office anymore, and he wondered why the informant bothered to send him through it.

Come see Texas. Well, he had come, he had seen, and he had no doubt that he was about to conquer.

4 Escapism

All Virginia would talk about was how excited she was. They had been in the room with a real-life murderer. Should they have introduced themselves?

All Willis could think about was, did they leave any evidence behind? What about that ticket for speeding?

So, they did what they always did, they talked about the first time.

The first person they pranked was in their hometown of Austin. Bertram Gates was a midlevel manager at a local software house. Willis had done some consulting for them and got to hear Mr. Gates in action. It was his first chance to use the Program, and Gates was a ninety-eight percent match of a target. What made Gates a real winner was his approach to women. He would look over any document that a woman had prepared—technical reports, feasibility studies, whatever— and begin with a five-minute commendation of the typing and formatting of the document. Then he would go over all the spelling and grammatical errors he could find (he had a gift for this; his mom had been a high school English teacher), then he would say, "But as to content . . ."

He'd tear any of their ideas to shreds, he would lampoon

their reasoning, question their competence. He enjoyed making new women cry. Office rumor said he was this way about dating, after the first (and only) bed tussle, he would compliment his date on her makeup, and then savagely critique her lovemaking ability.

Willis had had to sit through two critiquing session before he gathered target data on Gates. Sure enough, no wife, no kids, no dependent old people, no socially redeeming activity like working for the environment or feeding the poor. He was a one hundred percent shit. Willis gave the profile to Virginia and she came up with the plan. Willis had to go to one more meeting with Gates, to prepare.

Bert's sole social activity was his model train club. He would spend Friday nights with the boys making the little trains run on time. On the way back to his apartment, Virginia gently bumped his car at a stop sign. He flew out of his car to yell at her, and Willis, who had been waiting at the curb, put an ether-soaked rag to his face. It took him longer to pass out than they had read (on-line). They left his car with its door open. When they got to the warehouse, Virginia put on the costume, and Willis roped Bert to a chair, stripped naked in front of a PC.

Bert came to and saw Virginia dressed as the Angel of Death. She wore a black see-through teddy, and she had painted all of her skin black with very thin blue vertical stripes. She had a necklace of Tibetan skull beads and black opera gloves, but it was the wings—a six-foot span of black feathers—that drew the most attention. Her eyes, however, held the attention: she was wearing specialty contacts that made small skulls flicker in her violet eyes. Her raven black wig was partially covered in a black silk scarf with silver skulls on it. She was stroking his neck when he woke up. Willis stood behind him with a sap in case Bert needed a good rap. Both Virginia and Willis had expected supernatural awe at this minute; however, they handled the unfolding scene quite well.

Bert: "Who the fuck are you? What the fuck is this?"

Angel: "I am the Angel of Death, come to see if you should live or die."

Bert: "You're that freak who hit my car. You better let me go right now, or I will get your goth ass up on kidnapping charges faster than you can say *Lestat*."

Angel: "Mortal, I am Kali, Shakti, the lover of Shiva. I am all you fear and despise and long for, yet I have not but contempt for you or your world, which I could kick aside as a ball in my endless dance of ending."

Bert: "Help I am being subjected to bad theater! Get this crazy bitch away from me."

Willis at this moment sapped Bert because things were not going according to the script. Learning to improvise takes time. Years of hard dedicated displaced work can make you spontaneous. When Bert came to again, it was played differently.

Bert: "Look, you are clearly crazy, but if you will let me go, I'll give you some money for your therapist. What's your problem, daddy fuck you?"

Angel: "I may be crazy, but you are tied up. I do have the power of life and death right now. I am merely curious as to whether you should live or die. We crazy folk don't worship your minor god of money, we worship life and death. Much more power there than money. Do you want to live?"

Bert: "Of course, I want to live, your crazy cu—I mean, yes, ma'am."

Angel: "You are familiar with PageMaker?"

Bert (uncertain and afraid): "Yes."

Angel: "Then make a report for me. Tell me what you have done and what you hope to do. Give me your dreams and victories, and I will judge them on the scales of life and death. Neatness counts. You have an hour."

She undid his hands so he could use the keyboard. He seemed to have writer's block at first, then as he started to write it was fitful, coming in bursts. She went behind him, beyond where his head could turn, and started a metronome. Tick. Tock. Tick. Tock. He whimpered a little. After about fifteen minutes, Willis, aching from standing statue-still, reached over and patted Bert's skull. Bert screamed rather nicely.

After forty-five minutes, he said, "I'm done now."

The Angel walked to where he could see her again. She pressed a few keys and the almost silent sound of laser printers could be heard in the stillness of the warehouse. It was about three o'clock in the real world, but it was endless midnight in hell.

Willis and Virginia read the papers far behind Bert.

Then the Angel walked forward. Willis activated a tape recorder of Bert at his last meeting. Where the name of the female unfortunate was mentioned, they had dubbed in Willis saying "Bertram."As the tape played, the Angel lip-synched the lines. Willis aimed a flashlight at her mouth to emphasize the words.

"First, I must say, Miss Bertram, that I am very glad that you have good PageMaker skills; these are an important part of today's job market. The title could have been a tad larger and better centered, but the first page is all right. And that second page—boy, howdy! I see that you managed to number all the pages quite well, in sequence and everything. If I were giving grades for neatness, I suspect, Miss Bertram, you would be getting a hundred percent—well, looking at that title again, at least ninety percent. But, speaking of grading, I can't help but wonder about the grades you got in spelling. There is a difference in *principle* and the *principal*, you know. The *p-l-e* is an ideal, and *p-a-l* ran your high school. . . ."

The diatribe had nothing to do with the document the man had created, of course. What mattered was Bertram hearing his weaselly little voice calling himself Miss Bertram. He had begun to cry long before the live-action part. The tape played its last words, "But as for the content of this document."

As the tape ended, Virginia stopped lip-synching and began speaking, "You call these achievements and aspirations? Why,

I've seen people with half your IQ who do twice as well, have more money, and you're still unmarried yet pitifully unaware that you are a woman-hating faggot? Was it because your daddy fucked you? Or is it you want to fuck your daddy? Look at this so-called dream of a beach house. Oh, I'm so impressed—you dream of owning property in Galveston. You pathetic little schnauzer, a real man could have just bought even with the dead-end job you have. It's not like you have a social life other than two hours with train geeks, all of whom consider you a bore, by the way—our methods are nothing if not thorough. You even think of that piece-of-shit car you drive as showing some status—we sold that to a junkie that needs a ride for twenty bucks and felt we were cheating the little whore. You think getting a bachelor's degree from that jerkwater college matters squat? There are tougher high schools here in Austin. You even keep a little plastic cup with your school mascot on it in your little piece-of-shit car—I know, I took a pee in it when I saw it, then I felt bad because my pee is a little too precious for such an ignoble cup. You want to help humanity in your old age? Well, I tell you, you little weasel, you're helping humanity as much as you can now by not breeding, not that you would have much luck in the playing field with that little dick of yours. You are glad you gave money to the Cancer Society? Oh, that's very fucking original: we get ten people a week here that hope they'll live because they dropped their fifty bucks in the coffer—oh, I can see by your startled look on your weasel face that you have not dropped *fifty* bucks in. You're cheap and selfish in addition to . . ."

Virginia went on for twelve minutes of pure brilliance. Bertram was crying and sobbing, and then Virginia's voice became formal and strange again.

Angel: "I am the Angel of Death. I am the Judge of what was and what is-to-be. I find you, Bertram J. Gates, to be unworthy to draw upon the resources of this beautiful world any longer. You are too wretched to live; it is sad that the netherworld should be fouled by such as thee. But it needs must be!"

Then Willis sapped him again, and they dragged his unconscious form to their car. They drove him to his office and dumped him in the parking lot. Virginia had wanted to leave him naked, but Willis was worried that they might cause too much shock. His big idea was to put these people on the right and narrow path, hers was to punish. Both of these ideas were born deep within themselves.

The story of Bertram Gates was always the place of refuge. They told it one to the other, interrupting excitedly, punctuated with "I loved it when you . . ." and "I will always remember his face when we . . ." This story grew in might and main until it became the greatest myth of mankind. This was the source of their endless honeymoon: the ability to tell each other their shared adventures again, and by telling them, separate themselves from the mass of mankind, much as other people use politics and religion or fantasy role-playing games. Their stories always sent their troubles packing and filled them with a great sense of election, of being different—really different—in a time when that was the thing to be. It mattered little that their self-narratives stretched beyond the bounds that the gray world calls *truth*.

They probably would not be telling one another the Ice Palace tale. There, they had wandered away from the prankish world of freelance performance art and into some cosmic game played by giants and gods. This would leave them with only thirty-five great stories in their hoard, which would not prove to be enough against the stresses and horrors they were about to face.

That night as they went to bed, Virginia thought they had escaped the worst of all possible scenes and that with skipping only a month (or perhaps two, she pouted to herself), all would be fine. Willis suspected the worst, but given his suspicions, he proved himself an optimist.

5 There Were Things

Where Abel Salazar lived, it smelled bad because the refrigerator wasn't working well, and there were things in the refrigerator. Probably—hopefully—things that aren't in yours.

The house had six phone lines. Five were devoted to data transmission. Currently Abel was playing four chess games against opponents around the globe. He was also running a very sophisticated search program that looked to see who was looking at what other people were researching. Abel's little infobot did several high-level things on the Internet that even the operators of the nodes in question would have thought impossible. It was a formidable piece of software. The NSA actually had a lesser version of the program. But software is not enough for certain types of game-playing.

The phone rang. Now all six lines were in use.

Abel ID'd it as a pay phone in Houston and picked it up.

"Good afternoon," he said. "What do you have for me?"

On the other end was slightly whiny male voice, a voice that Abel despised, but one he needed.

"That's it? 'What do you have for me?' No 'How are you?' No, 'Sorry I haven't called?' Nothing personal. Just 'What do you have for me?'"

"I am sorry, John, you know that I am excited by the chase," said Abel.

"I know what excites you," said John, a small threat concealed in a friendly wrapping. "I have something really nice."

"How nice?"

"Emm, pretty nice. They may have found the SK."

"You've phoned that news to me before."

John said, "This time they sent an agent out, the buzz here says that this is the do-or-die mission. They want to close the case because they don't believe."

"Well, why the fuck is that good news? If they close the case, I may have to close up here."

John tried to mollify Abel, "Some people feel that the SK's partner has ratted on him. This time the case will crack wide open."

"You idiot. The SK has no accomplice. I know who he is. He works alone. They are barking up the wrong tree. As usual. Who covers the case now?"

"Bill Mondragon."

"You're fucking kidding, right? That kid is great on straightforward cases that can be won by keeping your unimaginative butt in the surveillance van, but he doesn't have the instinct. What's the matter there, Shepard just hate Mexicans? You know I ought to kill Shepard and make it look like an SK killing. He qualifies as a shit, anyway. That would keep the case open. So, where are they sending the young caballero?"

"Texas."

"You are in Texas. Where in Texas?"

"North of the town of Fort Worth. A town called Doublesign."

"As in *D-o-u-b-l-e*-sign?" Abel was typing on another computer. There were ten computers in the room, and this one was a Sparc station.

"Yes," said John, "Have you heard of it?"

"No. Never in my life. But they are right. The SK is there.

I guess it was just a matter of time. How did he contact the Bureau?"

"I heard it was a letter. Addressed to you," said John.

"Of course, it was addressed to me. I am the only adversary worthy of him. Get it for me."

"I can't do that, Abel. It is evidence."

"With your smarts, you can do anything. A single letter gets lifted from a file, big deal."

"This is an ongoing case. Mondragon will notice when he comes back."

"He won't be coming back. The SK will kill him, or I will kill him, or I will get him to work for me."

"Speaking of working for you, how much is this worth?"

"If you get me the letter, five grand. If not, nothing."

"What the fuck do you mean, nothing? This is the most important piece of data I've ever got for you."

"No. The letter is important. The investigation is a bore, a nuisance. It won't let me win. It won't stop me from winning, but it is not the key. When you get me the letter, send me a photocopy of it. I'll send you a thousand for that, the other four thousand upon receipt of the letter itself. If all you can get is the photocopy, you'll still get a thousand. That's pretty cool cabbage for running a photocopy machine."

"I can get you the photocopy, but this is going to be the last time I do anything for you. You didn't used to talk about killing agents. If you fall, I will be obliterated."

"Why, my dear Mr. Tyrell, I long ago arranged it so that if I fall you would fall, too. In fact, if I fall, I've got files on many, many people that will be e-mailed to thousands of the most interesting addresses on the planet. If I fall, you go, I go, businesses go, and perhaps government may topple. I have lived my whole life to have such secrets, and every day I have more. But don't worry, John, soon I won't need you. If this lead lets me catch the SK, I will give you twenty thousand, and you need never see me save in your dreams. So, pray to whatever gods or devils you pray to that I succeed."

"What gods or devils do you pray to Abel?"

"I acknowledge only one god: Abel T. Salazar."

"Good-bye, Abel. I will get you the photocopy."

"Get me the letter."

"I will get you the photocopy and after I spend your money I will lose this phone number."

John hung up, and Abel looked at the map displayed on the terminal before him, which centered on Doublesign, Texas. It was fifteen miles from a rather insignificant Texas village called Comesee.

According to Salazar's profile, the SK had been born in Comesee. July 4, 1933, in fact. Most serial killers would have retired at that age and drawn their benefits from the Serial Killers Retirement Fund, but not the SK. His mission was just as strong as it ever had been. If there was a killing there, it was probably for sentimental reasons. Then Salazar's smile faded. He had to make the call. Although Salazar acknowledged no god but Salazar; there was an authority of at least equal power that he had to consult.

She answered almost at once. "Hello, Abel. What do you have for me?"

"The Bureau thinks it has a good lead on him. For once, I think they may be right."

"Oh? Why this time?"

"It's next to Comesee, Texas."

"Where, Doublesign? Terrell? Noaccount?"

"Doublesign."

"Was there a victim?"

"I don't know yet. There was a letter to me, sent to the Bureau."

"Why do you think this has anything to do with him?" she asked.

"Ninety percent intuition. Ten percent despair."

"Why despair, oh, brave one?"

"The Bureau is thinking of closing the case—that would make it harder to track him."

"We could still do it. It's not like they have been any real help."

"It would be hard."

"Oh, Abel, don't despair. I am fated to see his death before I die, and heaven knows there is nothing that I want more than to die."

This was an old litany, and he didn't have the desire to hear it now. He wished that she would say something that might help, some clue that she had forgotten.

"I promised my man seven thousand dollars for the letter."

"I hope you are spending this wisely."

"It's the Doublesign connection. I mean, what are the odds?"

"Please don't use that expression in my presence."

"Sorry, ma'am. I forgot."

"What is your plan?"

"I am going to go to Doublesign and meet the agent there."

"Meet him? Did you say meet him?"

"I know the guy. I have some influence with this boy. I got him a lot of good assignments as he was coming up through the ranks. He owes me a lot. I am going to get him to help me smoke the SK out. I will call you from Doublesign. But you will already know I'm there, by your usual means."

"What name are you using?"

"Bobby Fischer."

"Adios, Bobby."

"Adios."

He could have used her name, her real name, but she wouldn't have liked the fact that he had pieced it all together. If he fell in battle, everyone would know. It is the duty of a god to make the world end with him.

He ended two chess games, a victory and a draw. Then he made his reservations. Lastly he took some of the things in the refrigerator to bed with him.

Tomorrow would be a long day.

6 Two for the Files

Virginia took the passing of a full week after the unpleasantness in Doublesign as a sign that they were out of the woods. She went dancing with a girlfriend, while Willis buried himself in reading at the John Henry Faulk Central Library downtown. It was a Friday night in July, and it was hot. Austin hot. They planned to rendezvous at their house about ten o'clock for iced green tea and chess.

While Virginia danced and Willis read, they were being read about. It was cool in the reading chamber. Cool as melting snow. It was always so. The cool of the chamber preserved a dream for decades.

The reading chamber was far away, on the island of Manhattan, in a natural cave that had been discovered around the time of the Civil War. Much of Manhattan is honeycombed with tunnels and caves, wine cellars, foundations, subway lines, power line tunnels, sewers, gas and water lines—and many hundreds of people live in these tunnels. Most live in a state of poverty that is beyond the imagination of most Americans. They live as hunter-gatherers, their minds often devolving into strange systems of magic and religion ruled by the forces of their sunless world. Most of them remember the world of light, but believe that they will never return to it. Some fear it.

When Amos Dundee discovered the cavern, he had it enlarged and lined with brick supported by steel pillars. He intended it as a wine cellar and surrounded it with a shell of pipes full of fresh water supply around the chamber, keeping it nicely cool. The Dundee family owned the brownstone above for many years. A nearby subway line ran very close to the chamber, and James Dundee arranged (as a folly) for the chamber to have a small window that looked out on the passing trains. The family's fortunes changed and the house left them. The deep basement was briefly made into a distillery during Prohibition, producing a brownish vodka that killed a few people in New Jersey.

Various owners found the deep basement (with its steep narrow stairs) to be more or less a pain in the neck, until William Seward, a right-winger who had no doubt that the bomb was going to be dropped any day, bought the brownstone in the late 1950s. He had the brick covered with lead foil and an inner shell of concrete added. He also began erasing any knowledge he could about the cellar, lest hungering hordes of postnuclear mutants should attack. In 1963, sure that the coming of British rock 'n' roll signaled the fall of the West, he went to the chamber to die. His family had not known about the chamber—suddenly mad Uncle Bill seemed to disappear, and after years of legal troubles they were able to sell the house to Tawny Tabori, British rock 'n' roll star.

Tawny had discovered William's skeleton and posed with it for her *Eternal Vacation* album. She had dressed William in a yellow velvet Edwardian topcoat and hat. When she was finished with him for photographic purposes, she returned him to his bomb shelter, which she repainted in psychedelic colors. William languished in this strange land until the current owner bought the brownstone in the mid-seventies.

He had the chamber fitted with lamps of brass and crystal,

overstuffed chairs in red mahogany, dark cherry wood furniture, decanters of brandy, bookcases with old beautiful books, and a node of the Internet. The only distracting note was a collection of ten cardboard boxes. Their official labels indicated brands of scotch, gin, and vodka, but written in bold letters on the outside of each were **THE ERASER #1, THE ERASER #2, and THE ERASER #3.**

He had been one of the architects of DARPA-net, and as soon as he left, the Department of Defense patented a handful of useful hard- and software products that kept him one of the richest men in the world. He had also achieved something else. He was invisible to most of the world. When he wanted to be the man with the bionic credit card, he was. When he wanted to be off the tax rolls, he was.

He envisioned his underground chamber as something rather like Verne's *Nautilus*. He moved about the bottom of the data sea, which was growing deeper every day, free from the very world that created the sea. He taped a quotation from Captain Nemo on his sumptuous rolltop desk.

I am not what you would call a civilized man. I have broken with the so-called civilized world, and I do not live by its laws. Please do not mention it in my presence again.

He didn't hate that world.

He loved it.

He spent every waking moment working on his one-man scheme to improve it.

The small things changed everything. John Chadwick, his father, had proved it was so. He had proved it so in the fifties, while his skeletal companion was huddling against nightfall. "Long before Chaos was a theory," he liked to say when he shared his drinks with Skinny Bill.

Skinny Bill wasn't finishing his brandy, so Mr. Roy Chadwick, otherwise known as the ShitKiller, finished it for him. Roy had been able to find out about Willis and Virginia by looking for traffic incidents involving a blue Taurus speeding away from Doublesign the night of the Fourth. It wasn't the first piece of data he searched for, he had begun by looking for owners of a blue Taurus in the Doublesign area. He had tried crime reports, checks on his work on Velma MacPhearson. He had looked at wig sales in Texas, checked out killings involving fast food. It was a stroke of genius to think of speeding, but genius stroked Roy Chadwick regularly for many decades.

When their car had shown up, Roy began looking for them. He had expected for a long time that someone else might have copied his methods, but he had not been expecting the sucker dart. Did these people just play with the Misery Makers? That was disappointing. He had hoped for an heir. Maybe he could find them, turn them to his way of thinking.

But there were two of them. One could keep the secret, but not two.

It made him think about too many things.

Things he hadn't thought of in many years. The root of his deed . . .

At that moment a subway train thundered by. He had cut through the concrete and lead to reinstall James Dundee's subway window. He could sit and watch people speeding by, knowing that he had personally made each of their lives better.

He could always break up the Spencer team. One way or another. He read their files and he waited for genius.

Spencer, Virginia M. Age 29 BS. MA Sociology University of Texas. Height 5'11" Blonde 135 lbs. No criminal record. Married once before Anthony Night. Divorced after two years. Interests: painting, line-dancing, avid book reading. Buys extensively from catalogs. Generous to family and friends. Dances at lesbian clubs. Works out at gym three times a week. Employed: Freelance tech-

nical writer, has worked as an exotic dancer, museum docent, costume manager. Extreme extrovert. Intuitive reasoning. Member ACLU. Former member Mensa.

Spencer, Willis T. *Age 32. BS. MA Applied Mathematics Rice University. Height 6'6" 165 lbs. Criminal record: shoplifting in college, apparently some computer crime (?? there's a reference or two, but it has been erased from systems ??), Married to Virginia for three years. Interests: marksmanship, recreational mathematics, old computers. Buys military surplus from catalogs. Works out at gym three times a week. Employed: Freelance consultant on intranet statistics, data mining, data relevancy algorithms, has worked as Y2K consultant, private investigator for insurance companies, taxi driver. Mildly Introverted. Rational-judgmental. Member various MIT clubs. University of Texas Juggling Club. Subscribes to half a dozen recreational math lists.*

Both had small insurance policies, the usual shots. Both had passports that they had used to go to Scotland the year before. Both had great driving records. They seemed to spend a little more money than they had coming in. There didn't seem to be any drug or drink problems. Both had both parents living. Virginia was an only child, a bit of a hellion in high school. Willis had a brother and a sister, both older. He had graduated valedictorian.

Willis was easy to suss out. Virginia, much harder. He was one of those men who lived in a world of models and games that would have stayed there all his life—except that love had brought him into the real world. Such men become unpredictable, because love is unpredictable.

Fate threw them together just before Virginia's brief marriage had broke up. Tony Night had been employed by Wisconsin Data, which, despite its cheesy name, had an office in Austin. He had moved Virginia there from Portland. There was something strange about her marriage to Night—there were no credit card purchases, no hotel bills; she must have stayed home a great deal. It didn't match her marriage to Willis.

Well, Willis was the one who must have found the Program.

Roy didn't know how he felt about that. On the one hand, Willis was no doubt among the very few people on the face of the globe that could truly appreciate Roy's genius. But on the other hand, he was trivializing the approach. He didn't burn with the fire, or perhaps Virginia had trivialized the whole thing. Willis seemed the smarter of the two, but they both had intellects that could make them real opponents. He had never fought against anyone with actual brains before. Maybe he should simply leave them alone—but that didn't seem right, either.

He just didn't like the idea of Virginia.

He had sicced the FBI on them, but that was a minor test. He could discover if the new man in the Bureau was going to provide any interest at all, and he could see what the Spencers were made of. He hoped the Bureau would try to find out about the Spencers, but that the couple would elude them— that would be a sign that these people were worthwhile.

"What do you think, Skinny?" he asked. "Still worried that the Ruskies are going to drop the bomb? You know, I had predicted to the very week that the Berlin Wall would fall, but nobody listened to me except that sci-fi geek . . . suddenly they thought *he* was a genius. They thought I was some kind of crank. They weren't ready for me, Skinny. They were just like you. Afraid of the big things. Big things are never unpredictable, Skinny, because you can suss them out. You can get the facts and figures and you can tell what they are going to do. There is no indeterminacy at the biggest levels. It is only on the small scale, the human scale, that there is freedom and unknown things. Skinny. You can't tell what the man behind you on the bus is going to do. But, here's the key. Change what the man on the bus does at the right time and you can change the way the biggest things go. If enough Berlin cab drivers had been a little nicer, East Germany would have remained Communist for another year. You looked at the big things, but not at the thousands of crucial little things. So, you're here with me. You hid from the future, but I make it."

Skinny, as usual, had no comment. Soon Roy would go back upstairs to sleep and Skinny could contemplate the late-night riders of the subway.

7 Fugue in Doublesign

The autopsy of Velma M. MacPhearson had proved useless.

As in other ShitKiller slayings, the .22 had shown up, cleaned with special care. The SK had dropped it in front of the only dive in town, a bar called the Shamrock fitted out in a cigarette-murky green and black with industrial wire spools as tables. The gun had lain in the doorway on the night of the fifth; under it was a crisp twenty-dollar bill.

The gun had seldom been fired. It had been purchased by one Dr. Blind in Albany, New York, ten years ago. Dr. Blind's address was a long-defunct mail drop in New York City.

William Mondragon sat in the Shamrock, observing the pyramid of empty Guinness bottles, from which cockroaches occasionally crawled. The aged sheriff rambled on about what a good time he had the night of the Fourth down at the American Legion Hall listening to the recorded voice of Elvis singing "Dixie." When he wasn't talking about the recent blowout gala, he pondered the disappearance of his deputy Mason Aldones, which seemed unconnected with the case at hand, and lastly (as in SK slayings) the sheriff told him how nobody hereabouts was likely to be upset at Velma's death.

She was the meanest dried-up prune of a person that you

ever wanted to meet. She spent half her time writing to the Doublesign *Significator* complaining about the damn state of the world. Over the years she took her neighbors to court for building a fence an inch inside her property line, or having their Christmas decorations up in July. She kept all the dirty books out of the library, using it only as an excuse to practice freelance censorship. She had tried to get the town clerk fired because he smoked at his desk. She even let the air out of the tires of someone parked too long in front of the parking meter at the library. Everyone had a story about what a shit she was. He couldn't for the life of him think why Washington had sent two young fellers out to Doublesign to look into a no-account murder that frankly was a good piece of social pruning, if you wanted his opinion, not that . . .

Mondragon had been playing with the lightweight green aluminum ashtray in front of him, scarcely listening. "Wait a minute. Did you say two fellers came to investigate?"

"You and that other Mexican boy that was here yesterday," said the sheriff.

"What other Mexican boy—er agent?"

"Now, you know, I don't rightly recall his name. No, he gave me an Anglo name—Fischer. I took him out to Miz Mac-Phearson's. I ain't seen a Fed since I was a deputy and they came during the Kennedy assassination. There was a raid here then, on Dr. Chainey's clinic. I would guess that you read up on that."

Mondragon had no idea, and no interest in the ancient raid, but did want the sheriff to keep talking. "Sure. I noted what a good job you had done. When did this other agent arrive?"

"I didn't do a damn thing. I was against them being here. They wouldn't tell us squat, and they got the Bureau of Drugs to stop Chainey, anyway. He could cure cancer, you know, but the Feds didn't want him curing it. They had their reasons. You couldn't tell me those reasons, could you, son? I worry a lot about that as I get older."

"I need to know when the other agent arrived."

"Oh, he drove into town about ten yesterday morning. He had me unlock Miz MacPhearson's place. He told me to wait outside, so I went across to the library and got me a book to read. Rex Hull's *Little Gardens of Happiness*. Do you like Hull? He turned up dead here a few weeks ago, at the Chainey place. Anyway, I was reading, and snoozing a little, and this guy came back and asked me a lot of fool questions like, did Miz MacPhearson have grandchildren, and did I know about the blue paint on the back of the library, and I told him that Miz MacPhearson didn't have no grandchildren 'cause she didn't have no children, and that, therefore, ipso facto, they didn't paint no graffiti on the back of a library building. He looked at me like I was crazy and then went and stood in the middle of the road between the library and Miz MacPhearson's house and smelled it. Smelled the damn road. He walked around the library a few times. I told him about the gun being found here, and he said that the Bureau was sending another man, and that when he got here, I should take him to the Shamrock, so that you can talk to Isidore."

"Isidore?" asked Mondragon.

"The barkeep."

Mondragon spoke with Isidore as briefly as possible, learning only that Isidore had a theory about the Kennedy assassination, and had been waiting twenty-three years for the Bureau to answer his letter about it. Isidore had by now connected Velma MacPhearson's death with the Dallas slaying and, being very talkative, would soon process Mondragon's presence into a thing of epic.

The sheriff left during this silly interlude, and Mondragon had to track him down again, this time by finding a greasy spoon called the Kuntry Kitchen. The sheriff was adding sugar to his iced tea as Mondragon stormed in.

Coolly and quietly, Mondragon asked, "So, Sheriff McGranahan, could you take me to Miz MacPhearson's?"

"I was wondering when you were going to ask," said the sheriff.

"What do you mean?" asked Mondragon.

"I went and called the Bureau, after you was so upset. So, I know they just sent you. I didn't get the license plate of the black Ford Escort he drove, but it was a rental from DFW just like yours."

"You're not worried that you were showing around an impostor?" asked Mondragon.

"That's almost a philosophical question, son. Everybody in this cafe might be impostoring right now. Most folks spend their whole lives impostoring themselves, scared shitless that somebody will find out. I can only guess the other fellow was a bounty hunter, but could be anybody, I guess. Maybe a reporter. But whatever, not my town's problem. It would be the Feds' problem, and you know, the gubment has shared so many problems with us, I don't feel the need to take on any more. Now, sit for a spell, have some coconut meringue pie and a tall glass of ice tea, or you'll burn to a fritter in that heat."

Waiting for the sheriff to leave was an eternity. Halfway through the eternity, the sheriff had announced that he was "fixin' to get ready to go."

The house smelled like an old woman. There were afghans on the couch, and the fixtures were decades old. Not antiques, but cheap clocks from the seventies. There was little blood upstairs. The sheriff showed him where the wires were cut for the phone, and the little lock that had been put on the power supply. No one had reset the clocks when the power had been turned on. The VCR flashed midnight and the clocks were six hours slow. A small jewelry box was open in the upstairs bedroom, and Miz MacPhearson had kept her cash in the purse that still sat on the kitchen table. The telephone answering display (atop the piano) was blinking rapidly, unhappy for its hours without juice.

Mondragon went over to the answering machine. Salazar's initials, *A S*, and an arrow were drawn toward the machine. He asked the sheriff to wait outside. He pushed play.

"PLEASE RECORD A GREETING. YOU HAVE ONE MESSAGE:"

"Hello, amigo. I see that you have been given the shitty job of finding the ShitKiller. You won't find him, but you will find me if you look behind the library and put two and two together. If you are that smart, I will gladly talk to you. Adios."

"PLEASE RECORD THE TIME."

Mondragon left the victim's home and ran behind the library. A short blue streak of paint marked the library wall. It looked like a car had brushed the wall, probably peeling out. Tire marks seemed to back that up. OK, someone had to leave fast. Who? The SK? Did he need to leave quickly? Didn't seem likely. The scenes of all the SK murders were chosen because the victims had no one who would interfere. They were all bitter, isolated people. But that meant he (or she) had been surprised. Someone must be after the SK. Well, Salazar clearly was. But why would he be seeming to show up a few days later. No. Someone was here. Someone might be near catching the SK. This would fuck up Salazar's plans. What were his plans, anyway? Ah, he wants help. If I can show him that, I've got it all figured out—or at least this much—then I can join him. Not that I want to join him. Unless he can help me find the SK.

Of course, Salazar is so crazy, he might just *be* the SK. Maybe all the agents that have wigged out on this case simply become the SK. Maybe it's a contagious mental illness.

The sheriff was staring at him. He did not want to provide amusement for the sheriff. He wanted not to look like a freak. Mondragon composed his face and strode purposefully back to the MacPhearson house as though hot on the trail of a clue.

Visiting the upstairs bedroom, he did find the sucker half

of a sucker dart. Salazar had asked if MacPhearson had grand-kids. None. OK. That means that he had found this toy and realized that it was out of place. OK, so it is a clue.

It was unlikely that anyone would let such a dried-up prune baby-sit their kids, especially not on the Fourth of July. So, if the toy belonged to a child, the child was not supposed to be here. A child might scare off the SK, given his record of killing people without dependents. But where was the child now?

Was the kid traumatized? Did the SK take the child with him?

Smell the street. Salazar had smelled the street.

So Mondragon went and smelled the street.

It smelled like a street. The sheriff was openly laughing now.

OK. OK. OK. That didn't help.

Since the sheriff's opinion of him could go nowhere but up, Mondragon asked some more questions.

"Were there any pieces of evidence that the other man saw or took?"

"The wig."

"The wig?"

"A cheap black woman's wig, the kind a kid might wear on Halloween to impersonate a witch."

Ah, so there *was* a child involved.

"Now did the other man take the wig, or is it still in your custody?"

"It's still in my custody. It had been partially under Miz MacPhearson's bed."

"Did he *smell* the wig?"

"Come to think of it, he did smell the wig."

"Did he allow you to smell the wig?"

"No. I reckon he thought I was untrained in wig-smelling, being as I am only a sheriff."

"Are there any children missing in Doublesign?"

The sheriff's tone lost its sarcasm. "Well, we have one little girl missing, but we think her father kidnapped her."

"Is this a recent case?"

"No. It happened in April."

"Has there been anything unusual in Comesee, Texas?"

"Nope. Heck there ain't that much *usual* in Comesee. It's pretty near a ghost town."

William Mondragon went to the Mirabeau B. Lamar hotel and got a room. He would need to figure out how to show off his smarts to Salazar. It was too late to trace the phone, but he called the Bureau to start some traces on the rental of black Ford Escorts from Dallas–Fort Worth International Airport in the last three days. He asked that the file on Agent Salazar be sent to him.

The last action cracked him up. When he had been given the SK file, they told him that the warning sign for going crazy was asking for the file on the agent before you. He laughed for a while, until it bothered him that he was laughing.

That night he dreamed of skeletons and little girls dressed as witches dancing around them.

8 Night of the Locust

It was Hiroshima Day. August 6. The day that controlled all of the world's mythologies for nearly fifty years.

The facility called itself *assisted care*. For most of its inhabitants it provided clean, thoughtful, and reliable housing. For Tony Night, it provided a bug-free environment. Before he would see Dr. Chadwick, the room had been cleaned of bugs. The nurses and FTTs didn't do this just to humor Tony. He had become quiet violent even at the sight of an ant. Moths, in particular, loomed large in his phobia. There had been a terrible row when an assistant wore a shirt featuring the Yellow Moth, back when that comic strip had turned into a movie that sank to the bottom of the box office. Tony screamed for days.

The room was small and had less of the retirement home smell than most of the Phoenician Arms.

Dr. Chadwick had immaculate silver hair, a string bow tie, and almost merry blues behind his round tortoise shell glasses. He carried a doctor's bag, which was empty, and a walking stick with a golden coin in its head. He had a little pad with little questions written in his very neat engineer's script (which was the only flaw in his medical costume). He had flown into Springfield on a twelve-seater plane after taking the big jet to

Memphis. He was so satisfied at having tracked down Tony Night so quickly that he actually purred. He usually purred after a particularly satisfying kill.

Dr. Chadwick smiled his most benign smile as they escorted Tony in.

Tony looked a good deal older than his thirty-six years. There were heavy lines under his brown eyes, and his light brown hair had began to grey in ugly blotches. Tony hated Chadwick on sight because he knew that Chadwick would ask him questions about the creepy-crawlies, and that would be bad. Then there would be Preparation H, the retirement-home code for Haldol, and what little remained of himself would slide into the cold oily sea within. Before sitting down, he thought, "The North Sea is inside me."

Dr. Chadwick talked about the weather, and Springfield, and nearby Branson, Missouri. Then he mentioned Mrs. Chadwick, and asked Tony if he'd ever been married. Tony talked throughout the interview, but Tony couldn't remember what he'd said. All Tony saw was an old movie that starred somebody who looked like him.

He saw the night his lazy wife, Virginia, didn't finish cleaning up the kitchen. She playfully offered him her butt to spank, like she had when they were dating, stupid slut. He got out the handcuffs like before, and then he got his father's shaving strap. He showed her. Later he had made up and said he was only playing. Then he saw the night that they talked about their fears and he told her about his fear of creepy-crawlies, and she told him about her fear of a hand reaching up from under the bed and a clown dragging her down into the darkness. Said she could not watch *Poltergeist* because of the scene. Then he saw himself working hard that weekend she was at her mom's, making the special trapdoor under their bed. He waited till the next weekend. She was asleep. He sneaked off to the guest bathroom and put on whiteface and the clown costume, and then went into the basement. He opened the trapdoor and moved his body up between the bed and the hole. He hit the remote control, and the circus song started playing, and then he reached up and pulled her down into the basement. They had fun for two days. It was a three-day weekend. Then he saw himself telling her it had all been a joke, that he didn't realize how seriously she took it all. He gave her flowers and he got some pills that made her happier from the doctor.

Dr. Chadwick was asking him how Virginia made a living.

He saw himself paying off the doctor, who told Virginia that she was pregnant and should stay at home because she would have to save her strength for the baby. Tony made so much money. Much more than that old boyfriend of hers, Willis the nerd-hole. They fit out an entire room as a nursery. Bright elephants and giraffes for the walls. She took the pills the doctor had given her, so she didn't bleed, and they made her a little fat. Then he gave her some different pills, and she bled a lot, and he blamed her, blamed her for losing the baby. He made her sleep in the nursery. In the baby's bed. He wouldn't let her see anyone. She had been very bad.

Dr. Chadwick asked about how he had made a living.

It's easy to make a living when your daddy owns the biggest Midwest grocery store chain. Daddy gave me my own software house in Austin, because of some article he read on Austin being one of the ten best places in the country to live, and since I was already living there and married, it was easy, and he didn't have to see me. Daddy hasn't seen me in years. Paw-paw had told Daddy how to handle people. Paw-paw told him that he had to find out what scared people, and then *be* that thing. Paw-paw had scared everyone out of business before the War, and that was where the money came from. Paw-paw said that he scared some people just by running a twenty-four hour store in towns that pulled up the sidewalks at eight o'clock. Tony always wanted to see the sidewalks pulled up.

"Did your daddy not want you at home?"

Tony saw a movie about something that happened to the family dog. It wasn't a very nice movie.

"Does your daddy ever come see you?"

Tony was bored, and he wished the doctor would go away.

Dr. Chadwick asked why Virginia liked Tony.

Tony taught Virginia how to play games. She had played silly little games like D&D, but he taught her real games. Games for sex, games to play on shopkeepers, games to play in public. All the other girls he dated wanted him because he was the heir to Night and Day Groceries, but she liked him because he was A. Night. She didn't really know what A. Night meant, but he showed her. Her daddy had played some games with her, but his games were better. Virginia was the only girlie who ever called him Anthony rather than Tony. He still loved her. He just hadn't scared her enough, so she never knew how much he loved her.

Dr. Chadwick asked when creepy-crawlies began to bother him.

When Paw-paw began to lose his marbles, Tony had to take care of him. Daddy whipped Tony good when he told Daddy that Paw-paw was crazy. Paw-paw used to catch cicadas in the summer and put them on Tony. Let them crawl on him, because Tony would get scared like a girly-whirly. Are you going to cry, little girly-whirly? Sometimes Paw-paw would smash the bugs on his face. He had to take it, to be a man. As soon as he could get away from Paw-paw he would run and hide and read a lot. He read everything he could about games. He could play anything. He didn't have friends, because he had to take care of Paw-paw, and Paw-paw was where all the money came from. So, he played games in his head all the time. He played games about Paw-paw. When Paw-paw died, they got a German shepherd that they named Moses after Paw-paw.

Dr. Chadwick asked about Willis.

There were many movies about Willis. They were all bad.

The first one was Willis doing some work for his company. Willis gave a big speech or something, and everyone was applauding (after looking to Tony to see if it was OK to applaud). He was so smart, he was going to make Tony a lot of money. So, he was going to be good to Willis. Everything fades in this movie except a spotlight on Willis and a big close-up . . . then the time came when Virginia had been good and he let her go out and they went to a big company get-together.

She kept looking at Willis, and she was talking too much, and she mentioned the baby, and that was bad because she was never supposed to mention the baby, and Willis looked liked he was thinking real hard, and Tony took her home and told everyone that she had a headache. She didn't want to put on the diapers, but Tony made her, because she had been very, very bad and she said that it wasn't fair, so he made her not be able to talk, and the next time she said she wasn't going to do it anymore, and so he left for a long time, so she would get thirsty. He had her tied up and he left for work, and when he got home she wasn't there. Someone had got past the security and stole her. He called the police, and Daddy's lawyers were there by dawn, but she got away, and there was a divorce, and he couldn't go to that, he had to go to Mexico and take lots of medicine, and he wasn't allowed to go back to Texas for a year, and he had to keep signing things for his software house, and he didn't own it, but Daddy said that was OK, he wasn't cut out for business, anyway. He had to give her a lot of money, despite the prenuptial, so she would be quiet. Then there was the bad movie. He tried never to play that movie.

Tony told the doctor, he needed to *go now.* He started to get up, but suddenly he felt very relaxed, and he fell back in his chair, and the bad movie played.

He was at one of the warehouses that serviced Daddy's stores in Oklahoma. He was vice president. Nobody liked him, but he didn't like them, either. Everyone was at a meeting. He didn't go to the meetings, so he was sitting in his office, playing with the paper clips. He heard some sounds. They were working in the air-conditioning. They better get it fixed. It was so hot. A guy in overalls stuck his head into Tony's office. Tony yells at him. The guy grins. He looks familiar, he pulls his head out of the office. There is a sound outside. They are supposed to leave him alone. He will get them for this. He goes to his door. It is locked shut. It is locked from the outside. He yells at the sons of bitches. They will all be fired. He goes to his phone. Everything he does gives him Muzak. When the meeting is over, he will give them all hell. Then he hears Virginia's voice from above. "God, I love you, I can't believe you are doing this for me." Tony knows he's crazy now, hearing his ex-wife's voice. He is scared. The air-conditioning comes on. At least something is working right. A stinky fog blows into the room. It's syrup. Corn syrup. All his papers are ruined, and he's filthy. Then the AC shuts off. He knows he must be going crazy. Corn syrup. Crazy just like his mama did after the dog. It's in his blood. The vent to the air conditioner falls onto the floor. He wants to get away, but he's so fascinated he cannot move. Then a garbage sack full of live grasshoppers is poured down. They jump all over everything. They jump on him, all over him, he's making messes of them trying to get them out of his hair and eyes, and they are on everything, and he's screaming so hard that his voice gets really high and weak like a little girlie-whirly, and then the lights go out. The last thing he hears is Willis's voice saying, "Next time it will be worse. I know when you are sleeping. I know when you're awake. I know if you've been bad or good, so be good for goodness' sake." Tony rolls on the floor to get them off, and that crushes them to him. He can't get them off, and they are even in his mouth, and he's tasting bug guts, and it's dark, and there will be a next time, next time, next time—

Dr. Chadwick tells him that he can forget the bad movie,

but Tony is too far inside himself by now. He will be a particularly troublesome patient when he wakes up, but Dr. Chadwick will be far away by then. He won't even be a doctor, and where he's staying he won't be Chadwick either.

His admiration for the Spencers is growing like a sequoia.

9 Cities of the Plain

William Mondragon had managed to track down the Ford Escort, and prints of Abel Salazar had been found within. In fact the prints were very easy to find, Salazar having taken a good deal of time to press his right hand on the dashboard. What Mondragon hadn't been able to find was a missing child who owned the wig. But traces of short blond hair had been found in the wig, as well as some roadside debris. He was beginning to think that Salazar had been trying to tell him that the SK was a woman, but he couldn't think of a way to contact Salazar. He was back in Houston when it hit him—then he felt dumb.

Obviously, Salazar had a contact at the Bureau. Salazar had known he was coming. Mondragon simply hung a sign up in his office: I WANT TO TALK WITH ABEL SALAZAR and his home phone number.

His phone rang the next night. The caller ID box displayed ERROR. That was amusing. Salazar must have some tech support, as well.

"Hello," said William.

"*¡Hola!*" said Abel. "I see that you are ready to call me, my young apprentice."

"Oh, great, one of the sharpest guys in the Bureau, and now you think you're Yoda."

"I was thinking more of Don Juan. But you've only seen enough of my sorcery to want to call me, not yet enough to be truly impressed. When you see what I can do, you will follow me, because you will want my secrets."

"What secrets?" asked William.

"In good time, *mi amigo*, in good time. Think about this: I walked away from the Bureau in the middle of some big investigations, and they can't find me. Can't trace my phone or my money, and I live just as I want to live. I live much, much better than I did when I worked there. I know what I want to know. Think about it."

"If you are a free man, why are you still looking for the ShitKiller?"

"A good question, which is the beginning of wisdom, my friend. But I will let you ponder it longer."

"Why did you want to contact me?"

"I want an apprentice. My hobbies are dangerous. I have no heirs. I don't want to vanish without a trace. Simple enough, really."

"No, not at all. Why me?"

"I gave you a very simple test: to contact me as soon as you figured out what was behind the library. Did you figure it out?"

"Maybe, but I want to talk to you some more," said William.

"But I don't want to talk. I am not seeking you as a companion."

"You have to answer some of my questions before I'll answer yours."

"You are confused, Mr. Mondragon, I do not have to answer any questions at all."

The conversation was over. William Mondragon hoped his father's advice about never giving people what they want too quickly was good advice. He looked over the Salazar file. There weren't any indications of mysticism. His only weakness of mind was a love of conspiracy theories. Toward the end of his career, he had begun collecting notes about the authors of math text books. Perhaps they were the source of all of society's ills with their story problems. There was a quote about math, about how really mysterious it was that the phenomena of the universe could be described in math. Mondragon couldn't follow where Salazar was going.

Salazar had begun to suspect that math teachers and the writers of math books were involved in a dreadful conspiracy. The SK was probably just a member of this chalk-dust-covered brotherhood that had gone too far. Only at the very end of his reports came the suggestion that math itself was alien to the Earth. It seemed to come from a galaxy called M-31. His last note, written in large letters on his desk blotter was, *Do we know what cities are really for anyway???* It had been a day or two before his disappearance was noticed. He was looking into some very humdrum cigarette smuggling; the SK not having definitely struck for a while. He was on assignment with a team from the Secret Service, who were tracking down a tobacco stamp machine. The Secret Service had called the Bureau asking for him, and no one knew what to say.

A lot of speculation surrounded Salazar. He wasn't hard to get along with, but he was by far the least-liked person on the floor. He didn't seem to have any friends. When his apartment was checked, the landlady remarked that he never entertained. She hinted that he hired a hooker every couple of months, but that he otherwise paid his rent on time, never complained, and was in all ways a model tenant. No one at the complex seemed to know him at all—other than the fact that he was touchy when someone parked in his reserved spot.

He hadn't taken any money out of the bank. His apartment was full of clothes, the fish needed to be fed, there was food in the refrigerator. In no way did it appear that he had planned a departure. The only bad news in his life had been the cancer death of his mother a few months ago, leaving him with no close relatives in the United States. There were some uncles in Mexico, who had no idea that Salazar was working for the Bureau, having had no contact with him for more than fifteen years.

For months it was assumed that the SK had nailed him.

His car turned up months later in New Orleans, wiped very clean and parked in a No Parking zone.

This did not dispel the notions about his demise, but opened yet more questions about SK lore. Perhaps the SK could spirit people away. The SK case was considered an even worse assignment than it had been before.

Salazar's calling him made Mondragon sure that the path to Bureau legend had begun. Today he began to break with regulation. He took down the small photo of J. Edgar and his heart began to pound.

A week passed before Salazar called again.

"So, my friend, what do you wish to tell me?" asked Salazar.

"The mark on the library was made by a car of people fleeing the SK," said Mondragon.

"How do you know this?"

"The librarian parks there. She had not seen it on the third, and it's impossible to miss, considering how she has to exit her car to walk into the building, so it was made the fourth. I can't pinpoint the time, but no one in the neighborhood seems to have heard the sound of a car scraping a building, so it most likely happened during the fireworks show," said William.

"Good, you are almost halfway there. How do you know it wasn't the ShitKiller's car?"

"He had nothing to run from. He wouldn't be scared of anything, his killings are well planned out, and in twenty years of killings by this guy, we don't have any eyewitnesses."

"Well," said Salazar, "that's not true, but the Bureau's files say so."

"So, that's all I know," said Mondragon.

"You should not lie to me. You know it wasn't the SK because he sent me a letter in care of the Bureau."

"I don't know what you are talking about," lied Mondragon.

"You are not ready to work with me yet. I will give you one more try to come clean. By the way, why didn't you place the 'Desperately Seeking Cinderella' ad?"

Salazar hung up.

Special Agent William Mondragon hadn't placed the ad because he hadn't wanted to play someone else's game.

Mondragon had recorded both calls. If need be, he could go to his superiors tomorrow with proof that Salazar still had a connection in the Bureau, but for all Mondragon knew, his supervisor was Salazar's connection. It was four days until the next call.

"So, Special Agent William Mondragon, what do you know?"

"I know who the car belonged to."

"And that would be?"

"That would be something that I will only tell you in person. You don't need an apprentice, you need some data that your contact can't get you. You need traffic reports for the surrounding area on the night of the Fourth. Somebody peeled out of there, somebody good and scared. I am betting that it was somebody who either saw the murder, or at least was startled by the killer. Somebody who dropped a wig in the street, but the wig wasn't there when you came. No. Somebody walked out of the house and carried it into the house. You know a great deal more about the SK than the rest of us, but you don't know who was in the house, why they ran, and most important, you don't have any idea where they are now. So, you need me. Now what I need is more than what you need. You need to know where the SK is. I need to know that and I need to know who you need to know for. Who is paying you?"

"Very good. You are very close to being correct, but you

are wrong about my not needing an apprentice. I have many needs you probably can't understand."

"You're not the mild-mannered quiet type that your file would say you are. Nobody like that steps into the Void. They continue their humdrum little lives until they die in some very predictable way, maybe a heart attack or cancer. You don't want that life or death. It hurt when it took your mama."

"Señor Mondragon, you are brilliant. You think slowly, or you could have contacted me the first day, but you are brilliant. This leads me to my great paradox. Do I make you my apprentice, or kill you? Brilliant men are dangerous—when they achieve a certain level of brilliance they are free from the odds. It is as if you have become a star and are affected only by other stars, not by the lesser gravity of earth. Now I must decide if you are my star pupil."

"You want the information I have. I want your secrets, Abel Salazar."

"In the French Quarter of the city of New Orleans, there is a wonderful restaurant called the Court of the Two Sisters. I love the coffee there. You can be there in two days, enjoy the coffee about eight in the evening, then stroll through the Quarter to Jackson Square. You'll find me walking beside you. It is a short distance to the Cafe du Monde with beignets and tourists. We can talk there."

"That is one of my favorite spots in New Orleans."

"I know you were there last Easter. Actually the Saturday before with a young lady. How is she doing?"

"She's quite well. Thank you," said Mondragon.

"You see, I do have powers that you don't have. I just don't have the instrumentality you have. I look forward to seeing you."

As Salazar hung up the phone, Mondragon thought of Julie. It might have been a—no it must have been a lucky moment for him. Salazar had known him briefly in the Bureau, if New Orleans was his base of operations, he had merely seen Mondragon and Julie doing the tourist thing. It was slightly above the odds, but not anything truly weird.

Mondragon knew that he had crossed an important line. He had begun investigating the case for fun. Murders aren't fun. The thrill of danger and of the mysterious is not how real agents operate. At least not agents who stay alive.

He had allowed Salazar to move him into Salazar's way of thinking.

"I'll only go this far and no further," he told his cocker spaniel, who wagged her tail, glad at the news.

He called around for a date that night, but everyone was busy.

10 A Badly Written College Essay

Virginia stood at the wrought-iron gateway and looked back at the three-story home she and Willis owned. The windows threw back the rosy light of dawn, and they reflected the radio antennas from the nearby canyon. The house was the cream color of local Edwards limestone, its trim a light sea green. The etched glass dragon that dominated the double doors to the house looked as though it were about to leap down into the koi pond across the bridge and make a meal of the large slowly moving fish. Perhaps it was jealous of the other dragon—the wrought-iron dragon that served as the gate to the estate. Gentle southern breezes came out of the canyon and turned the green grasshopper windmill atop the tower, and lightly shook the red-and-green and green-and-white caladiums at the base of the mimosas and the post oaks. Two months had passed, and Virginia had even convinced Willis that all was well.

She was in her running outfit, ready to jog down to the post office.

Like most wealthy people, the Spencers used a P.O. Box to give them another layer of protection from the world. As she began her jog, Virginia was once again glad that she had insisted that Willis make a fortune before marrying her. She had money, lots of money, from her divorce to Anthony; but she felt that Willis might not have been happy if he were dependent on her all of his life. It had been a good call. Not many couples had a castle in their early thirties.

Willis had been one of the first people to raise the alarm about Y2K. His high school in Lubbock was surely one of the last places to teach COBOL programming, and even better, he was very much a geek growing up. Willis was the last member of that generation of computer hobbyists that tried to control everything in the house from the home computer. Willis's dad had been one of the first of that same tribe. So Willis had a certain satori that all those little microcomputers wouldn't know what century it was either, and (with a little help from Virginia) he made very dire predictions early on, while selling Y2K compliance services. The millennium had made a mint for him. Of course, that was also how he discovered the Program.

She talked him into running the Program again soon. She had heard of a mechanic in Dallas who had made a small fortune selling needless repairs to old ladies on fixed incomes. One of her bridge partner's grandmothers had her Toyota treated for "cancer of the fuel line." This sounded like a good bet for the Program. She could take a day off from volunteering at Planned Parenthood and drive up to Dallas. She could wear the white wig and put on a few wrinkles and crow's feet. She was beginning to plan what problem she would claim for the car. It would probably be safe to use one of their own cars for a change rather than a rental.

The post office was sleek and new, all gleaming metal surfaces. In the box was a *New Yorker*, a couple of bills, and a large brown envelope hand-addressed to her. It bore no return address, but its stamps had been canceled in Doublesign, Texas.

The envelope had four things inside.

1. A stamped addressed postcard. The postcard showed two women in full-length bathing suits riding in an "open--air" or rather "open-water" mini-sub (perhaps the scene was shot through a glass bottom boat). The caption on the back of the postcard read: "Just two of the lovely mermaids at Florida's Weeki Wachee cruise the depths during the Mermaids' all new show, 'MERMAID FOL-LIES.' " A handwritten note on the back read, *I choose to meet you at the Mirabeau B. Lamar Hotel in Doublesign, Texas.* The address was a P.O. Box in New York.

2. A menu from the Ice Palace in Doublesign, Texas.

3. An old-fashioned punch card with a note written on it, in the same handwriting as the postcard.
Dear Virginia,

Yes there is a Santa Claus. I know if you've been sleeping, I know if you're awake. I know that there is some business you need to finish up alone, and I know I am the only one that can help you. If you just mail the postcard ten days in advance, I can make every-thing all right. If you tell Willis, I will have to make everything bad for him. I know you love him too much for that. He has done more than what a husband is supposed to do. He rescued you from the dragon. But we know the dragon still lives inside you. Let's kill it together.
Love,
Your Fairy Godfather

4. An essay in dot matrix type on yellowed computer paper. It was one of Anthony's essays. Typically, it was pompous and rambling—often defeating the very points he was supposed to be arguing. Anthony had a pretty

easy time in school. UT had a dorm named after his
family. He got all A's. Only the first few pages were included.

Anthony M. Night II
Anthropology 401
Self Designed Study
Dr. Y. Tomas

PRANKING: AN AMERICAN WAY OF KNOWING

The American fascination with the prank as a way
of looking at the world in a new way is not a simple
manifestation of the trickster motifs. The prankster
is not simply Coyote, or Loki, or Hermes fulfilling a
simple role in the human psyche. This aspect of pranking had been examined elsewhere[1] and provides a useful
explanation of the effects of pranking within a psyche. America, however, began with pranks as a way to
destroying an existing order. Previous pranking was a
matter of social licenses. The jester could make fun
of the king, but he still remained king. The Boston Tea
Party was proof that you could play a game with the
king and the king could lose. The architect of the
prank was Benjamin Franklin, who had created the first
American prank. In 1747 Franklin created a fictitious
Polly Baker. Baker's letter to a London newspaper
talked about her trial for fornication in the States.
She claimed that she had been the maid of a magistrate,
who had instructed her that it was God's commandment
to "increase and multiply." [2] It was Franklin's first
prank, a small beginning that ultimately led to the
separation of church and state in America.[3]

Pranks may not always be beneficial in nature.
Abraham Lincoln pranked the North into believing the

issue that was most important for the Civil War was the question of slavery. Actually the big economic issue at the time was the control of corporations. In the South corporations were controlled by the state government, in the North a growing movement lead by Obadiah Marsh of Innsmouth, Mass., wanted corporations controlled at the Federal level, preparing them for national and later international power. The Northern plan won, and the corporation became the dominant force in American economics by the end of the First World War. Notably the first court case tried under the Fourteenth Amendment of the U.S. Constitution, which any schoolgirl will tell you is what freed the slaves permanently, was actually *Santa Clara County vs. Southern Pacific Railroad*, 1866. This case established the rights of the corporation as a "person" under law[4] an interesting remanifestation of some staged debates between Lincoln and Douglas just seven years before.

Orson Welles's famous prank of creating the illusion of a Martian invasion to increase America's pre-WWII tensions had a much deeper effect. America, unlike Nazi Germany, had not associated space science with defense, and it wasn't until Welles's pranks that the U.S. began to watch the skies. The effect of Welles's broadcast was to have the U.S. welcome Wernher Von Braun and crew with open arms and begin the space race. NASA tried to get a special pension for Welles, during his years as a bad wine huckster, but when they realized that they would have to let people in on the darker side of the joke, declined.

Another politically motivated prankster is Los Angeles-based José Luis Peña, leader of the Excluded Middle Commune. Typical Peña hoaxes have included the *Cathouse for Dogs* and the *Celebrity Sperm Bank*. These

are launched with a press release that is always
picked up on a slow day. Peña always calls the press
in afterward to demonstrate the hoax. Peña insists
that his motives in creating and then documenting
these hoaxes is to increase media literacy, create
social change, and creatively inspire people towards
self-empowerment.[5] These justifications lay Peña
open to accusations of elitism, since he assumes
that ordinary people need him to point out that not
everything reported by the media is true or accu-
rate.[6]

Interestingly both recent dream studies and chaos
theory agree---

The essay ended here. There was no grade on the paper,
but it showed that someone knew a lot about her life. She
would give the mailer an A for the sheer spookiness of it. She
put the envelope back in the P.O. Box. (She would drive down
later and put it in her car—she didn't want to carry it back to
the house.)

She was almost a hundred percent sure that Anthony
hadn't sent the essay. He was supposed to be off his rocker,
or as she liked to put it "in the bug-house." The essay was
disturbing because it meant that someone understood, or was
very close to understanding.

Night had saved her life, and then destroyed it for fun.

Even Willis didn't know that. Not the *saved* part.

In her first years at college, she had a series of bad dreams
involving a basement. Something bad had happened there. She
got some counseling and came face-to-face with a long-
forgotten picture of her father over her, fucking her, when she
seven or eight. "Don't tell Mommy. It's our little game." It's not
an unusual game, about half the women in America get abused
at least once. This was the same Daddy who was paying for
her education. Maybe he had even forgotten. Maybe it didn't

matter to him. Maybe she was just crazy. She tried a thousand times to call up her mom and tell her, and couldn't call. So, she decided to end it all. She got her roommate's prescription sleeping pills and went down into the basement under the dorm and took them.

It was Anthony who woke her up. He was playing a game called Assassin, where you took people out with sucker darts. He had just been killed.

He gave her a long talk about looking at anything in your life like it was a game. Even the worst things could be understood and accepted if they just weren't serious.

He also told her that he would pay for her education so she didn't have to see her father again.

"That way, he loses, see?"

Anthony taught her many games. Some of them were simple S&M games many couples enjoy. Some involved hurting other people, but not too bad. Some involved helping other people out anonymously. Anthony always said that it was more fun to be Santa Claus or Satan than to be ourselves.

Later, just before she married him, she found out that he hadn't been playing a game that night in the basement at all. He had heard about her problems from the school therapist and decided to watch her until he could play White Knight.

She took that as sign that he really loved her.

It was a long time until she realized that he just didn't care. She was a token.

She told herself for many years that she shouldn't be like him.

But of course, he was right: Loki, Coyote, Hermes always win out. They make you think like they do.

She would go to Doublesign.

11 At the Seventh Rank

Abel Salazar knew nothing but envy. It was the house, the other path that his life could have taken. He just stared at the Spencer's house. There it was. It was the other side of the chessboard. They still played like he played, but their game was OK. Sure they broke some laws—a little kidnapping here, a little breaking and entering there—but they could be written up in the papers and be exonerated. They could be filmed. They were *Natural Born Killers* without the blood. Their transgressions let them be bold, have a big house in a beautiful neighborhood. They had their pecan trees and their koi pond. They had their nice cars and they had friends who didn't twitch at the sound of sirens, or who dwelt behind as many layers as secrecy as his patron. They could walk in the sun, run in the sun.

They were good, too. So damn good. He could track down maybe ten of their pranks.

He had come across them when he was still in the Bureau. They weren't as careful then, a little too prone to letting Polyphemus know, but he hadn't thought he would ever meet them. He had a gut feeling that they had some connection with the SKiller. Both seemed to be Texans, although the SK didn't operate out of Texas (probably New York or Chicago). Since they had done a bad job fleeing the killing in Doublesign, it probably meant that they had been in league with him if only briefly. Probably they had tracked his career for years, and then found he wasn't the shining example he seemed to be. Salazar grinned at that one.

Their prank was one of the last things to cross his desk. It was, amusingly enough, the reason he had decided to play the Game. He realized what they were up to. It was the same sort of thing the SK did. Maybe millions of people did it. Maybe all those dreary people you see at airports are just pretending to go somewhere. When he was growing up, he had read Chesterton's *The Man Who Was Thursday*. At least he thought that was the title. It had been about a conspiracy that had been so thoroughly infiltrated by the police that every member was a cop, a detective, a spy, and so forth. The Spencers' pranks had made him start wondering: How many people are always pretending to be something that they're not? How many honest people are there?

The prank was a beaut.

It looked like a SK exploit, because the target, Vernon Labrador, was a guy without family, no one would be hurt, but then in a certain sense, Vernon wasn't, either. Vernon owned a thriving health food store in Charity, Texas. It was odd that such a small town could support the luxury of a health food store, odder still for it to have had so many stress-related deaths. But Vernon saw to each . . .

Whenever anyone died of a nutritionally related disorder— and face it, short of car wrecks, all deaths are usually nutritionally related—he would send the bereaved families information on how the dear departed stiff could have eaten better, particularly by avoiding that killer of killers, *M-E-A-T*. The bereaved would read the horrible literature and, fearing everything from mad cow disease to cancer, patronize Vernon's Health Hut for a few months until the taste of tofu and sprouts could no longer feed their Texas-size appetites. When they fell off the vegan wagon, Vernon would make sure they got more literature or he'd rely on his gestapo to frighten them with unpalatable facts about the amount of undigested red meat in the gut of the average adult male. People grew so fearful of Vernon's predictions that they died of guilt when they would succumb to a candy bar or a Big Mac. Of course, their guilty dead hands clutching the nonkosher poisons fueled the fears of others. Vitamins sold. Herbs were bought, and tofu was barbecued. (Texas is still Texas, you know.)

But Vernon began getting little things in the mail. At first it was mildly threatening things like bumper stickers saying I EAT VEGANS. Then cut-out articles on the growing threat of urban cannibalism. He received the full FBI files on cannibals. He got the Hannibal Lecter books and *Alive!*, with certain passages highlighted. He went to the police, who laughed him off.

Then the phone calls started. Voices whispering in the night, "You know vegetarian flesh tastes so much sweeter, I can hardly wait until I can sink my teeth into your thighs." The police tried tracking the calls, but no luck. Vernon began telling the callers that he wasn't a vegetarian.

Then he got a letter saying that all they wanted was the confessions of Vernon's nonvegetarian status. They would leak to the local newspaper if he didn't pay them two thousand dollars at midnight at the old slaughterhouse. The whole idea of cannibals was just to scare him.

Vernon couldn't afford the scandal of being exposed as a meat eater, so he got the money in small bills as instructed and drove to the old slaughterhouse. Surely the irony of the location was not lost on him. As he stepped into the dark building, a powerful flashlight blinded him. He heard a thump and felt a pinprick in his chest. He looked at the tranquilizing dart before everything went black. When he awoke, he was cold. Mainly he was cold because of his nakedness, but also because of the cold steel hook that had been duct-taped to his back. Or more precisely his back had been duct-taped to the hook, from which he dangled about three feet off the floor. It was night. A man and a woman had erected a small tent on the floor of the slaughterhouse. A bright lantern burned, and the man and woman were well-lit in their safari clothes.

"I do believe he's awake," said the man. "Oh, jolly good, I so much more wish him to see the flashing of the knives."

"What are you doing?" asked Vernon. "I brought you the money."

"Oh, bother," said the woman. "You're quite slow. Look at our equipment. Do we strike you as the sort who would need money?"

"Are you going to kill me?"

"Yes, old chap. Kill you and eat you," said the man. "We gave you many chances to run, you know. We were quite sporting."

"You can't eat people," said Vernon.

"Of course, you can. And with the equipment here, it is so easy and so automated," said the woman.

"What are you going to do?" asked Vernon. "I can get you more money. I could help you get people more tender than me."

"I know you could do that," said the man, "Titania and I have studied you greatly. You are very good at preying on people."

"Yes," said the woman. "You are a frightfully good predator, preying on their fears and guilts. We thought you would certainly be the most dangerous game."

"But we caught you so easily," continued the man.

"Wait!" said Vernon. "Let me go. I'll run a merry chase for you. I really will."

"Well . . . normally we would," said the woman. "I mean, the chase is very important, but, well—frankly, we're hungry and you drove the McDonald's out of Charity, so where else are going to get a bite to eat at this hour?"

"I could fix you something at home," began Vernon, until he realized she was joking.

"Oh, don't put yourself out on our account. My husband need only hit the switch over there." She gestured into the darkness. "And the hook will begin to move along the belt that way." She pointed up again into the darkness. "Then you'll circle the building, once, then be automatically gutted, your blood will be drained from your body with the help of your beating heart and then you'll be quartered. We'll pack you in dry ice and take you back to Austin."

(According to Vernon, her voice had trembled when she said "Austin." She hadn't meant to do that.)

The man walked into the darkness and there were sparks as a big switch was thrown. The hook jerked and Vernon began rising. The man and the woman turned off the lantern. Vernon began screaming.

The hook rose, but the conveyor belt did not take him to any automatic gutting program. Instead he merely went around and around the top of the building, growing quite hoarse from screaming. It was two days before anyone found him. That was always true in SKillings. Since people hated the victims, no searches were mounted soon; there was always just relief.

When Salazar had read about the case three things stood out: Titania, a character from Spenser's *Faerie Queen*, the mention of research, and the inadvertent mention of Austin. So when looking for the fleeing car, the name *Spencer* and *Austin* made him remember the case. He doubted that Mondragon could ever find his way to Austin, even with the car clue. Maybe he should simply call him. As he resolved to do this, some afternoon activity occurred at the Spencer home. Willis Spencer walked into the front yard. Poor guy looked so down. His wife had left him two days ago. He was covering up for her on the phone. Getting a tap into his equipment had been easy. Salazar had just borrowed a Southwestern Bell truck and went to the nearest box. People like Willis don't ever take security steps like having their phones encrypted. They think that since they are smart, they are invulnerable. Smarts save very few people. Salazar had seen a lot of smart agents die.

Salazar was just waiting for Willis to ask for help—admit to a friend or to the police that Virginia had bolted. He had a plan for that.

He didn't know where she had gone, and he didn't care. All he needed was to get Willis on his side, and then Willis could explain his connection to Chadwick. He would wind up killing Willis, which was a sad thing, since he owed his entry to the Game to Willis. Willis had inspired him with the Charity slaughterhouse caper.

He would make it up to him, he would tell Willis everything just before he killed him, and he would kill him real cleanly, and then he would immortalize him by writing a book about Willis and Virginia and putting it on the WWW. He would call it *Endless Honeymoon* and paint their pranks as endless fun, playing the god game. It would let other people figure out how many people there are playing the Game, it would let them in on the real secret of cities. It was a damn shame he couldn't publish it under his own name, but that was part of the rules of the Game. If you play on the black side of the chessboard, you play a masked figure. But as he watched the worried look on Willis's face, he felt that there were some benefits to the black side of the board. It had been a long time since he had ever felt as passionate for a person as Willis did. Poor stupid bastard, staring off at the road.

12 Ashes to Birds in Doublesign

When she checked into the Mirabeau B. Lamar motel, she knew that she had lost a battle. Virginia wondered why she had abandoned her smarts on her second day at the hotel. She didn't check to see if Anthony was still in his asylum, and she hadn't told anyone where she was really going. If she called Willis now, he would be mad and worried; although it was a matter of time until he figured out that she wasn't out researching a new prank. She had told him that she was looking into a female minister in Milando. He would check his files when she hadn't called back, and see that the woman had either died or had ceased to be a source of woe.

The first day hadn't been too bad. She figured that whoever had sent the note would be watching, as anxious as herself to meet. She knew that—no, she hoped that—she was the object of someone's prank, someone's active prank. She even wondered if it was Willis trying, in some strange dysfunctional way, to say everything was OK after the murder in Doublesign. Of course, mainly she thought it was the murderer. It did not worry her that the person had killed. Whoever he or she was, he or she was smart enough to find out about Anthony. That kind of smarts means smart enough to kill. She could die very easily every day in Austin while jogging down to the mailbox. No, the killer wanted something else and was relying on a powerful cocktail of fear and curiosity to make Virginia give it up. The first day wasn't bad because the anticipation at every sound—every phone ringing in another room—made her think the moment of revelation was near.

She ate pizza. There was one pizza delivery place in Doublesign, so she ate noon and night, skipping breakfast. She told herself that this was silly and tried to make herself walk the few blocks down to the Kuntry Kitchen. But, no go. He could come and tell all.

She guessed it would take Willis a day to doubt her story. She wanted him to do so, but she didn't know why. On some level, she suspected that she wanted to punish him for picking her in the first place. There had to be something wrong with him for sticking with such a fucked-up girl. In the early days of their marriage, she always worried that he was going to send her away. Every time she was bold enough to say something she really thought, he would agree, but she always feared that someday she would reveal too much, and it would all be over. It had to be this time. She couldn't tell him about this trip, because he might have said no. Well, of course, he would say no, it was a stupid trip, a dangerous idea. But if she hadn't made it, it would eat at her every day.

The second day was very bad. She found that the room was ten by fifteen. She could pace the shorter distance in four long steps. Step, step, step, step. She could pace the longer distance in six long steps. Step. Step. Step. Step. Step. Step. She resolved to pack it in on the third day.

On the third day, she resolved to leave by noon. At one, she resolved to leave by three. At four, someone knocked loudly on the door.

She looked through the peephole for a long time.

On the other side of the door stood a short thin man with

silver hair and a neatly trimmed mustache. His turquoise blue eyes matched his impeccable suit. He carried a small black briefcase. He had a polite smile. He looked right at the peephole with a very patient (and, Virginia thought, *kindly*) expression. He had no nervousness in him; he knew what he was about.

Virginia opened the door partially, keeping a chain in place. "What do you want?" asked Virginia.

"To talk with you, Mrs. Spencer, about some property of mine that you or your husband may have found."

"We don't have anything," she said.

"Of course, you do, and you've been putting it to a remarkable usage, not one I quite approve of, but I am sure that's no fault of your own. It probably didn't even occur to you that it could belong to someone. Believe me, I have no ill intentions toward either of you, but I will be insistent that the property be returned."

"Go away. I shouldn't have come to see you."

"Yes, that's exactly what the Program said you would say. I've updated it a few dozen times since the very primitive model you have. But you are really wondering about what is in my case. Capital. I'll just leave the case here and you can join me for dinner at the quaintly named establishment down the road at six. I'm sure that you will find them a delightful alternative to your endless round of pizzas."

"Who are you, if you are, indeed, the sort that tells names, and why don't you think I'll just drive the hell away from here when you are gone?"

"My name is Roy Chadwick. You came here because you hate your husband for his loving you, and you'll stay because you love him and have begun to hate me on sight. You know that you should just drive away, but you'll make the mistake of looking in the briefcase, and you'll stay. I don't know how long you'll stay, because that is built on questions of free will, but I know what your programming will make you do for a while. That's why I had to time my entrance. Now I will leave you with the case and the paradox of free will."

He laid the case down.

Her next awareness was that she stank. She had been afraid to shower, some of that due to fear of missing a phone call, the rest a gift from Mr. Hitchcock. When she had counted fourteen *mississippis* she opened the door and grabbed the briefcase. She intended not to open it. She was going to get in her car and drive home and tell Willis everything. She just wanted Chadwick to see her pick up the case. She didn't see him watching, but he could be anywhere—behind a bush, a car, a thickness of air. Once the case was inside the room, she began packing up her things to leave. She would take the case with her. Willis and she could view it.

But what if it meant some kind of problem for Willis? What if it would make his life sad, bad, or mad?

It was light brown leather, an old case like her daddy used to pack when he went on day trips. It had been scuffed and worn over the years, yet some care had been taken to keep it clean, its brass fittings shiny. It could hold a large number of secrets, or perhaps a bomb, or maybe a plague, or maybe nothing at all.

She could just throw it away. But then she would never know what was in it. She could just drive south toward Austin and toss it into an arroyo. But then someone else might find it.

She could just leave it here for Mr. Chadwick.

She could do many things, but Chadwick was right about what she did do.

She opened it.

It contained two documents.

One was printed on yellow, stained, brittle, green-barred continuous-feed paper. It contained a printout of a COBOL program decades old, the same program that Willis had found on an ancient spool when he made Monolith Insurance Y2K compliant. The Program that found their victims for them.

The other was a nicely formatted spiral-bound list of the crimes committed by Virginia and Willis since the days of their courtship. It was listed chronologically, first a citation of the laws they had broken, then a description of the events. It was mainly guesswork using a series of police reports and newspaper clippings—several of their pranks had made it into syndication in those columns dedicated to weird or humorous crime. The guesses were good. After each crime description was a list of confirming information such as credit card charges, car rentals, hotel rooms, and so forth, that showed how likely it was that Virginia and Willis had been in the area of the crime, and that they had bought the odd items (from makeup to tents). Since the list was merely a printout bound nicely by some copy shop, there could be any number of them. She had to see what Chadwick wanted.

It had all been her fault, she had talked Willis into the Game, once he had explained the software to her.

She showered and showered and went to the Kuntry Kitchen, which smelled of wholesome chicken-fried steak and black-eyes. Chadwick sat at the booth near the back, sipping iced tea and looking as dapper as before. He smiled when she walked in. She had left the case back at the motel, at least some symbol of rebellion—although his Program had probably told him as much. She tried to look him straight in the face as she crossed the room, but she collided with an apologetic waitress delivering a tray full of German chocolate cake. Unstained but undignified, she made her way to Chadwick. Just as she sat, another waitress brought their food. He had ordered for her: all her favorites. Chicken-fried steak, broccoli-rice casserole, Texas caviar and jalapeño cornbread. Iced tea to drink, served (as it so often is in north Texas) presweetened.

"Are these all in my dossier?" she asked.

"No. Some of them are just what's good here. I know you

won't believe it, but I don't like having to resort to high drama. I am a minimalist. I was a minimalist before being a minimalist was cool. But everything I have simulated about you suggests that high drama gets through. You are, I would guess, an adult child of an alcoholic? I'm sorry. I'm far too blunt. You know, it's actually been nine years since I talked with anybody face-to-face. At least anyone that could talk back, my manners have grow rusty through nonuse."

"I hope your brief outing into the world of the quick will not be taxing for you," she said.

"It won't be a brief outing. You and I have a good deal of business to do. I want to see if you are the one to take over my life work, or if I will have to kill you. I'm being too blunt again. The cornbread is quite excellent, isn't it?"

"Since you know that my husband and I are already using your Program, what do you want?"

"You are not using the Program seriously. You are kidding around, and you don't kill your victims. You hope that they will reform. You don't do metrics on your operations. How many of your targets get better, how many keep going, how many get worse?"

"We've tried to check up on things."

"And your results?"

"Well, we haven't been scrupulous."

"No, you haven't been rigorous at all. Because it's a goddamn game to you. Oh, you both play the Game very well, you might be the greatest artists of the late twentieth, early twenty-first, century. I bet it makes you crazy, doesn't it? Your well-hatched plots, your great theater, and the only press notices you get are in 'News of the Weird.' "

"It's not exactly an artform you can share. So have you done our metrics, are you here to give me the science of our art?"

"Yes, I have, as a matter of fact. I estimate that I have correctly traced about eighty percent of your feats, and of these slightly over half of your targets give up their bad behavior, with maybe half of those becoming exemplary citizens, that feed the poor and visit those in prisons. Of the remaining forty-five percent, about half stay the same and half become more sadistic and worse to their fellow man."

"That's quite a recovery rate, don't you think? One half saints, one fourth the same, and one fourth worse. I take it you just kill them. One hundred percent give up their evil ways, but no one gets better. Unless you feel we are cutting into your market, what's your worry?"

"I am not in competition with you. You are the closest thing to my way of thinking I have seen in over forty years. If you and Willis were to keep doing what you're doing, I would think it is a good thing. But that is not what my Program leads me to believe will happen. I have seen your fate, and unless I can motivate you to alter it, it will be the downfall of mankind in less than fifty years. I know this as strongly as I know what you are about to say."

He pulled out a standard business-size envelope from his vest pocket.

She said, "That's just cheap theater. Predicting what someone is going to say is just mentalism. So-fucking-what?"

He handed her the envelope. One a single piece of typing paper were the words: "That's just cheap theater. Predicting what someone is going to say is just mentalism. So-fucking-what?"

She shrugged. "So-fucking-what?"

"My predictions are too dire to risk testing them. You and I are going to go on a little road trip, and if I get you to betray your husband and kill an old defenseless woman, mankind may be saved."

"If I don't go?"

"I'll kill you."

"Doesn't your amazing Program tell you if I am going to go with you?" she asked.

"No. That's a real decision point. There is such a thing as free will, I discovered it in nineteen sixty-six. The future is not fixed, just more inflexible than we would like to believe."

"What do you think I'll do?"

"I think you'll meet me here in two hours with your bags packed, checked out of the hotel. I think you'll want to find out how you might endanger the human race, not because of your love for them or for yourself, but because to endanger them would be to endanger Willis, and you owe him your life and love him more than all things."

"What do you think I'll do if I find out you're full of shit?"

"That's simple. You'll kill me. I don't need a Program to simulate that one."

13 The Decline of the West

The Decline of the West is a bar in downtown Austin on La-
vaca Street. The north-south streets in downtown are named
after rivers, the east-west are numbered. The bar shares a
block with the New Atlantis bookstore and a high-rise. The
old brick building has been at various times a copy shop, a
grocery store, a martial arts academy, and a coffee shop (also
named the Decline of the West). Willis Spencer walked in a
little after six on a Tuesday evening. Virginia had been away
for four days, and he had broken down and called Virginia's
mom in St. Paul to ask if she was there. He assumed that either the marriage was over, (because he was timid about
playing the Game) or that someone had abducted her. The
first seemed by far the most likely, since she had taken her
car with her, but the latter could still be a hope. He feared
losing her more than he feared anything in his life. He had
been a timid little geek all his life, and it wasn't until meeting
her that he had felt the pulse of life. It wasn't just her beauty
or the way she laughed or the fineness of her mind, it was
something so rare he never could have imagined it before he
had met Anthony Night. Right after he had called Virginia's
mother, and thereby scared her mother (who had never trusted

her daughter since she ran away briefly when she was sixteen), he got a call from a man who identified himself as Bobby Fischer. All Bobby had said was that it wasn't a mystery to him where Virginia was, and if Willis would like to be in the same mental space as he, he should meet Bobby at the Decline of the West at six.

Other than rescuing Virginia from A. Night, Willis had done little on his own. Only now did he realize that without her he was timid and a bit thick. What magic she must've worked to have kept him from knowing that.

Downtown bars are always full at six. Full of people wanting martinis before their rides home, gathering a little courage to meet their spouses, their kids, their lives. Bars are a little too noisy, since loudness is an old human technique for banishing self-denial. Bobby hadn't mentioned what he looked like. Willis thought he had caught a trace of a Hispanic accent, so he looked hard at the few Hispanics in the bar. Older men mainly, in overstuffed suits, probably bankers. Willis wondered if he should have called the police. Probably not. Since he had never come to this bar, he didn't expect that anyone would recognize him.

He was wrong.

John Reynman, owner of the used bookstore, was there with his wife, Haidee. They hailed Willis as he walked in.

"Hey, stranger. Ain't seen you in a while," said John. "Want to sit with us?"

"No," said Willis. "I am supposed to meet someone."

"Well," said Haidee. "You can wait with us until they show."

"I, em, told him I would be alone," said Willis. "I only know him through the Internet, so he's looking for me as a single type."

"You know," said John. "I don't think I've ever seen you single. You and your wife always shop for books together. I was telling Haidee the other day, I always think of you as the mystery couple. You still love each other so much, it's like you're honeymooners and that high-tech stuff you do seems to give you a bunch of free time to be in love, something that most of the world only dreams of doing. Can you tell me again what it is you do?"

"Look, I really need to make contact with my client. Virginia will stop in next week, and we'll chew the fat."

"Well, we're heading back to the shop to update my credit files tonight, so we'll be there until late. Bring your client by if you like, and I'll give him a discount. I came across a copy of that exposé of the Yellow Flower cult you were interested in. I've got it under the counter for you, but I don't think you came in all summer."

Willis smiled and walked away, but was able to hear Haidee say that he didn't look good. Willis tried to be obvious, to send out the "I'm here" vibe. Bobby hadn't told him how he would spot Willis. Maybe the fact that he knew people here would queer the deal, or (of course) maybe the whole thing was a prank, and there wasn't anyone here. Willis took a booth near the front. He ordered a Shiner and took out a paperback copy of Rex Hull's *Little Gardens of Happiness*, a mystery set at the wildflower research center in Austin. He was too nervous to read and felt too self-conscious not to have a prop in his hands. He held the book a moment or two before he realized he was holding it upside down.

A pale chubby Chicano with a nervous tic above his left eye walked up to Willis. He wore a pinstripe suit slightly too small and few years out of date. He had a gaudy tie with Daffy Duck painted on it, scuffed ostrich skin boots, and stained teeth. He put something on the table to introduce himself. A white pawn.

"Mr. Spencer?" he asked. "You can call me Bobby Fischer."

"You look more like a Lopez or a Capablanca," said Willis.

"Do you play?" asked Bobby.

"I am just a dilettante."

"Pity, I am always looking for serious players. So, your wife has been missing for four days. I assume this is a major worry for you."

"Yes. I think it would be a worry for anyone."

"You would be surprised. When people go missing it is sometimes a great joy for everyone else around. Could you imagine that—a person so vile that everyone in their little town might hate them? A real shit."

"Well, my wife would scarcely be that."

"Of course not, Mr. Spencer. We know that. We have a dossier on her. I just asked if you could imagine that, a person so horrid that everyone in the town might hate her? Perhaps a mean old widow who derived her kicks out of making little kids suffer for frozen custard. You know what frozen custard is, don't you Mr. Willis? What some folks call soft-serve ice cream?"

"I know what frozen custard is. Look what does this have to do with my wife? Who are you? Who is *we*?"

"We are the Federal Bureau of Investigation, Mr. Spencer, and we know who your wife is with—we just don't know where. I wish I had some reason to tell you who your wife is with, but I can't give away free information. You're in the information business, aren't you, Mr. Spencer? Been in the information business since you were a hacker named Bloodaxe, haven't you? Now I am in the interesting position of having some information that you'd pay dearly to have. Oh, don't insult me by offering money. I know you have a good deal of that, even more than you let the IRS know you have. Oooh—that stung, didn't it? Not the reference to your past crime but the Infernal Revenue Service. I guess that shows what demons we fear nowadays."

"What do I have that you want, Mr. Fischer?"

"Oh, you have many things I want. I want your dragon doorway and your koi pond and your skill with advanced data mining. I want your marriage and your happiness and a place in this pleasant town that O. Henry named after Athens, 'the City of the Violet Crown.' I want all those things, but they are beyond your ability to sell—or, sadly, of me to buy. I do, however, want to talk to you about soft ice cream and Doublesign, Texas."

"I guess it's time for me to get a lawyer."

"Mr. Spencer, I am not the DA, I am not the police. I am not here merely to gather information on your activities on the night of July Fourth. I am here just to help you out. You see, I want to reunite you and your wife. I just want her traveling companion. You can decide if you want to take her back, now that she has run off with another man. You may want to get a lawyer then, to sue the bitch for divorce, but that is not my concern."

"So, what do you need to know? You want me to confess, and then you'll tell me something terrible?"

"Oh, I want much more than a confession, Mr. Spencer. I want your aid. You seem to have some unusual abilities at creating dramatic scenes, and I may need a drama coach for the things I need to do. But I'll give you something you may have always wanted, a chance to ride along with a G-man and see how real justice is done, not your playacting bullshit."

"You'll let me go along?"

"Not merely let you, amigo, I will insist on your presence. I don't think I would sleep well at night knowing that you were, no doubt, using own vast resources to track down the man I am looking for. You might fuck it up, or—worse still—you might find him first. So do you want to tell me about Velma MacPhearson's murder?"

"Well, to begin with, I didn't kill her, nor did Virginia. She had been freshly killed when we found her."

"How did you know the kill was fresh?"

"Blood was still coming from her head wound."

"How had you entered the house?"

"I broke in a downstairs window."

"Had you looked at the front door of the house?"

"Yes. It was closed as we approached."

"So if it was—as you say—a fresh kill, the killer was in the house. Did you interact with him?"

"No. I figured out that the killer must have been in the house, and I told Virginia we must leave."

"Were you familiar with other killings with the same MO?"

"No."

"Have you followed the careers of serial killers?"

"No."

"Does the name Roy Chadwick have any meaning for you?"

"No."

"That's a very nice beginning, Mr. Spencer. We'll talk soon, perhaps in a day or two."

"You can't just walk out on me. You have to tell me who my wife is with."

"I already did."

"But that name doesn't mean anything to me."

"So you say. You may wish to think about it. In any event, you know more than you used to, and all it cost was a confession to being at the scene of a murder that you did not report to the police, and some breaking and entering. You see, I am very easy—I always give good payback."

"You bastard. You can't leave."

"Yes, Mr. Spencer, I can because I fully appreciate your position."

Bobby handed Willis Spencer the white pawn and sauntered toward the door.

Willis held the pawn tightly. Without the oracle of his wife, he didn't know whether he was doing the right thing.

It was a bad time to discover that it was Virginia and not the Program that made his life comprehensible.

14 My Daddy

It was a black Cadillac from the seventies. Virginia didn't know where Chadwick had gotten it from. As they were speeding north toward the Texas panhandle, Chadwick was sporadically talkative. At first he didn't talk about anything remotely related to the trip, other than hint at nightfall; he had big revelation. At first he wouldn't let her drive, but after about an hour, either trust or fatigue set in and she drove. A few hundred miles south of Lubbock, his tone changed. Virginia thought he was reciting a speech long rehearsed—one of those speeches that we tell ourselves in the shower or when driving in long empty spaces. She asked little and let him talk. She was listening for some clue, some doorway into this strange man that could make him tell her whatever it was he knew. She was also listening to her own heart's reaction to the words, hoping to find some interior clue as to why she believed his predictions of doom.

"My daddy was a genius. He taught math at M.I.T. right after World War One. He tried to interest investors in his electronic calculating Program, but he was pretty clueless at selling things. He had invented the theory of the computer like Von Neumann or Turing, but he couldn't explain the importance of his idea.

At the time of the crash, he began by studying pattern recognition problems. Everyone wanted an explanation of the crash. He invented a good part of catastrophe theory and a lot of chaos theory by himself to explain recent economic conditions. Did this get him the Nobel Prize? No, it pretty much classed him as some kind of nutcase. He couldn't explain what he was doing. He lost his position, and to feed his wife and child he went to work for the insurance industry. He was respected there. He was a whiz at actuarial tables and risk assessment. He practically revolutionized the field. Not that you get any statues for that. He knew what he had done. He knew that he had taken maths to a new level, and toward the end of his life, he was hoping for big number-crunching Programs to work with his models. But he was bitter and sad. Every setback he had he attributed to himself. He would spend hours in the basement crying his eyes out. He moved us to a little hick town called Comesee, Texas. No one could bother him there because no one there understood his work. He drank a lot. He smoked too much, and he knew exactly how much each drink and each cigarette shrank his life. He made this mechanical display board that could recalculate his life expectancy after each drink. He would make a martini and hit the button and—*zoop*—there it was. Three point two minutes less. There was even a little alarm that would ring when he had calculated an hour. Mom and I had to deal with that. He was an early convert to home schooling. He kept me at home. In fact, he got very paranoid about records. Social Security, driver's license, bills—you name it. He made sure that we had as few records as possible. Now, this was in the old days, before you could hack into a system and make things disappear. So, it was all social engineering. Mom—well, mom died before him. I don't want to talk about that. His last action was to get me a job at Stone Mount Insurance. A small company that got sucked into a medium-sized company then into a large one, and then into a giant one. I did great. Better than great, because I had math tools that were simply way beyond anyone else. I am not a genius. I am smart, but not a genius. When the old man died, he told me that I had a special destiny because I could foresee the future. Now you can't really see the future, you can only see probabilities if you've got enough data. But the old man said that the time was coming when there would be a lot more data than anyone had ever dreamed of."

Chadwick fell asleep at this point in the story. She could've just pulled over, probably killed him with ease. He seemed pretty frail. But she simply wanted to know more. The Program that she and Willis used to find their victims was way beyond anything that Willis had ever seen thought out. She had to know how this little maniacal man knew so much and what else he knew. When he woke up a few miles down the road, he looked a little sheepish, but he didn't seem scared. Maybe his Program told him that she wouldn't kill him just yet.

"One of my first big jobs for Stone Mount was to look at certain types of death. Deaths related to anxiety and depression. I asked for the job, you understand. I wanted to find out why my dad had died. I wanted to know about cancer, about alcoholism, about slow suicides. I produced a lot of data for the industry. But I discovered something as well. I discovered that there are true shits in the world. I called them 'psychic vampires.' These people make the lives of everyone around them miserable, and they seem to flourish on the misery involved. You can spot them. They outlive or run off their mates and make no attempt to remarry. They run businesses that are marked by a high death rate of their employees. Their houses are surrounded by deaths of a certain sort. Stress-related deaths stalk their Sunday schools. They are bringers of cancer, of alcoholism, of strokes, of certain pneumonias and flus. Now, it wasn't news to any thinking person that there are people that actually live on the misery of others. What I found out is that a lot of these people have no dependents—taking them out has no cost to anyone. Emotionally, financially, and so forth. So after a few months of internal debate, I issued a report in the company showing that it would be economically advantageous for the insurance companies to provide a group fund for knocking these people off. I was fired. I was threatened that if I ever spoke of any of my findings that Stone Mount would lock my ass up. No one listened to me. No one. Now, think about it? If you shot a sniper before he shot four or five people, you would be given a medal, right? There is no question that our society lives on this principle. I realized that I had merely taken Dad's ideas to the next logical level. He probably knew I would."

"What happened after you were fired?" asked Virginia.

"At first I just slinked off with my tail between my legs. Then I heard about DARPA-net, the Department of Defense's linked computer network. It was just being made. They needed people with an in-depth understanding of emergent principles in linked computers. In short, they needed my daddy, but they got me. I was one of the architects of the Internet. So, I saw what could happen. I saw that certain sorts of data mining could occur, long before anyone else thought of it. The idiots that put it together were just interested in communication, so that they could survive the Cold War if it got hot. They didn't even see that they were building a nervous system, one that looks at everything it touches. Only in the last few years, with their primitive search technologies, are they getting the point. Even now, they are mainly looking at refined data, not data in the raw. They don't know what questions to ask."

"Do you know?" asked Virginia.

"Probably not," admitted Chadwick. "But I know that questions can be asked. One of my earliest questions was about finding psychic vampires. I was using a versions of the algorithm I had written as a COBOL program for the insurance company. A much more advanced version, and I got answers pretty easy. I looked at those names every night, and I wondered how many people they were making miserable. How many lives were being poisoned by their mean remarks, their gossip, their stupid and demeaning rules for their employees. One of them lived less than three blocks from my house. Ralph Matusac, a jeweler. He had had a very unhappy and short marriage and had developed an evil attitude to women. He managed, unconsciously, to plant certain messages in the minds of every couple that bought their wedding rings there, or in the minds of every man that purchased an engagement ring. There was a ninety-three percent chance of divorce if you bought your rings from this guy. At first I thought I could just help him out, give him an ear to spew his venom in. So I broke my granddad's gold watch and took it in to be fixed. Matusac was a decent guy, loved to go out for some beer, liked the local teams, and knew a few good jokes. So, I decided to put it to the test.

"There was a woman that I was seeing. Her name was Alesia. I proposed to her. It was an experiment. I loved her—well I thought I loved her—no, I really loved her—but I wanted to see Matusac's reaction. I thought that if I could show him an example of how happy Alesia and I were and would be, as well as being his friend, I could change him. Murder wasn't necessary. It would let me know that people could be changed for the better, and that here was a hope in my cold equations. Besides, I felt that my love for Alesia was strong enough to withstand anything that he might throw at it. He smiled when I told him, but his jokes got more bitter. He seemed to have this radar: when I had had a fight with Alesia— even a minor one like whether or not to tip a waiter, he had some story about unhappy married people that he had seen. Every negative emotion that I had, no matter how well I concealed it, he zeroed in on and pushed. As the date grew closer, I realized I couldn't change the way he was. I began to see changes in myself despite my intentions. I no longer wanted to marry Alesia. In fact, I stood her up on our wedding day. While she stood at the church in the wedding gown her mother had made for her, I was shooting Matusac. I couldn't let him do to anyone else what he had done to me. My original idea of killing the psychic vampires was the right one. I went underground after that. I knew I had to make certain changes in the world. It wasn't easy at first. I was a protohacker. I was one of the first people that got money from nowhere that banks thought was real. But I got better. I got very good at hiding behind dead people and neglected accounts. And I got good about finding appropriate targets. I always checked up, unlike you and Willis. I always saw to it that people were really helped by social surgery."

"Did you ever go back to Alesia?" asked Virginia.

"No. I couldn't rekindle my feelings. I felt too bad at having listened to all the poison. I knew I was too tainted. I'm sure it hurt a great deal being stood up, but I saved her from a greater hurt. I simply disappeared, dropped off the face of the earth, as far as she was concerned."

"But what about friends? Family?"

"My family was dead when my father died. I haven't had any close friends. They would be in danger from knowing me. In fact, you are the first woman I have spoke to since Alesia's time."

15 Mondragon's Career Flashes Before His Eyes

Willis kept burying his face in the pillow of room 204 at the Mirabeau B. Lamar hotel. The maid hadn't changed the bedding. He had arrived with Bobby Fischer less than two hours after she had departed with Chadwick. Fischer had tracked her to the hotel with a credit card. The clerk had no ideas about her leaving, other than it had been a morning phenomenon. Willis had not freaked out at the news, but was excited at Fischer's tracking expertise. When he smelled her Eternity on the pillow, he entered a sort of blissful trance, believing that his FBI man had something akin to supernatural powers, and that soon he would restore things to their Eden-like order. Willis had always believed that in matters of the heart, the FBI was really on your side. He even thought that someday if he just had the chance he could explain his activities to agents and they would applaud. The only problem would be if they caught him and shot him before he could speak. He felt that now, all was well. He was still bothered by the man's fake name of Bobby Fischer, but being the sort of creature that he was, Willis felt the need to forgive him. In fact, he even thought that the playful pseudonym might be a sign of kinship, which could only lead to a serious bond. Willis rolled around in the bed, dream-caressing the form of Virginia, breathing deep her smell. He would not leave a single molecule of her here.

Bobby, meanwhile, was sitting bolt upright at the little table, his mind lost in thought. He hadn't decided on his next move. His employer would want results soon. His guess was that Chadwick would merely kill the woman. There were many indications over the years that Chadwick was misogynist. He had thought to bring Willis to the scene of the crime, have Willis kill Chadwick, and return to his underground existence many times richer and free of his employer's control. Chadwick had never transported a victim before. So, the victim idea crumbled. He had to figure out what to tell his employer, what he was going to do, and what to do with the idiot rolling in his wife's perfume.

Fischer's cell phone rang. He stood up and left the room, standing where Chadwick had stood yesterday with his briefcase. It was his man in the Bureau.

"Mondragon is off the ShitKiller case. In fact, he's on administrative leave, and you owe me for this."

"I want that guy active on the case. What the hell are you talking about? Tell me everything."

"Look, I saved your Mexican ass and you owe me big time."

Fischer took a deep breath to control his anger. He knew Tyrell was a jerk, but this jerk was his only fleshly connection to the FBI. "OK, I'll pay you, we'll talk about that, but tell me everything."

"Mondragon wrote a report about you. He decided that you were, or more correctly had become, the ShitKiller. He recorded his calls with you and was attempting to trace them."

"I can't be traced, that isn't a problem."

"No, but you can be identified, and the more they look at you, the more you look like a convenient corpse. An agent gone loony is bad, but a corpse that ties up the loose ends of many killings is good. And there are people who are out to get you."

"O'Brien."

"O'Brien, yes. He's a field supervisor. He's Mondragon's supervisor now. He was eating up the whole Salazar-is-the-SK argument. Hell, I was beginning to wonder myself."

"Wait, now, . . ."

"Oh, for godsakes don't tell me—like I would believe anything from you except a cashier's check. Anyway, Mondragon took his recording to be transcribed, which, as you know, is under the control of me, your little guardian angel, so I just made sure that only one half of the call exists. The transcript reads Agent Mondragon: Blah, blah, blah. Then silence, then Agent Mondragon: Blah, blah, blah."

"So, what—what about the original tapes?"

"They were delivered back to his office—here's the beauty part—and Mondragon's dad had given him a big-ass lodestone years ago. His father was full of half-baked mysticism and given to aphorisms right and left. The stone is supposed to be about the pull of mystery or some damn thing. Anyway, so he's got this ugly, big magnetic rock on his desk. He's got in trouble with it before. Anyway, it just so happened that the tapes were laid on top of the rock and were erased. Of course, I had actually erased them as soon I could. The little prick had already told me that he hadn't made copies. In fact, I bawled him out about it. I made him promise me that as soon as he got the tapes back he was going to make copies."

"So, everyone thinks he's crazy?"

"Sure. We all know it's a matter of time before this case makes people crack up, anyway. He was given the case because he was too young and smart and everybody hates him."

"So, how did it go down?"

"O'Brien called him into his office after the transcripts were delivered. O'Brien was pissed. He suggested that the kid had made up his story about you because the kid knew how much O'Brien hated you. Mondragon got real Latin and talked about his honor and made a little ass of himself. He said that he shouldn't have told the Bureau anything, just given them the head of the SK on a silver platter. He would play the tapes for O'Brien himself. He practically ordered O'Brien to get a tape recorder forthwith. Then he marched his little Mexican ass down to his office, where the tapes had been delivered atop his hunk of lodestone. He snatched them up and marched back to O'Brien's office—this is so beautiful: he didn't check them out. O'Brien had got the tape player, since he does really want to catch your butt, and then there was nothing but this hiss. So *I* get called to the office. Did I know anything about these tapes. I identified as coming through my office for a standard transcription, and that they had been delivered back to his office. Mondragon starts yelling that I'm out to sabotage him, and O'Brien tried to get him to calm the fuck down. I'm expecting it will be a day or so before the lodestone comes up, and I am going to promise a full examination of my staff— when Mondragon himself brings it up. He says something about his paperweight. O'Brien asks what the paperweight is, because he's trying to calm Mondragon down, and Mondragon says it's a lodestone. I roll my eyes, while O'Brien points out that data is erased by a magnet. Then O'Brien lashes into me. How could any of my staff be so stupid as to deliver tapes atop a magnet? 'A magnet?' I ask, 'A magnet, sir? We are to be on the lookout for lodestone keepsakes on agents' desks? I'll start a memo right away. I'll also mention looking out for giant incense braziers that might burn paper, and buckets full of acid.' Well O'Brien shuts up and tells me to get out of his office, so I waltz back to my desk. About half an hour later, Mondragon crawls out of the office and heads to his desk. I intercept him to apologize for making things worse for him, and he tells me that he is on administrative leave and asks me what I really think that means for his career. So I take him aside and I make my voice all gentle and low, and explain that A.L. is the first step out of a job. It takes a good six months to fire most federal employees, and that if I were him I would get my résumé tighter now. He wanted to know what would happen to the SK case, and I told him that they would find someone else to make crazy. I explained that the job was the Bureau's way of forcing people to retire by making them crazy. I said if there were something like the *X Files*, this would be it. He asked if I thought it would negatively impact his law enforcement career. I said that he should have no prob if he aimed to be the sheriff of some little city, but that if he intended to work for a larger town they would check with the Bureau and that his employment chances were diminished. I took him down to the cafeteria and got him an iced espresso and a cookie. He asked if I really hadn't heard your voice on the tapes. I told him that I didn't do the transcripts, and that it was possible that some recording flaw had simply screened out your voice. He asked if I knew you. I said we had met while you were with the Bureau. He then asked why you had been assigned the case in the first place. I got real confidential-like and told him that the Bureau just plain doesn't care for Hispanics. I told him to look around the cafeteria. There were some black men like me, and lots of Anglos, but he was the only brown motherfucker here. So he went back to his desk. I saw that he took his lodestone with him, but hasn't quit, at least not yet, anyway."

"But I need him at the Bureau. A live case will produce clues for me."

"They'll get some other schmuck, don't worry."

"No, I need results now. Even Mondragon was apt to undercover something."

"What do you need results now for?"

"I'm just plain sick and tired of the case."

"That's a fucking lie, man. You live for this case. If you ever caught the guy, you would die at having the game over."

"Did Mondragon say where he was going, or anything useful like that?"

"No."

"Can you find out if he used the Bureau's travel agency for a flight?"

"Sure. I can look into that. But it will cost you."

"You'll get your usual fee."

"I am beginning to think that my usual fee is not good enough."

"Tough shit. You don't understand, document boy. I do keep a recording of all of our conversations. That would be on O'Brien's desk tomorrow, with a copy hand-delivered to the *Washington Post*. You can't find out, I don't have anything to lose."

"I could just stop working for you."

"And miss the thrill of having a life through me? You would sell your mom not to be a glorified file clerk. With me, you've got your revenge and I would guess about twenty thousand a year to aid me in ongoing investigation. No, you will remain happy with what you get, and if someone doesn't replace Mondragon very soon, you will not be getting very much."

Fischer hung up. He went into his room. Willis had dozed off.

"So, tell me, Mr. Spencer, what was your wife's first husband like. Was he an older man?"

Spencer woke up. "Why do you ask? Night was older than Virginia but only by a year or two."

"Well, she seems to have run off with an older man, so I need to know about her relationships with older men, with her father, with people radiating authority."

"Virginia did have a problem with that."

"What do you mean *with that*?"

"Letting authoritative men walk all over her. But that's all over. That was why I encouraged her to do the pranks. I figured if she had some role reversals, it might cure her of caving in."

"I'd say she's caved. If I were you, I would worry."

Willis's own worries were different. Maybe he hadn't radiated authority. Maybe the model of a game-of-equals both for and against the world wasn't the right model. When he was seventeen, his mom had caught him playing with a GI Joe long since exiled to the garage. He was ashamed of not having put away childish things.

He was ashamed of lying in bed, ashamed of trusting these men with clues. He would stop listening to them and he *would* get her back.

16 The Helium Monument

Roy Chadwick and Virginia Willis were standing beneath a four-pronged metal sculpture overlooking a pleasant park with two lakes. The park was surrounded by hospitals and doctor's offices. Two less grim buildings stood nearby: one an observatory and the other garden center. The sculpture consisted of three aluminum cylinders joining like the edges of a trihedron and a fourth aiming straight upward above the suggested pyramid. In the niche formed by the three support cylinders was a metallic model of helium. Amarillo, Texas, is the site of the largest storage facility of helium in the world. The wind was chill, it came off the lakes, and the monument seemed strangely futuristic for the city. Virginia couldn't make out Chadwick's purpose in bringing her here. Mainly she wondered if Willis had gotten her message. It had been so slow getting here. The weeks she had to wait before going to Doublesign made this more unreal.

Chadwick looked dapper as always, with a gray suit and an old brown hat with a little feather in it. Her granddad had worn hats like that. They had paused in their sweep north for her to buy clothes at a Lubbock department store. He had so deeply hacked into the credit system, it was clear that money was no longer an object for him. Its only real interest was as a marker that he studied through his data mining, a way to see who bought what, what patterns were out there. He could live on any amount of cash.

He had been carrying a cane since Lubbock. At times she thought he was pretty old and tired, but mostly he kept up his mask. He was deeply worried about something, and compensated by displaying his mastery of arcane knowledge. As a tour guide, he was awesome, his mind full of facts and stories about things they saw on the road. When she realized that it wasn't just some Texas thing with him, that he could rattle off amusing tales and strange anecdotes about pretty much anywhere in the U.S., Canada, and Mexico, she wondered briefly if he was wired to the Web by some invisible machine within him. She just as quickly disposed of this cyberpunk notion. She was surprised that his car didn't have any datalinks associated with it, and that his logging on at the hotel where they stopped seemed a rather simple affair. He had an off-the-shelf laptop, certainly not the best of the line. He didn't seem to have any complicated security protocols going on and used standard servers. He didn't mind her looking over his shoulder, but did say that he wouldn't answer any of her questions until they were finished in Amarillo.

She watched while he had looked at a couple of humor pages and then went to an area of his own. There was some highly dynamic representation of data there, which appeared to be crystalline structures growing and crashing, and he made a very few clicks, which seemed to aid some of the crystals and hurt others, but what surprised her most was not the weird interface, but how little work he seemed to do. Either he needed to do little to effect his changes, or perhaps there was little left for him in the world; each created alternating senses of depression and awe in her. Depression set in at thinking that Chadwick was just plain operating on another level of being and that she and Willis were merely ants that had annoyed him. The awe stemmed from the same basic perception, except that instead of being an annoyed or angry god, perhaps Chadwick was interested in passing the holy fire onto them, or at least to her. She didn't know how she felt about that last thought. She had no intention of leaving Willis; in the long run she'd go back to him, but the possibilities of what this could do fascinated her. In the long run she and Willis had planned on a family, and if she could pass on Chadwick's secrets to them, it would be great. Unless such knowledge came with some sort of damnation. After all, his knowledge and his self-imposed mission had separated him from the world. He hadn't even spoken with a woman since he ditched his fiancée. Her plan with Willis was that this sort of playing with the world was just for fun, a lagniappe that gave another layer of play beyond what their money and investments had brought them. Certainly they had not planned on carrying on with their adventures after having a child. It was one thing to prank some evil old fart every month, another entirely to risk their kid's safety and sanity. What would she eventually tell her son or daughter about this? "Gee, I remember the day in bleak October when I stood at the Medi-Park in Amarillo, Texas, with a genius-madman-killer and looked at a monument to the most common noble gas in the universe. Boy, was that a formative moment for me. Let's see it was October sixteenth, Oscar Wilde's birthday. Oscar once said, 'It is better to build a monument to a noble gas than to no gas at all.' "

Finally Chadwick broke the silence. "Helium," he said, "is a symbol of happiness. It rises up the moment it is made, and if no place is made to collect it, whether a big salt dome like Amarillo has, or a zeppelin, or a child's balloon, it will rise up forever. Now I have studied you and Willis Spencer. You are truly smarter than most people. I don't mean smarter in the book-learning sense—of course, you've got that covered and have learned that those kinds of smarts don't buy happiness or success. I mean that you and he are smart enough to come up with a scheme to be balloons, to have some way to catch your happiness. Few people figure out a method for this, most people may find happiness—Camus is right in his call that happiness is inevitable. You even chose a rather noble way to be a balloon, you try to get the balloon prickers before they can prick too many balloons. You don't know how much it bothers me to intervene. I didn't want to come along and prick your balloon. I have dedicated my whole life to protecting other people's happiness. I am sad to be, in the end, perhaps one of those people that I have struggled against. I don't want you to think that I don't know how unhappy you are that I have taken you away from your husband. I am not unconscious of my actions. I know that what is about to happen is going to be pretty devastating to you, and I know, because I ran simulation after simulation, that it has to happen this way. All I can do is apologize in advance and confess my true state. I chose this weird little monument so you would remember my words, whatever happens."

"Don't your simulations tell you what's going to happen?" asked Virginia. "Aren't you the little know-it-all god?"

"No," he sighed. "I don't know it all. If I knew it all, everything would be good in my actions. I know far too much. I am like a doctor that knows what will happen if the fever is untreated and doesn't stop on its own. I know how little the chance of it stopping there is. I know what a small chance there is that the patient is allergic to penicillin. But that isn't the knowledge of the odds-breaker that the penicillin will kill the patient or that fever would have stopped on its own in an hour. That's the knowledge that I deal with. If I had to do it all over, I doubt I would choose to know what I know. But I do know, and therefore I must act."

The wind had begun to pick up, and Virginia was cold. He had told her to buy a warm coat in Lubbock, and in a silly rebellion she had refused. She didn't want him to see her shiver, and she felt even stupider than before. How dare this old man give her these sententious speeches? He had ruined her life, and now he was trying to make himself feel better. Bastard.

"So, Dr. Chadwick, what is the nature of the cure you are about to perform on me?"

"I am going to have you perform a murder."

"I don't do murder."

"You will. All of my simulations show me that you want to. I know what a really bad life you have had. I know more than you've told Willis, because you are afraid he would leave you or just be plain unable to deal with things. I know you really want to kill somebody. It probably should have been your first husband, but now he's too pathetic for that. What joy could you have in that? Knocking off someone in asylum? My simulations indicate that you probably tried to do it once— can you tell if it is so?"

"I never," she began, and then realized that he might have records of her making the trip to Springfield, actually driving up to the asylum. Maybe he had some way of knowing about the pills, Daddy's heart medicine that she had saved, years ago, if she ever had to kill herself. Maybe his simulations would tell him that was the first time she had ever lied to Willis, the first big lie, the one she knew would kill the marriage, at least before this lie. But he was wrong if he thought she would help him commit a murder. Fuck him and his simulations. They had probably killed him as a human being. You probably died when you ran these things on yourself. It is so hard to make the big choices without help. Most people turned to religion or to their friends, or to pulling Tarot cards, anything to make the choice for you. It was only now as she was freezing her butt off, so many hours from home, that she realized that Chadwick wasn't someone to be admired. He wasn't like them. He had become a killing machine. Now no one mourned his victims; his ideas of saving lives by killing the sources of human misery might even make sense on actuarial tables. The point was he didn't have a choice. She wasn't going to do the killing. She would go along with it and then escape. Or maybe she would kill him—well, not really kill him, but prank him in some way, if she got a chance to find out what he thought was so horrible about her and Willis having the Program. She didn't think of him as crazy. He processed data well enough. He was just like the machines whose company he had chosen over mankind (apparently over womankind, especially). If he thought something bad would happen, he was probably right. She didn't know how much of his power over data she wanted. Perhaps just a taste of it could still leave you happy. She did want to be rich and happy and make her kids rich and happy, and she really wanted to be home, and was already thinking that she couldn't explain any of this to Willis, and that it was probably too late. It was probably too late when she drove to Double-sign, and by now he probably had the car back and was so worried and scared that it was too late, and she didn't want him to think she was just having an adventure, because she knew that he had always thought she would just go off somewhere on an adventure, that she didn't really love him. She loved him. She loved him. She loved him. Why did she fuck things up this way?

She also realized that she had read the speech about happiness before, that it was out of a book, which probably meant that Chadwick got his models of human life from books. It was a good omen, though, considering what she had written to Willis.

Chadwick was just staring at her with his stupid old-man smile. The worst thing that men do to women is stare at them. It makes them self-conscious, assessing their own worth in beams of the man's gaze. It makes them things. It makes them data.

17 Comesee, Texas

It was at breakfast at the Kuntry Kitchen in Doublesign, Texas, that Bobby Fischer's tone changed toward Willis Spencer. Fischer was practically inhaling a plate of chorizo and scrambled eggs, while Willis was trying to make himself swallow oatmeal with brown sugar and raisins. Suddenly Fischer put down his knife and fork.

"I thought you might work as bait, but you didn't, and that is that. I found your car for you, where your wife abandoned it. Just drive your Anglo ass home, If I find her, I'll send her back. I thought you would be useful, but we just got here too late. She's already caved, unless Chadwick has put her in a trunk somewhere. You can go."

"Just like that. This is the help I get from the FBI. You just want me to leave. I'm finding her without you."

"If you don't leave, I'll give you to the local sheriff. I've got the evidence that you were at the crime scene. I can't believe you never even had your car repainted. She parked it at the hotel. It's, what, five blocks from the crime scene with a nice big spot on the right fender where you grazed the library fleeing the murder."

"But you know I didn't kill the old woman. You need me to testify when you catch Chadwick."

Fischer laughed. Then he said, "I don't need you. You are a little weasel-man. I thought I had some use for you, but Chadwick is too quick. He's probably already ruined her. She was no doubt attracted to his party line, and besides, having been cooped up with you for three days, I suspect that he's more fun than you. So, go home, little man, or I'll have your ass in the little jail here."

"You're not the FBI at all. Who the fuck are you?"

"I can prove that you were at the scene of the murder. You couldn't get out of this if you had Jesus Christ as a character witness. That's who the fuck I am."

"I'm going to follow you."

"Then you will learn what a forty-five caliber frangible bullet can do. It could bring down a galloping horse, it could leave quite the hole in you."

"If you're so murderous, why is Chadwick alive?"

"Touché. I've only had two chances to shoot at him, but neither was close enough. Chadwick, however, is a master at avoiding detection. I was able to find you because of some paint on a building. You leave too big a trail. You stumble along like a cow. *Blam!* I make you into hamburger. Go now. I'll pay for your oatmeal. Take your things from our room and drive your little getaway car back to Austin."

Willis went to the hotel room. Fischer seemed to hold all the cards. No, that was mixing metaphors. Which Alice book was cards and which one was chess? Well, either way, it grew curiouser and curiouser. He would have to try to find Virginia on his own. If he tried to follow Fischer, he could only follow him to an airport, or some other place where Fischer would get away, while Willis would be trying to buy a ticket. Virginia could wing it. She was at her best making do with what she had. She was the one who could best handle the unexpected.

Given a minute or two more, she could've handled finding the old woman's body three months ago. Dammit, Fischer was right. Willis was just a minor player, and not very smart. He hadn't even thought to get the car repainted.

He threw his things into the nice old Samsonite briefcase they had scored at a junk shop in Taylor, Texas, and he went down to the car, filled it up, and headed south toward Dallas and ultimately toward Austin. The car smelled dusty.

The first little town south of Doublesign is Comesee. It has three junk stores, a karate academy, an Old Fashioned Kitchen, a drugstore and post office—and some nice old buildings from the turn of the century that haven't had a business in them in twenty years. It's the kind of town you speed through, just as fast as the world itself has left it behind. As he passed through town, a Champagne colored Celica was zooming north. A small dark Hispanic man was driving. He looked at Willis and then, to Willis's amazement, made a 180-degree turn behind him on the highway. Willis put on the gas, but the other car was faster, since its driver was not slowed by surprise. Willis sped up, but soon the Celica was alongside him with the driver signaling him to pull over. The driver showed him some sort of badge.

I'm just screwed, thought Willis. He pulled over, and the other man was right behind him. The other man popped out of his car as soon as it stopped. He was the opposite of Bobby Fischer in many ways—he was dark, small, and very lean. His clothes were newer and less flashy, and he was running up to Willis's window. He said, "Are you Willis Spencer?"

"Yes."

"Do you know where your wife is? I think she may be in danger."

"I have no idea where my wife is, I am sure that she is in danger, and I don't have a clue about who you might be, except some other rude asshole that will get my hopes up."

"I am Bill Mondragon. I doubt that knowing me will get

your hopes up, but I may be able to help with your wife's danger."

"Who are you with?"

"I am, well, I sort of am, with the FBI," said Mondragon.

"And why should I be any more happy to see you than the last guy who claimed to be FBI?"

"The FBI hasn't sent anyone to you. They don't even have your name. The man you interacted with is a dangerous man called Abel Salazar."

"He told me his name was Bobby Fischer."

Mondragon shook his head. "That's so pathetic. When he worked for the Bureau he used to brag to everyone about what a great chess master he was. Nobody would play him because they figured that he would just beat their ass. Finally, one day they got a Russian defector to come by to challenge Salazar. It turns out that he couldn't play for shit. So he has retreated into his fantasies. That makes him dangerous. Where did you last see him?"

"Look, I don't like this guy, but why should I talk to you? What do you mean you are *sort of* with the FBI? I don't think I'm familiar with that rank. Is *sort of* beneath Special Agent?"

"The Bureau pulled me from the case I was working on. They don't like me because I'm going to solve the unsolvable case. I am on vacation without pay, while they think about me. Boy, if that doesn't give you reason to talk with me, I don't know what would. Look I don't know anything about your wife. I know a few things. I know that I was researching a bizarre serial killer. I know that you and your wife and this car were near one of the killings. I know that Salazar is investigating the case, presumably for some rich persons that are paying for his expenses. I know that he went to Austin to check out you and your wife. Did you know your whole neighborhood thinks you're weird? I found out your wife disappeared with this car six days ago. You left with a man answering Salazar's description three days ago. I know you have tons of money, do a little contracting work when you just plain want to, and I know that you and she are a loving couple. The last card is the one I'll win this hand on."

"How do you know we are a loving couple?"

"All your neighbors talk about how you are so often hand-in-hand."

This made Willis feel good. It was the first time he felt good since July 4.

"OK. I saw Salazar in Doublesign, Texas. I had met him in Austin, Texas, and he had hinted that he knew the whereabouts of my wife. He said he needed my help, so I went with him to Doublesign. While we were there, I moped around the hotel room and he got calls on his cell phone. I was a pathetic jerk hoping he could solve things."

"Can you drive me to where he was?"

"I drive. You follow."

"I'll want to talk to you there."

"I may want to talk, I may want to mosey down the road. I'll think about it. Salazar was in a motel called the Lamar, room one-eighteen. If I decide I want to talk to you, I'll hang around the restaurant nearby. But I'm not staying long. It's called—"

"The Kuntry Kitchen," said Mondragon.

"You've been to Doublesign before."

"I only go for the food."

Willis laughed. He began driving to Doublesign. He wanted to talk with Mondragon. He hadn't had any of the sick, worried feeling that he had in dealing with "Bobby Fischer." It's easy to work with someone if you know you're really on your own. Time to put some of those contracting lessons to work. He drove to the Lamar's parking lot; he could see that Fischer's car was gone. He was going to let Mondragon handle it. Willis was through being helpful for a while.

He drove down to the Kuntry Kitchen. He was beginning

to get hungry, the depression that had made him hate his oat-meal was leaving. He felt a little embarrassed about going in. After all, less than an hour ago, he had been yelled at by another man and had slinked out with his tail between his legs. He would wait a few minutes and see if Mondragon would join him.

He looked around the car for something to read. Finding nothing, he started to clean the car, so that he would look purposeful.

He found a brief series of numbers and letters written in the dust on the dashboard. He knew it was Virginia's finger writing, they loved little games like this. He memorized it and then erased it.

Now, if he could just figure out what it meant.

18 Breaking In and Out

It was cold and dark, and the two story house was in a well-to-do older neighborhood. Chadwick actually let her carry the gun. It was much less fun than any of the pranks, and she realized that the stakes were much higher. She had to get away from Chadwick, and she didn't know for sure that he wasn't armed. The break would have to give her plenty of space to run back to Willis. Willis clearly hadn't figured out her message to him, she regretted using a cipher, even a simple one, but she had been afraid Chadwick would inspect her car. Of course, since Chadwick gave the impression that he could figure out most of what you were going to do—ninety-five to ninety-eight percent of most people—it was hard to do anything around him. You either thought he knew and already planned for it, or worse, that he wanted you to do it. She would keep humming that Christmas song about Santa Claus coming to town . . .

Chadwick parked the black Cadillac at the end of the block, near a public park. People used this area as overflow parking whenever they had parties in their homes, there wasn't much park usage on a cold October night. She wished she were back in Austin, where not only was it warm, but the Halloween decorations would already be up. The thought of orange Christmas lights being subverted for Samhain made her giggle, but Chadwick's cold stare quickly ended that. He went over the plan again. He was trying to sound calm, but this first collaborative job clearly unnerved him. That was her hope. Maybe he had his calculations, he didn't have experience of how the human heart actually worked, that being somewhat beyond his Program. The instructions were simple. He had told her that all his jobs were simple. Simple jobs, you walk to them, you do the deed, and you walk away. It was ten-thirty. Their target, Mrs. Hahn, always went to bed after the evening news.

Her attacks on the local population were twofold. The first was simple gossipmongering, usually centering on the bad health of others. If one of her neighbors had a minor surgery coming up, for example, she would contact the neighbor's children and friends to let them know how *very bad* things were. This was all confidential, of course, your mother wouldn't want you to worry, et cetera. The children and friends would drop everything and fly in to see Mom, who was getting her hangnail fixed or whatever. Mom would like the visits, but be a little shaken up about the trouble everybody went to. This usually deeply worried Mom about the real state of her own health. Meanwhile, the children and friends couldn't believe that Mom's trouble was merely the bad hangnail, or whatever, and they'd come to the conclusion that something *really* was wrong with Mom. So they would end every phone call or e-mail with a query about her good health. These queries planted the notion of sickness in Mom's head, and either her denials or her speculations about her growing illness made the kids and acquaintances worry. The kids might even lose their jobs coming to see Mom so often, and Mom would be ready to check into a retirement home long before her time. What made this attack (which Chadwick said was one of the most pernicious he had ever seen), especially bad was that all of her victim-agents had actually thanked her for the information and gave her candies and cards at Christmas time. Mrs. Hahn was still getting candies from families whose father or mother she had knocked off years ago by the power of suggestion.

Her second attack was anonymous. Now Chadwick admitted that he didn't know for one hundred percent certain that she did this one. Someone did, and the Program picked her. Every month on the fifteenth, like clockwork, there were anonymous letters that were mailed from a downtown snorkel box. They were typed on an old manual typewriter, whose lower-case *e* skipped up. They were simple notes like, "Do you wonder why all the wives laughed at you, when your husband took Sally Ballentine home? But I guess you're too slow to put things together." Or "It must be sad to watch your oldest son get so screwed up on drugs." The factual content of these notes was pretty small, and both Virginia and Chadwick suspected that they probably repeated gossip already floating around—since Mrs. Hahn, like most psychic vampires, had no discernible creativity, only cunning. The letters had various effects, some ended marriages, while others merely planted the seeds of suspicion, many grounded kids (and certainly ensured that when the kids escaped Amarillo for college, they didn't return—at least not until Mrs. Hahn called them about their parents illnesses).

Virginia knew that Chadwick had picked such an over-the-top case so that it would be easy to kill her. Virginia did want to pull the trigger. She read the reports that Chadwick had on deaths, divorces, broken families, stress-related illnesses, alcoholisms. The woman was a plague.

He was in full-on lecture mode, and he probably would be until they left the car at 11:00. The question of house defenses came up.

"Most psychic vampires come into sorts of house protection extremes. The most common has defenses out the wazoo—alarms, guns, and connections with guard services. This is because they are aware on some level that they are a menace to society, and that someday the jig will be up. These PVs are not hard to track to their lairs, since they are so used to relying on others. For example, their main line of defense may be a guard service contacted by a silent alarm. Since they believe in the goodness of others, they think the nice people at the alarm company will help them out. They will likewise have talked all of their 'friends' into getting the same service, since spreading paranoia is pretty much a standard tactic for these people. This will give you a good deal of information on the defenses, since most houses in the immediate area will have the same defenses, which usually means finding a single point of failure is not a hard thing to do. The second type of PV, such as our mutual friend Mrs. MacPhearson, is convinced of their moral superiority above all other humans and they feel extremely safe in their lairs. For example, had you and Mr. Spencer merely tried her front door in Doublesign, you would have found it open. I simply walked in quietly during the rockets' red glare. Mrs. Hahn would seem to be in the smaller second camp. She sees all of her poison-spewing as being the Lord's work, and would most likely draw gardening metaphors such as weeding to explain what she does. She probably thinks she is helping out families by exaggerating illnesses of certain members. However, Mrs. Hahn does have something that most PVs don't have—several thousand dollars' worth of precious gems. Mr. Hahn, before he disappeared in Mexico some years ago, was a wealthy jeweler. His greatest joy was trying to find the best gems available for his wife. She would always look at his rare treasures and sigh, 'Oh, another one—like I have any place to wear this.' But after he arranged his disappearance, she fixed up one room of her house like a vault. Here," he pointed to the floor plan, "the back bedroom. It is where all the alarms are, and there are bars on the back windows. I suspect there may be movement-detection alarms in the room as well, but I couldn't find any record of her purchasing them."

Eleven o'clock came and they left the Cadillac. Virginia was glad for the cold night air, but especially for the silence. They walked up to the Hahn house, and Chadwick used a shim on the door. It was open in less than forty-five seconds. They went in.

The front room was quiet and dark (Virginia had seen it that day when she had faked being a seller of magazine subscriptions), and it was furnished by Ethan Allen. They went through it quickly, past the stairs and through the elegant but unused dining room. A light came on in the kitchen and they froze. They were expecting Mrs. Hahn to be asleep in the smaller of the two bedrooms on the first floor. They edged back to the front room. They heard a microwave, which beeped after two eternities (or about three minutes). The light went off in the kitchen. They saw Mrs. Hahn emerge from the kitchen heading toward her bedroom with a teacup. She entered her bedroom and partially closed the door behind her, turning on the light.

"We'll do it now," whispered Chadwick.

"Let's wait until she is asleep," said Virginia.

"No. The longer we wait, the more chance things will go awry. *Now.*"

"OK. But I'm scared you go first."

He walked ahead into the dining room and then into small hallway that connected the two bedrooms to the rest of the house. She was very close behind, carrying the gun. As he passed the open door of the bigger bedroom, she pushed him with all of her might. He fell, and, sure enough, a motion-detector alarm went off. She kicked him all the way in and pulled the door shut after him. As she had seen from the front room when she sold Mrs. Hahn a year's worth of *Cosmopolitan*, there was a lock on the door. She locked it quickly and yelled, "Call 911, you self-righteous bitch. There's a famous killer in your gem room!" Then she bolted.

She had asked Mrs. Hahn about her sleeping habits earlier

that day. Her recommendation that the old woman try a cup of Sleepytime tea about half an hour after going to bed, if she was still restless, seemed to have worked out rather well.

She slipped the gun in her pocket as she ran. She intended to wipe it for prints and ditch it in the public restroom in the park. She was also going to call 911 from there as well, in case Mrs. Hahn failed to follow her recommendation.

She didn't have the keys to the Cadillac, but she didn't want to be associated with it, either. After ditching the gun, she called the police and told them that a serial killer was in Mrs. Hahn's gem room. They wanted to discuss the matter with her—for example, how did she know it was a serial killer—but she felt she should move on.

She took off down Western Street. She had seen a place that sold coffee and doughnuts. She wasn't going to run in looking distraught, calling for a cab. That would be a little too memorable. She went in, had coffee and a couple of doughnuts, watched a couple of police get the call, and when they were gone, she started flirting with the counter guy. When the place closed at 1:00 a.m. he took her home. No sex—well, not really—and she left his house for the airport at eight.

She tried calling Willis from the Dallas airport and then the Austin airport, but he was gone. She took the shuttle home and wondered if her leaving had fucked up things for good.

19 Two Plus Two Plus Two

Willis was waiting for Mondragon at the Shamrock Bar in Doublesign, Texas. He couldn't understand why the barkeep kept asking him questions about the Kennedy assassination. No, he didn't know who the umbrella man was. It could have been Hunt, if he knew or cared who Hunt was. The barkeep pointed at a spittoon on the floor.

"That's my moneymaker. You want to know how?"

"Sure," answered Willis. All he really wanted to know was what did 2N2P2E stand for.

"Well, you see, I git people to bet with me that they don't know how many doors the Shamrock has. They can see a front door and a back door, so they always say 'two' and I say, 'No five. There's the front door, that's one; and the back door, that's two; and the refrigerator door, that's three; and I'm named Isidore, that's four; and that's"—pointing dramatically at the spittoon—"a cuspidor, that's five."

For reasons unknown to modern psychology (for who can truly say where run the roots of man's mind), this weird little performance suddenly freed Willis's mind to know the meaning of the message; unfortunately William Mondragon walked into the bar at the moment. Unfortunate because now Willis had to decide quickly if Mondragon would be of any more use to him than the crazy ex-agent had been. It sounded like Mondragon was well on his way to being an ex-agent himself, and nothing about what was going on suggested to Willis that Mondragon would be keeping his marbles. Hell, Mondragon probably didn't even know how many doors were in this place.

"Hey, Mondragon, come over here," he said.

William Mondragon walked over.

"I don't have any useful news. I found out that a woman resembling your wife left town in black Cadillac, which you and Salazar already knew. I haven't found accounts of such a vehicle being abandoned or any killings that fit the pattern of the SKiller, and nothing to indicate that your wife has interacted with any law enforcement people."

"That's bad. What do we do next?"

"A lot of that depends if she gets a signal to you. Maybe you should've just gone home and I can call you every day."

"Are you a betting man, Mondragon?"

"Sure. Why do you ask?"

"I'll bet you twenty dollars that you don't know how many doors there are in this bar."

"What?"

"Well you're an observant guy. You told me that you were one of the youngest special agents the Bureau has ever had. It's not a hard problem. And you can make twenty bucks." Willis pulled a twenty out of his wallet and laid it on the bar. "You game to try?"

Isidore was grinning hugely and walked to the other end of the bar to serve some local patrons. Willis hoped that he had not told Mondragon about his little game. Mondragon pulled out his twenty and covered Willis's and then walked around the bar carefully. He peered over the bar and checked for cabinets. He checked to see if either the front and back door had screens, and then he walked back to Willis and pulled up a bar stool. "OK, but I get your twenty if you don't know, either."

"OK," said Willis. "How many doors?"

"Three," said Mondragon. "Front, back, and refrigerator. I thought there might be some cabinet doors, but I find that those have been ripped away over the years. I would guess the joke depends on people not noticing the refrigerator door."

"You are wrong, my friend. There are five doors. The front door is one. The back door is two. The refrigerator door, which you were smart enough to spot, is three. Our noble barkeep"— Willis pointed at Isidore, who puffed up with exaggerated pride—"is four and that"—he pointed at the spittoon—"that damn spittoon just cost me twenty bucks."

Isidore almost doubled over laughing. Mondragon looked very concerned and said, "I know this must be rough on you." His gaze kept moving back and forth between the spittoon and Willis.

"No," said Willis. "No. It's funny because that's a spittoon. You see, that's funny."

Mondragon tried to force a little laugh. "Oh. I get it, it's a *spittoon*."

Willis was handing the forty dollars from atop the bar. Mondragon took the money with evident dread.

Willis tried again. "You're a good guy, Mondragon. You see, I was trying to figure out whether to tell you that I had figured out the cipher."

"What cipher?"

"I found a note in the dust of the dashboard of our car. Virginia had written 2N2P2E. I didn't know whether or not to tell you."

Mondragon was still staring at the brass spittoon. He said, "Well, I'm glad you shared that."

"No, it tells me where she is. It's helium," said Willis.

"She's on Mars?" asked Mondragon.

"Mars?"

"Helium, John Carter, warlord of Barsoom?"

Now Willis looked at the spittoon with alarm.

Mondragon said, "Never mind. Kids' books. You were saying helium?"

"Yeah. Two neutrons. Two protons. Two electrons. She's in Amarillo, Texas."

"I was following the subatomic particle list, but you've lost me."

"A few years ago, Virginia and I took an informal class at UT, Classics of Texas Fiction. There were these novels set in Amarillo. *The Cellophane Fawn Trilogy* by D. B. Bowen. Never mind that, the point is that he makes a big deal of the fact that most of the helium in the world is stored in Amarillo, and most of the plutonium, as well. Anyway, for a while we made jokes about Amarillo because we thought that maybe everybody talked like they had just taken a hit off a helium balloon."

"Well, that's very ingenious and all. But did it occur to you that she might have simply written 'Amarillo' or 'Willis, I'm being kidnapped'?"

"She may have been under observation."

"Oh, sure. Writing a description of an atom isn't odd in any way if people are watching you."

"Look, it's all I've got to go on. I am going to head to Amarillo. I've got a car, and I'll feel better grasping at straws."

It takes ten hours to drive from Doublesign to Amarillo. They made Amarillo by morning and were treated to Amarillo's greatest natural resource, a sunrise. It was very different from the busy environs of Austin or the closeness of Doublesign. It was a place where the sky determines so much.

The plopped into a Ramada Inn and got half a day of shuteye. When Willis opened his eyes, Mondragon was already on the phone, very excited.

"Wake up. They caught him."

The police station was downtown. The locals were not as

overawed by the FBI badge as Willis thought they would be. He guessed they would be even less overawed if they knew how close Mondragon was to being fired from the Bureau. He distinctly heard someone say something about a Mexican as they were being escorted to a small interview cell on the fourth floor of the city jail.

The man they had caught gave his name as Brother Juniper, which was a literary reference, but Willis couldn't place it. Apparently, he was a sexagenarian jewel thief. He had no idea why Mondragon thought this was the man.

Willis and Mondragon stepped into the interview cell. The officer told them they needed only to press a red button and he would be back at once. He was clearly contemptuous of the fear that Mondragon seemed to radiate. Brother Juniper was in orange prison fatigues. He looked shrunken and awful, and Willis was immediately embarrassed for him. It was like seeing someone's grandfather in jail for DWI. Brother Juniper had silver hair, old skin, blue eyes, and slight palsy. He looked scared, defeated, and sick.

Mondragon began, "Good afternoon, Mr. Chadwick. I have wanted to meet you for three years."

Chadwick replied, "Good afternoon. I am sure that the pleasure is all yours. You are—let me think, my memory is not as good as it once was—Abel, no, William Mondragon, Special Agent of the FBI, but I don't know your assistant."

Willis began to introduce himself, but Mondragon cut him off. "You're quite the celebrity, you know. It will make my career for having been the one who has caught you."

"Caught me at what? Some local police caught me in the process of trying to stop a jewel thief, an impetuous young woman, who overcame me due to my advanced age. I admit things look bad for me, but my impeccable record as a citizen will set me free. Who could put a doddering old man away for a brief folly?"

Mondragon said, "A doddering old man would scarcely know my name."

"You are wrong, Agent Mondragon. Keeping tabs on the boys of the Bureau is a major hobby of seniors. There are many Web pages about agents, as you no doubt know, although I fear some of them may not be officially sanctioned."

Willis asked, "What about giving the police the name of Brother Juniper?"

Chadwick said, "The narrator of Thornton Wilder's *Bridge of San Luis Rey*. He is interested whether we live by accident and die by accident or live by plan and die by plan. That has been my interest for many years."

Willis understood that this was the man who wrote the Program. A minor point compared to the fact that Virginia had been with him.

Mondragon said, "You are wrong if you think you can walk away from this. My files on you are huge. Even if you were held innocent of every murder we suspect you of, you would still spend the last years of life simply sitting in courtroom after courtroom."

"Well, it will have to wait until the good people of Amarillo can decide whether or not I am a heroic senior citizen, or a hardened jewel thief."

Mondragon said, "You'll be extradited out of this little town in forty-eight hours."

Willis said, "What happened to your—er—accomplice?"

"I didn't have an accomplice. I was merely taking the night air when I saw a woman in a black Halloween wig entering a respectable-looking house at eleven at night. My keen instincts told me that she was up to no good, so I quietly followed along and stepped through the doorway she had left opened. She pulled a gun on me and forced me into a back bedroom, but one which was fortunately wired with motion detectors, which were her undoing. She fled into the illicit night, while the poor widow—whose home we were such unorthodox guests in—indulged in paroxysms of fear and calling the police, who came quickly to her aid. Unfortunately, they had captured me, an honest but foolhardy citizen, but I have great faith in the judicial system to work things out."

"That's the biggest load of bullshit I ever heard," said Mondragon.

"It is but god's honest truth and certainly good newspaper copy" said Chadwick.

"I am going to get you out of here today, and your doddering old man doesn't impress me at all. Sure, you may be old and doddering—I'm sure decades of serial killings really take it out of a guy. I'm going to start the ball rolling now."

Mondragon motioned Willis to step out of the cell.

"Look, I'm going to make some inquiries about extradition. We'll be the ones to move him, and that will give him plenty of chances to talk to us. You go back inside and visit with him for a while. Don't tell him who you are. Just say you're my assistant, what a hard-ass I am to work for, whatever. He needs to trust you."

Willis stepped back inside the interview cell. Chadwick was sitting at the interviewer's side of the table. He reached his hand underneath and touched something.

"You are Willis Spencer. I am afraid I have let things get dangerously out of control. Your wife may be in the hands of my enemies, who are playful, but not like you and she. I can help get her back. You must aid me to escape. Say nothing to indicate you have heard me."

He stepped away from the table and back to his chair. He had remained the old and feeble man that he seemed, yet there was a strange fire in his eyes.

Willis had no trust in this man, but he seemed to be a chess-player rather than a chess piece. Willis knew that he had to move into the player role to protect his queen.

20 Diagonal Capture

What Virginia Spencer wanted most was a hug followed by a warm bath. She had been afraid to bathe while she was with Chadwick. He looked too old and feeble to hurt her, but she couldn't relax enough to take off her clothes. The shuttle dropped her off and she saw Willis's car in the driveway. Hers would still be up in Doublesign. The house looked dark, and her calls had failed to rouse anyone, neither of which gave her much confidence. She didn't know whether she should go on inside. It might simply be time to go to the police. She would take all of the responsibility. The games had been her idea, Willis could have just sat at home night after night, his only big excitement making the Gold Club of the nearby Block-buster video store. He may have thought she deserted him, or perhaps he was doing something heroic and was trying to rescue her. That would be very bad, he was terrible at improvisation and always looked to others for clues. He was born to be a sidekick; although she hid this fact from him at any cost. She had thought that she would deal with the strangeness in Doublesign in a day or two. Now it was a little over a week. He would probably never trust her now.

She had been hesitating in the orange light of sunset at the dragon gate. She thought for a moment that she was being watched and then laughed that off as paranoia. Who was left to watch her? She had been the one responsible for putting Chadwick away. Heck, maybe she was due some sort of reward. He might be on the FBI's Most Wanted list or something, if they were even clever enough to see who he was. He would probably break out of the jail in Amarillo. Somebody who had killed more than three hundred people and not been caught was apt to be fairly resourceful. She went through the gate and up toward her spacious house.

There is a special quiet in homes that are missing someone. A silence that is thicker. It touches your body, especially your ears, and you feel like you can pull it away. But you can't. It's just there, covering everything. The house was a little cool. It had been such a mild October that they hadn't even turned on the heat yet. It was hard to accept what a big state Texas is: that she could be freezing her buns off just yesterday, and know that her neighbors are out for a dip in their unheated pool.

She went to the phone to check her call notes. There weren't any. That meant that Willis had received them. Let's see, she had called from Dallas less than two hours ago. So, where was he? Either he knew she was coming and just split, leaving his car, or he was out with a friend. He couldn't have gone for good since his car was here, so she decided that he was thinking about what to say to her, what to ask her. He was probably in the canyon near the house. He liked to take long walks among the broadcast towers to think.

She could meet him in various ways. She could go wait outside, and be demure and guilty. That would work good unless night fell first. She could be on the Internet, acting like nothing had happened. No, that wasn't a good idea at all. She could be freshly washed and naked and kneeling. Yeah, that might be the best. Even if he was mad, he hadn't had sex in seven days, which was a minor eternity for them. They could talk afterward.

She ran to the black sunken tub in the master bath. She poured out a special blend of oils that included rose, tuberose, vanilla, and myrrh and filled the big tub. She lit two red candles to help her get in the mood. Besides, she wanted the scene partially made up no matter when he came home. She stepped into the warm water and grabbed her loofah. She needed to scrub like crazy to wash off the smell of the airplane, the Cadillac, and the crappy hotels. She hoped the scrubbing didn't spoil the effect.

She wanted to plunge in, but she knew she didn't have time to do her hair. She risked a semisleep just above the waterline, breathing in the heady smells. She really needed to spend the night in here, but that wouldn't be very fair to Willis. She was trying to think of what to say to him. Explain why she ran off, that she thought she was saving him, saving them, saving the little baby girl they wanted in the future. She wished the sensuous herbs held some answers.

She heard the back door open. Oh. He must have been in the back. Sometimes when he was nervous, Willis would do the real scut work of gardening like raking or even building a flower bed. She tried to position herself in the water. He must not have heard the shuttle drop her off at the gate, but their lot was pretty deep, and that was no surprise. He would be coming in here to wash up, so that he could wait for her. It was very important to greet him in low, even tones so that she didn't scare him. Early in their marriage they had played pranks on each other, but they hadn't liked the sense of guardedness that resulted. So they treated each other with exaggerated care and gentleness.

She could hear him making his way through the house. He was checking the phone now. He was seeing if she had called from the airport. God, he was such a sweetie, she really hoped that she hadn't fucked things up.

The door to the master bath opened. In the doorway was a short overweight Hispanic man, clearly surprised to see her and quickly reaching for a shoulder pistol.

"Holy Mother of God, she was right. He didn't keep you." he said.

"Who the hell are you?" she asked.

"I am Bobby Fischer," he said.

"Glad to meet you, I'm Boris Spassky. Now, why the hell are you in my house?" asked Virginia.

"You're very bold for a naked woman. I am here to interview you. I know that until recently you were with Roy Chadwick."

"Where would you be knowing that from?"

"Your husband shared this information with me."

"Do you mind if I get up and get dressed. I am sure my husband will be here soon."

"No. He seems to be on a quest looking for you. I am not expecting him tonight. Now, I have no desire to hurt you, but I am not interested in spending the evening in a long interview. You get dressed, join me in the kitchen, and we'll have a great little chat. By the way, although I am interested in what you may have seen and experienced with Mr. Chadwick, I am not so interested in it that I would hesitate for a moment in shooting you. I am not what you would call an ethical player, I have been in interested in Mr. Chadwick far too long to be at all willing to prolong my investigations."

There was a true tiredness to his tone, and Virginia believed him. He wasn't like Chadwick. Chadwick had been interested in putting forward a certain style; he really wanted to make a connection despite all of the "dangers of his life mission" grandiosity. He stepped out of the room. She wondered if he was gay—her nakedness didn't seem to interest him at all. She decided that she was too tired to try for any heroic escapes, perhaps the easiest path was simply to believe the guy.

She dressed, wishing she had the opportunity to get clean clothes, but decided that would be beyond her host's forbearance. She went in the kitchen. He had pulled one of the chairs away from the chrome and glass table. He gestured with his gun.

"I'm going to handcuff you to the chair. That way I don't have to keep my weapon drawn all the time, and there will be less chance of accident. Please move very slowly as I handcuff you."

Virginia did as she was told.

Bobby Fischer pulled a small recorder form his shirt and placed it in Virginia's lap. "Voice activated." He said, "Say something."

"Something," she said.

He played it back and played with the knobs for a moment.

"OK. Now when did Roy Chadwick contact you?"

"It was nine or ten days ago."

"Method?"

"He sent me a part of my first husband's college paper on pranks."

"Oh, that's good. I mean, how did that make you feel?"

"I was scared. My first husband was a crazy abusive man who hurt me in many ways. The thought that someone else might be working with him or for him scared me."

"Chadwick told you to meet him at the Lamar Hotel in Doublesign. Do you know why he picked Doublesign?"

"My husband and I vacationed there."

"Yes, for the last Fourth of July, where you attracted Chadwick's attention in a novel way. What did Chadwick want with you?"

"I have no idea. To talk, I might guess. He doesn't have many close friends."

"To talk. You want me to believe that one of the most prolific mass murderers in America wanted to chat with you?"

"I am a great conversationalist," she said.

"I am not amused," said Bobby Fischer.

"Well, some people think I am a great conversationalist."

"What did you and he talk about?"

"Chemistry, mainly. We talked about helium. It was his choice of topic, not mine. He may be a great serial killer, but he's a lousy conversationalist."

"Look, I could just shoot you now."

"Yes, you could, but you would miss the good part. You aren't wondering about how he contacted me, you don't care what we talked about, and you aren't interested in what we ate. Get to the stuff that does interest you."

"Where did you go?"

"We went to the town of Amarillo, Texas."

"Why did you go?"

"There was an old woman he wanted killed. He wanted me to kill her."

That produced a reaction.

Fischer asked very slowly, "He . . . wanted . . . you . . . to . . . kill . . . her?"

"Yes, surprised the hell out of me, too."

He sounded like he was in pain. "I've got to make a call. I'll be out there." He pointed to the patio beyond the kitchen window. "So I can see you."

He pulled up the miniblinds for a clear view.

"Hey," she said, "will you get me one of those bottled green teas with honey from the refrigerator?"

He looked at her like she was insane, then went and got the ice tea, opened it, and handed it to her free hand.

"Remember. I can see you. Don't do anything weird."

"I never do anything weird. I am Ms. Normalcy."

As he left to make his call, she was happy to have shaken him up. She had no idea who he could be. He clearly wasn't law enforcement. He said he had interacted with Willis, but that wasn't provable. Perhaps he was flunky for some rival of Chadwick's—someone else who wanted the Program. Maybe he had run his own simulation on the events, but clearly the idea of her being made to kill someone wasn't in the data. She decided to tell him all the rest, but only when and if he happened to ask it. She watched him through the window. He kept shaking his head no at the person on the line.

He turned off his phone and walked back in, clearly a beaten man.

"My employer demands to see you. We must leave now."

21 In Vino Veritas

Willis Spencer and William Mondragon found themselves in a downtown Amarillo bar across from the public library on Fourth. It was called Pages. It was decorated with library kitsch—books on shelves, posters reading BOOKS FALL OPEN AND YOU FALL IN. and READ ANY GOOD BOOKS LATELY? A few of the specialty drinks had bookish names like Nonfiction Martini (Pernod, vodka, vermouth), Pulp Fiction (sloe gin and Everclear), Sci Fi Martini (vodka and kumquat liqueur), and so forth. There were green ceramic bookworms, and bespectacled professor owls, and other symbols of the book-filled life. Despite the lofty tone of the joint, Willis could see only an average just-getting-off-work crowd. A couple of small truck drivers having a beer or two before they went back to their dock and closed for the day. A pair of female clerks from a city office fighting off loneliness by downing a couple of stiff drinks before a night of TV, an older man avoiding some horror at home that a couple of Nonfiction Martinis would give him the courage to face. No one seemed to look at the books, nor did conversations become literary; in fact, the conversations didn't even drown out the roar of *Wheel of Fortune*.

Mondragon, on the other hand, had misgivings neither

about the bar nor about anything in his life. He ordered Shiners for both of them.

"We got him. We finally nailed him," said Mondragon.

"That doesn't do a damn thing for me—I didn't get Virginia back," said Willis.

"I'll get her back."

"Look, this isn't helping. You got what you want, and you won't have the energy or the time. You aren't any different from that other guy. You're just a hunting animal."

Mondragon took a big pull on his beer. "No," he said. "That's just not true, and I highly resent your saying that. Salazar just wanted you as bait or something. I joined the Bureau to help people, and I will be sure to get your wife back."

"Probably in a goddamned body bag."

"No, that isn't his style."

"Then where's my wife?"

"Well, judging from Mrs. Hahn's story, your wife fled the scene after tricking Chadwick into that weird bedroom of hers. Hell, I've seen many penal institutions that don't have the security that place has. I wish I knew how your wife knew to do that. My instincts as a law enforcement officer tell me she's just hiding out, probably at a homeless shelter or something. You're still calling home for her, right?"

"Every four hours after we saw Chadwick—not a peep."

"She's around, what could happen to her?"

"Did Chadwick have any enemies?"

"Well, that's interesting. You wouldn't think so. As the SKiller, he only picked on people without roots who cause more than their share of human misery. You wouldn't really think that anyone would spend any energy gunning for them, except for people like me, who are hired to. But I know that Salazar must have some kind of patron because he spends a lot of money on the case, and we can't seem to find any source of income. So, somebody hates Chadwick."

"Maybe they're just jealous. I mean, Chadwick is sort of

the Napoleon of crime, you keep telling me—although I find it hard to believe that that pathetic old man in the cell could be the Napoleon of anything."

"Don't be fooled. He has eluded our best and brightest." During this exchange Mondragon had continued to buy beers for the two of them. Willis wasn't finishing his, but Mondragon sucked them down. There was something wrong here, but Willis couldn't figure it out. Mondragon should have been the happiest man alive: he had, after all, captured the guy the Bureau thought was uncatchable.

Willis asked, "Does your leave status put you in trouble with the Bureau? Does it matter for the extradition thing?"

"No," said Mondragon. "This is the kind of thing that Bureau legends are made of. A guy bucking the system (but only so much) does what nobody else can do. My name will be remembered forever."

"What you really mean is that you will be remembered as the guy that came along later and picked up the SKiller after my wife had imprisoned him in a feat of smarts and daring."

Mondragon killed a bottle in one long draw and ordered a Nonfiction Martini. "That," he said, "is exactly what I mean. Did you know the Bureau has lost six agents going after this guy. Five men. One woman. I'm not stupid. Not a stupid greaser, like some of them think. After they lost the first two agents—and when I say lost, I mean lost to lunacy, no one has died investigating the greatest killer in America—the Bureau only picks guys they want to run off. They picked Salazar because he was into conspiracy theories and cover-ups. It's a damn shame that he spent so little time with Isidore, they would have gotten along famously. The woman before him was a tad too aggressive in feminist issues than a special agent is supposed to be, so she was assigned the case. 'It's been too tough for our men to handle.' She met Chadwick. He simply convinced her that he was right—that there exists a small group of people who just plain deserve to die. She thought the only error in his thinking was deciding that it was a small group of people."

"Well, they won't run you off now."

"Won't they? I'll be on Domestic Terrorism when I get reinstated. I'll be driving to farm after farm and asking, 'Did you buy that ammonia nitrate fertilizer for your obvious fields of rutabagas, or are you going to blow up a federal building?' Then I listen to them about how the damn *gubment* is on their backs and they can't even fertilize their crops anymore without some suit from Washington showing up, and meanwhile I am sitting there thinking, 'Well if they weren't going to blow up a government building before, they're going to now.' And I fill a simple form that I saw the rutabagas and I drive another twenty miles to talk to the next farmer."

"But you feel that it will be worse this time."

"Of course. I look like an idiot."

"Is that why you aren't helping find my wife?"

"No, in addition to really wanting to find your wife—if I fail at that, look how incompetent that would leave me looking. Gee, this woman can solve the case and I can't even help her and you out enough to get you back together. There is no credit going on here. You figured out she would be in Amarillo. Chadwick was able to figure out that you and she had been in Doublesign, which Salazar had figured as well—and it was him who gave me enough clues to find you. I didn't even know that she was with Chadwick. Salazar figured that out. What have I done in this big high-profile case? I show up a little too late, and smarter people hand things to me. People not even in the fucking Bureau hand things to me. Smart Anglos hand things to me. You know, a few weeks ago, I thought people in the Bureau hated me because I was smarter than them. I was great at the Academy, I moved through the system fast. I did some good work on tracking stolen goods. But no. They hated me because I am pathetic. I don't know anything. I was put where I was put because I am a screwup. You know, that was why they put me on leave. I am a screwup, I kept a big whopping magnet on my desk that erased all my evidence so far. No backups, no nothing. Wouldn't you let someone go who can't think to make a simple backup? This isn't my ticket to success, it's my ticket to failure. Pretty ironic, isn't it? When I first got this case I thought it was my real opportunity, my chance to make it big. Then this little faggot John Tyrell explained to me what should've been blinding obvious, that the SKiller case was a way to run people off. You know what John does? He runs the document center for christsakes. He is cluing me, the smart guy, into how the cow ate the cabbage. I was rude to him and he got me back later. Why? Because I am arrogant and stupid, a dangerous combination."

"That's great, you're sitting here feeling sorry for yourself, and my wife might be dead somewhere."

"She isn't dead somewhere. She fled the scene. She's too smart to be dead. She's probably the smartest person in this. She's smarter than you, she picks winners to be with. You got two nuts from the Bureau."

"Like you said, you're going to be a total loser unless you can help me find her. You've got to come back to Austin with me."

"No, Chadwick is being extradited. He's wanted for four murders in New Orleans. They want him real bad, and I made sure they found out about it first. I am going to take him there tomorrow. You go home to Austin, and contact the local police. I'll be free in a few days, and can come see you, but I tell you that she will long have been free."

"You are a dick. Transporting a prisoner isn't a glamour job. Look, if you want to get your rep back, you've got to at least make sure the woman who caught the SKiller is OK. Someone from New Orleans will handle the transportation. You've got to help me."

"I won't help you with your wife."

"That was the same goddamn attitude of Salazar. Jeez, you

guys are the same. I tell you what: if I help you get the reputation you deserve, will you make sure that finding my wife is the number-one priority?"

"How could you help me?"

"Simple, I make you the man who catches the SKiller."

"He's already been caught, haven't you been paying attention?"

"So, he escapes, and after Virginia is safely back in our home, you catch him again."

"What makes you think he will escape?"

"We will help him."

"I'm not really in the business of helping serial killers escape."

"Think of it as a hobby. Besides, if you don't fulfill your dream of being the capturer, you know what the rest of your career would be like."

"But you can't guarantee that you can capture him."

"*Au contraire*, I've got two things you don't have. I know how he picks his victims, and once Virginia is back, I've got the only person who's ever caught the SKiller."

"But that doesn't help me look better."

"Mum's the word on our aid, man. All I want is my wife back, and I'm not driving back to an empty house in Austin."

"How could we do it?"

Willis began telling Mondragon his plan.

22 Salazar Shows Fear

This trip made the mild discomfort of being with Chadwick into a memory of heaven. Virginia was gagged, blindfolded, handcuffed, and placed in a sitting position in the back of a van. She knew they were heading north, because it was getting colder. Fischer had lost all of his cockiness. He apologized profusely the first night about the way he was transporting her. He had parked in the woods and he allowed her to relieve herself at gunpoint. He said it would be another two days before the trip would be over. He said he had never done things like this before. Murder was OK in his book, but not kidnapping. He let her lie down during the night, while he slept. She kept losing herself in memory. Sometimes she was hiding in the closet from her drunken daddy, sometimes she was back at Anthony's. She trembled all the time. Occasionally she whined; Fischer begged her to shut up.

The second night, Fischer asked her if she would be a good girl. He was going to let her stay out of the cuffs for a while. She nodded. He gave her a crappy red sports drink. It was freezing cold, and she had heard him stop at some truck stop to buy it. She wanted to be smart, to use her brains, but he had taken them away. Mainly she wanted something hot and a chance to stretch. At least somebody wanted her alive. Given her years with Anthony, this didn't make her feel any better. There is alive and alive.

She asked him, "Where are we?"

"I think Ohio. If not, almost in Ohio." Fischer replied.

She hadn't expected an answer, but she had to get him talking.

"Do you have to do this to me? I could just sit beside you. You've got the gun."

"I don't like doing this, Mrs. Spencer. But I have my orders."

"How would anyone know about your orders? Hell, I could help you drive—you look pretty beat." She lost it then and giggled at her own manipulativeness—she looked like death warmed over and she was trying to get this guy to let her drive. Jinny, you are a silly!

"My employer would know. She has ways of knowing things."

"You don't sound very happy working for him."

"It's a her."

"You don't sound very happy working for her."

"She lets me be me. She allows me to do anything I want and makes sure I don't get in trouble for it."

"She sounds like supermom. My mom was that way for me," said Virginia.

"She is my mother. I don't mean that literally, but she saved me, and cared for me and makes all the bad things go away," said Fischer.

"I need for someone to make the bad things go away."

"I know and I'm really, really sorry. There is nothing worse than being trapped against your will."

Virginia smiled a little. This pathetic little pudgeball was about to tell her how trapped he was. He didn't know anything. He had never been trapped and he was going to use the trivial sufferings of his life as an excuse to have them freezing their asses off in Buckeye country. She would make him talk, though. She could get anybody to talk.

"You've been trapped pretty often, haven't you?"

"I am trapped by having a superior mind in a world of mental pygmies. In school I was the only Chicano kid who did good. I went to school in a little Texas town, Thalia. There weren't many Chicanos, and the ones that were there revolted against the trap by being a stupid gang that the gringos just beat the shit out of occasionally. You know how hick Thalia was? They thought the kids from Wichita Falls were the arbiters of cool. My first trap was wanting to get a job that could make them scared. The only thing that made those bastards scared was a badge, so I wanted a fucking badge. It had to be a big badge, so I went into the FBI. That's the biggest fucking badge there is, Efrem Zimbalist Jr. and David Duchovny."

Virginia was flexing all of her muscles and thanking the goddess for taking those Tai Chi classes. Some of her brain was coming back. She asked for another sports drink—one which had guarana and gingko biloba. Why did the bastard buy cold drinks in winter? He was well off on his story. He must spend a lot of time alone—such people always have well-researched stories. She wondered if he were a superspecies of the psychic vampire. Please just let him show his button to her.

"But the FBI didn't help. All of my jobs were dealing with other Hispanics. I worked inner city crime, drug trafficking, immigration related issues, smuggling—you name it. I was made to scare the few people like me with brains and will. Now, mainly, they had will, because crooks with real brains never get caught as long as they don't get greedy. So I was actually an extension of the same forces I hated growing up. I tried to be political. I supported *la raza*. I helped out where I could—I supported local marijuana growers in the valley against the cocaine dealers from Mexico, who wanted to move in."

"This all sounds noble, but a little odd. I've got to go pee again."

He watched her less while she relieved herself. Her big goal for the next day was to get along without the gag. She would have to break his model of the omniscient employer.

She pulled up her blue jeans. He began talking right afterward as though this were the most normal of human interactions.

"It didn't really help. It didn't help them. It didn't help me. I was further and further from my desire to play with those poor dumb white kids from my hometown. I had to intellectualize my desire to get back at them for treating me so bad. They raped my sister, did you know that? No help from the dumb-ass sheriff. All little Mexican girls are whores."

"So, why didn't you target them? The badge is a pretty strong wall to stand behind."

She knew she had to be careful. She didn't want to identify with him. She needed to make him identify with *her*. Her only hope with him was to convince him that she was the only sympathetic listener.

"Because I was busy and timid about losing the badge I had worked so hard to get. You don't throw away eight years of your life on a whim. You've got to be sure it is the deepest of rivers."

"But you threw it away. You're pretty clearly not with the FBI now."

"No, I didn't throw it away. I lost my mind and my employer found me. I don't even have a rebellion to be proud of. You can't be very fucking proud of a breakdown."

This news wasn't as reassuring to Virginia. His voice had gone up at least half an octave, and he was pulling at his hands with a certain amount of violence. Careful, girl, don't let him get too roused up. Better not offer any more criticism.

"How did you start working on the Chadwick case?" she asked.

"The woman that worked before me on the case was the fifth agent to try his hand. All the others had been guys. Her name was Suzanne Wilson. She wasn't well liked. She was trying to inject some feminist theory into the Bureau, much as I was doing the Hispanic thing. We talked about it some, she was very sympathetic. She told me about the SKiller case. She thought that if she could figure the guy out, it would really help the position of women in the Bureau. You know—do what no man had done. But she came across the one big problem: she couldn't figure out where he would strike next. She studied case after case, trying to figure out the big question. She began studying the victims. She came to the conclusion that the guy was doing a big service to mankind. She decided that her ex-husband was a perfect example of the type of man who should die, except the SKiller was too merciful—he never killed anybody with connections—like living relatives. After a while she just took to sitting in her office thinking. I got transferred to Houston, so I lost touch. She decided that the problem with the world was not that there was this crazed serial killer out there, but that he just wasn't killing enough. It was all classic stuff—she had notebooks full of her plans, an apartment full of ammo, and then one day, she takes an assault rifle with her. She leaves it in her car, and when she goes to lunch she drives to the Mall and starts killing people."

"Wait—I remember that. There was a terrible scandal when it was discovered that she was an FBI agent, and that the rifle belonged to the FBI."

"It cost us lots of funding and was the beginning of my damnation. You see, I begged to be put on the case. I wanted it more than anything. My supervisor told me to lay off. He said that five agents had lost it trying to solve this one, and the last one had her head blown off by the Secret Service— on national TV no less. She became a sort of icon for various militia movements, and I can't even begin to guess how many antigovernment Web pages have pictures of her head being splattered. He warned me not to take the case. They wanted to close it, make it go away. They weren't even sure that the guy existed. Maybe he was a sort of demon summoned out of the massed minds of agents—a crook too smart to catch. The more warnings I heard, the more I wanted it. I would be the one. I would break the code. Me. This would be my ticket out of my trap. You know, I could write a book about it, there would be a movie, I could lecture, I could put any spin I wanted, I could finally push around the white trash that had pushed me around. It was all and everything. So after months of e-mails and calls, I got it. It came in the form of four big file boxes just waiting on my desk one day. My fellow agents even gave me a 'going loony' party. But I believed that this was it. Say, do you want anything more to eat?"

"I would kill for a microwave burrito."

He tied her up again, put her in the van, and set off on foot, inanely telling her to "wait right there." He was gone for about half an hour. She had never been so scared. What if he didn't come back? She would have laughed with the irony of waiting in the dark worrying about her captor, except it was cold and all the noises of the forest got so much louder. She wished she knew what time it was. She wished she wasn't bound in so uncomfortable a position. She wished she knew where the hell she was. She wished that Willis at least knew she was alive. She wished she were dead.

She smelled the burritos almost as soon as she heard him coming and the gag went nasty with saliva. He hadn't given her any solid food. She whimpered as he took what seemed to be an eternity to untie her, and she tore into the burritos like they were ambrosia. She didn't hear much of his story. The three burritos were the kind of food she wouldn't have eaten on a bet a week ago.

"I guessed his killings had something to do with chaos theory. But I couldn't grasp it. I read all the popular books on the subject—you know, like Kirsten Munchower, but I didn't get it. I tried asking the Bureau mathematicians, but they didn't help out. It was too tough for me. I had my one chance out of my trap, and someone smarter than me was laughing on the other side. I got a clue once, though. I went to a popular math lecture and this man described cities as vast 'computational arrays.' I knew then the city was the equation that the SKiller used. I knew that all I had to do was see the city as a bigger than average chessboard, and that mathematicians already knew this—but they were just fucking with me. They knew and they were covering up. That's when I walked out of the Bureau. I wasn't going to find anything. Zero equals zero."

"That's a pretty understandable frustration," Virginia said between bites, "I wouldn't call that losing your mind."

She, of course, actually thought he was bug-fuck crazy.

"That wasn't when I lost my mind. That came later. I am tired. I'll tell you tomorrow night."

With that her Scheherazade let her wash her mouth out and put in the wet gag. He, of course, had a coat—something she thought about a great deal that freezing night as he snored in the front of the van.

23 Aiding and Abetting

The restroom was cold, badly lit, and it stank. Willis's hands bled from the screwdriver slipping and making his hands tear against the grimy plaster around the window. He had about ten minutes to make a big enough opening for Chadwick to slip through. At least eight of those minutes were gone. Of course, it all depended on whether or not Mondragon had convinced the Louisiana State Troopers that the restaurant of choice to stop at on the way to New Orleans from Amarillo was the Barras Grill in Gilliam, Oklahoma. Mondragon had remembered four things about the restaurant. It had great burgers. It had fried rattlesnake tenders. It was on the route the troopers were taking, and it had big windows in the restroom.

The restrooms were behind the grill shared with the Chevron station, which was the major industry in Gilliam. Mondragon had hung a hand-lettered sign reading *Out of Order Use Women's* over the men's room door about ten minutes ago. He was watching for the troopers to drive up, while Willis was knocking the window out of the frame as quietly as he could. Mondragon was on the other side, ready to run interference if he had to. They were both sure of two things: Chadwick was an old man, and old men have to pee a lot. The window was three quarters done. Mondragon whispered into the cracks—"Go ahead and push, we've got to risk the noise."

Willis pushed and the window tore out. The pane fell on the asphalt outside and shattered. It seemed like the loudest sound that Willis had ever heard. But no one came running. Willis damn near pissed himself.

The saving grace that allowed them to get here was bureaucracy. It takes about four hours for a prisoner to be released. Since Mondragon had nothing to do with the capture, he could leave as soon as he wanted. He had never introduced Willis, so if the Amarillo cops remembered him at all it would be as some sort of assistant, or perhaps a witness who could identify Chadwick. Mondragon had visited with the troopers briefly, long enough to comment on their route and the restaurant. Not a smart thing, really. They might remember that the restaurant had been suggested to them. This was where the pumpkin-head mask came in.

The first thing that Willis and Mondragon had done was stop in a gag shop and buy a cheap Halloween costume for Willis. It was a big pumpkin-headed mask and black cape. If the troopers accompanied Chadwick into the restroom, he was to jump from out of a stall, pull a gun on them and order them into the stall. As soon as the smell of cheap plastic filled Willis's nostrils, he was in his element. He had made it a game, and now he felt in control. Even if the troopers shot him he would die as himself.

Willis and Mondragon knew that the troopers had told their dispatcher that they would be stopping at the grill, so Mondragon's part of the plan had been excellent.

It was the day before Halloween and unseasonably cold, the flip side of the warm fall that had preceded the millennium. Willis needed to pee pretty bad himself. He asked Mondragon if he could pee. Mondragon stood at the open window. Willis's car was just beyond, hidden from the highway by the Chevron station. Mondragon looked at him with disbelief, and then said, "Hurry, dickwad!"

Willis pulled it out and saw the steam rise as he watered the urinal. He saw himself in the mirror and jumped at the pumpkin-headed man. He was supposed to be the Headless Horseman, which was the oldest prank in America. He doubted that either of the troopers were, in fact, named Ichabod Crane. He finished his duty and hid himself in the stall.

He had called home several times looking for Virginia, he had called her mom and her friends in Austin. He told them that he and Virginia had had a fight and that she had gone off in a huff and that he wanted to know was that she was OK. Mondragon said he had put in a missing persons report for her, but he didn't believe him. He didn't believe in anyone associated with this business.

Mondragon *might* be helping him out. He seemed a nice enough guy, but if he saw some advantage in lying, he would do it. Hell, he had lied *to* Mondragon as far as that goes. He hadn't told him that freeing Chadwick was Chadwick's idea.

The oddest thing was that he believed *Chadwick*, the serial murderer with the greatest number of kills in human history. It had to be his respect for Chadwick as programmer. Willis could never have made the Program, certainly not in a clumsy stone age language like COBOL. There seemed to be some genuine desire to help people there.

Mondragon stage-whispered to him, "Act like you're using the john!"

Willis dropped his pants and sat on the dirty toilet. He could hear the wind whistle as the door was opened. He heard a man go to the urinal, and then flush a minute later. The guy washed his hands and pulled at the spooled towel. He wished he had some way of watching. The guy went out. Willis could hear him talking.

"It's colder than a son of a bitch in there. The window's been knocked out."

"Can we let the old fart go in there?"

"His legs are manacled. What's he going to do, fly out the window?"

"Was there anybody in there?"

"I didn't see anybody."

Things were looking up. Willis pulled up his pants and stood on the toilet seat so that no telltale legs showed from beneath the stall door. He pulled the door (by the coat hook) to block himself from sight.

The outside door opened again, and he heard someone shuffle in. The shuffle made its way to the toilet. Willis carefully pushed his door open a little so he could see the figure of Chadwick relieving himself.

He whispered, "Mr. Chadwick, don't be scared. I'm here!"

The old man didn't acknowledge the whisper.

"Mr. Chadwick, we don't have much time."

Of course, the old man was hard of hearing. Willis stepped up behind him and put his hand over the old guy's mouth. He turned Chadwick to him and whispered, "We've got to go now."

Confronted with the pumpkin-headed man, Chadwick fainted. Willis almost dropped him, but got a good hold on the belt buckle. He hauled Chadwick toward the window, not an easy task, despite the old man's light weight. He stuck Chadwick's head out the window and Mondragon pulled on it while he lifted Chadwick's feet. The old man was out with a *thump*, and Willis followed, his black cape snagging on the window as he fell out. He and Mondragon were running toward the car. The back was open, and they pretty much threw the old man into the backseat. They closed the door quietly and Willis was behind the wheel in an instant.

Willis pulled out onto a residential street that ran behind the station. He took quick turns and went into the parking lot of Compton's Pay and Save.

"Take the goddamn mask off," said Mondragon. "Stick with our plan."

Willis pulled off the mask. "With any luck, they'll think Zorro did it."

Mondragon flashed him a look of disgust. "Now, you stay here. They'll check out the immediate area, but since he can't run, the next thing they'll do is head for the highway. I am going to go inside and be buying Coke, and see whichever way they take off. We'll go the same way, because they'll get the locals to set up a roadblock on the way back. In the meantime, see if you can wake up grandpa, here. What did you do to him anyway?"

"I scared him, I guess."

"Oh, great. The big-time serial killer of, well, forever and you scare him. You better hope that you didn't give him a coronary. You and your damn mask that would startle the troopers into inaction. Get the bolt cutters out of the trunk."

Willis got the pair of bolt cutters. Virginia and he had bought them years ago working a prank that required them to cut through a lock and enter an abandoned carnival, and they had been so dang useful that they always carried them. Their handles were over a yard long and bright yellow. No one seemed to be watching him from the house behind the Pay and Save, but no stealth was possible at this moment. He snapped the connected chain for Chadwick's manacles. Chadwick was, at least, still breathing.

He put the mask in the Dumpster and began shaking Chadwick.

"Oh, god, it was you. Are you crazy? You could have scared me to death," wheezed Chadwick.

"Yes. It's me. We need to get moving as soon as the troopers leave. Where do you think my wife is?" asked Willis.

"Well, if my calculations are correct, there was a small chance that she might elude me and fall into the hands of my pursuers. Since that has happened, all I have to do is get to my machine and figure out where my pursuers are."

"You mean, you don't fucking know?"

"I haven't been sure if they are still active. I only have glimpsed their activity by deduction. Many of the people who have investigated me seem to have come to either a bad state or received unexpected money in their lives, therefore I deduce that someone is after me."

"You've never bothered to figure out who?"

"I knew as long as my method of target selection was unknown to them, I couldn't be tracked. I figured they would get me sometime by random chance, but as I got older, I tended to feel a bit invulnerable. But don't worry, my calculations are very plain on the idea that if you help me I will find your wife before they are able to get anything out of her that could endanger the Program."

"Why should I trust your calculations?"

"I predicted you being here. What are the odds of that? I'll admit I hadn't expanded my Program enough when you showed up in Doublesign, but I'm sure of things now. Except for small places where free will may warp things. I'm ready."

Mondragon came from the front of the store.

"They're on their way back to Amarillo, so we can go south."

Chadwick looked scared.

"What's he doing here?" he asked.

24 Salazar's Halloween Tale

He had not made the bonds as tight, but the gag was worse—cold and nasty. There was a lot more speeding up and slowing down, and many more turns. He cursed in Spanish a lot, mainly maledictions regarding the ancestry of other drivers or their incestuous habits. Virginia guessed they were heading toward New York or Washington. She tried to calculate how long it would take to drive to Washington, and they should already have been there. Her bladder was full and every muscle in her leg and back ached. She wondered how long before she would just want to die. She went over and over his story for some useful pattern, something she could turn to her advantage, but it was the usual "Poor, poor pitiful me!" The only other constant was fear of his employer, a powerful woman. There was sadness about his sister's rape, which might be some key there, but probably not one she could develop in a night.

She thought about Willis. Where was he? How was he? All she really hoped for was that he didn't blame himself for her disappearance. Perhaps she asked for it, by just playing with people—maybe that put her (and Willis) in some category of people that could be played with. Maybe the minute you wandered beyond the place with rules, vultures like this swept down on you. Pitiful creatures that are themselves prey.

She cried a lot.

Sometimes she was numb and black and still and she wasn't there at all, but the van would saw or a truck would pass and she could hear it, or he would curse some construction on the road.

It was getting colder. He had apologized that the heating in the van didn't work.

Fortunately, he pulled off the road almost as soon as it got dark. He had been promising to do so for an hour. He had bought food at some roadside place a few miles back. She smelled chicken.

When he pulled over, he said. "I'm going to give you more freedom tonight, because this might be your last night alive. But please remember, I am under orders and I won't hesitate to shoot you, if you should try to escape. Nod your head if you understand."

She nodded. She wouldn't try to escape. Even if she had the chance in her fatigued state, in the cold she couldn't make it very far. The cramps in her legs were so bad, she doubted that she could walk very well.

He took out the gag first, then pulled off her blindfold.

"Happy Halloween!" he cried. He had bought a bucket of chicken and a bag of trick-or-treat candy. There were fixings with chicken and soda, coffee and tea. It was a macabre attempt at a last supper. She knew she had to sound grateful.

"Wow! What a spread. Macaroni and cheese, my favorite! That's really nice," said Virginia.

"I am glad you like it. I wanted you to have something nice." Fischer said as he loosened her bonds.

She began flexing the pain out of her hands, so she wouldn't be too clumsy to use the plastic knives and sporks.

"Happy Halloween," she said.

"I always eat this when I am on the road."

"Do you have to travel much?"

"Thankfully, no. When I was younger I loved it, but you get older you want to stay at home. That was why I was always amazed at Chadwick, that he could still do it. I think I would have given it up years ago."

"Do you see chasing him as the rest of your career path?"

"No. Once I hand him over to my boss, I'm a totally free man. The boss just wants him bad, and she will pay through the nose for him."

"Why does she want him?"

"I don't know."

"But you must have guessed."

"I think she is either a victim that lived, or perhaps a relative that he didn't know about. He couldn't have been perfect. Didn't some of your pranks screw up?"

"Sure. There were a couple of close calls."

"You want to tell me about them?"

"Not tonight. Tonight is your night, you left me with such a great cliffhanger last night."

"Oh, thanks. I tried." He smiled like a schoolboy that had just been told he was particularly clever.

"Say, do you really think tonight will be my last night?" she asked.

He hung his head. "I don't know, but I would guess so."

"Well, could you tell me your real name?"

"I am not supposed to, but my real name is Abel Salazar."

"Like the film star?"

"You watch those crappy movies?"

"I loved Mexican black-and-white horror films. They were Saturday matinees when I was a kid. You any relation?"

"Not that I know of. Gee, you're the first Anglo I've ever talked to that recognized the name."

"Well, I may be a little different from most Anglos."

"I already know that, ma'am. I sure wish I had met someone like you when I was young enough to take a wife."

"You can't be that old now. How old are you? Forty, forty-two?"

"I'm forty-eight."

Jeez, she thought. She would have guessed fifty-five.

"See," said Virginia. "You're young enough to marry. It's probably hard to meet girls when you live an underground life chasing a supergenius serial killer."

"I've thought of calling Dr. Laura for advice."

"Well, you know, honey, what you should do is join a church and go to their Christian Singles class. Then someone would call in later and tell you that you can meet nice people at the grocery store on the vegetable aisle. Then Dr. Laura will tell you not to try bars, and above all don't try to meet people on-line."

Salazar laughed and Virginia laughed with him.

"Now, you were going to tell me the rest of your story," said Virginia.

"After I walked out of the office, I just drove until I was tired. Houston is a big city, and I drove around and around. I didn't want to go home because I knew there would be agents waiting for me there. The Bureau picks up its own and gets them squirreled away as quick as they can. I found a hotel, rented a room, and just checked myself and cried. I cried for three days. I realized that I had thrown my career away. Maybe if I was lucky I could become some sort of security guard. I had worked so hard and I just threw it away. All I did was order room service and cry. I didn't have shit, no girlfriend, no real friends—just contacts—I didn't own my house, I didn't have any transferable skills. I had just fucked myself up. On the third day I rose, and went to the lobby. I had meant to drive home and face the music—maybe the free treatment they would give me would help, but I just collapsed in the lobby. Then he came in."

"Who?"

"Chadwick."

"He told me he hadn't interacted with anybody for years."

"Look, he's full of shit. Don't buy any of his stories—he just likes to bullshit. He came in and sat down across from my chair. Of course, I didn't know who he was. This old Anglo just started talking about how sorry he was and how he knew that this case must be too tough for law enforcement, and how law enforcement was for the good of society and so forth. I was so zoned out, I didn't even know he was talking to me. I mean, I bet he rambled on for ten—maybe fifteen minutes, before I even bothered to pay attention, I was so depressed. Then I got it. He was the SK! He was just sitting there, all I had to do was get up and grab him. I could undo all of my problems. He smiled at me and gestured at his lap. Of course, the fucker had a piece trained on me the whole time. I could see its barrel poking out from beneath his coat. He was just playing with me. He asked me how long I thought it would be before the Bureau caught him. I told him I had no idea, but that was what they wanted more than anything. 'Well, don't take too long. I'm getting pretty tired of this.' He wanted to be caught. I told him if he really wanted to be caught he had to reveal his victim selection method. 'Oh, no, I can't do that,' he says. I completely hate the guy at this point, do you follow? I am thinking that I am going to risk his bullet, and then it hits me. How the hell does he know I was here? 'Your credit card. I was just waiting for you to use it.' The Bureau tracks stuff like that, but it has to wait for the companies to provide the information. This guy had to be hardwired into the system. I knew then he was some kind of computer guy, somehow the Internet or something helps him pick his victims. I want to get him to talk more. 'So you flew all the way to Houston, just to see me?' 'Sort of,' he says, 'I try to get a look at the agents that are trailing me. It gives me something to watch for so I will be careful, but when I went to the Bureau they told me you were already crazy. It usually takes longer for them to go crazy, you know.' I tell him that I am sorry to have disappointed him, and he starts apologizing again. He didn't want to make me feel stupid or weak. He was concerned. His real battle isn't with the Bureau. If he could find some way to totally hide the killings, he would do so. He felt for all of us. I ask him if he means that he has interacted with all the agents. He said yes."

"Before or after they go crazy?" asked Virginia.

"I asked him that, too. He said both. He keeps his identity a secret before they go bonkers, tries to warn them off. So I asked him why he really came to see me. You know what he tells me? 'Cost analysis. I have to decide whether keeping up my quest decreases the sum total of human unhappiness in the world. I need to get an estimate on how much unhappiness my actions may cause you. I social-engineered it long ago that the people investigating me would be loners, so it would minimize the damage.' He just needed an entry in his happiness ledger. There was no concern for me. I guess that if I had a poor dying grandma that would cry her heart out when I went bonkers then he might have just given up. He had just squashed me like a bug, and he didn't care. Or more precisely he cared in some engineering way. He had even set it up so that only loners would investigate him. He made me lose because I was a loser. Do you understand that? Do you fucking understand that? Every goddamned reason I had to pick my life to that point he had just used. I was the ultimate pawn. I was a pawn because he needed pawns. I went into shock as it all became clear. I saw this blackness descending out of the air and surrounding me. I heard him leave—he said other things, but I couldn't make them out. I was just in this blackness, and I saw it all. He had a great little scheme. Since there would be investigations of his murders, there would be danger. So he manipulated the Bureau to assign only rootless agents—people who were like him, obsessed in some way—and they would snap eventually, but it didn't matter because by and large they didn't take anybody with them. Well, Suzanne did, but who knows? Maybe she killed some shitty people. The point was, I was created. He created me so that he would have ineffective opposition, that I wouldn't hurt anything when I was gone. I was screwed by this guy way back when I was being beaten up in Thalia. I don't remember much after the blackness came down. I woke up in M.D. Anderson Hospital. I just sort of froze there in the lobby of a Ramada. I woke up—I mean I had been awake, I just hadn't known or cared where I was. I asked a nurse what was going on, and she told me that my aunt was waiting to hear from me. I told her I didn't have an aunt, and she said, yes, I did—my aunt in New York that was paying my bill. She'd drive me to her tomorrow morning."

Virginia tried to get him to say more, but he pretty much ended his talk here. She got it then. Just as she was playing him, he was playing her. He was under orders to tell the story of the evil all-powerful Chadwick and the mysterious other. Damn this. This was what she did, not what was done to her. But she had scored in her game. He didn't make her sleep with the gag.

25 Concerning the Saints

Happy Halloween," said Willis Spencer. "Here we are, driving randomly south, maybe to my home in Austin, on All Saint's Day, with you either the biggest killer of sinners—or the biggest sinner. I wish I knew where to put you. Are you a saint or a sinner?"

They had cleaned up Chadwick and gotten him some clothes at the Salvation Army. His dapper elegance was gone. He slept a lot, but mainly he looked off into space. He wanted to return to his machines, but he wouldn't tell them where they were. He was trying to steer them toward Willis's resources. Mondragon kept wanting to check in at the Bureau, but didn't want to show his hand in the escape of Chadwick, so mainly he rubbed his hands together and looked sick and guilty as hell. It had been silent for about an hour as Mondragon's car sped south. Willis didn't give a damn about the answer, all he wanted was sound, some sense they hadn't all just done the stupidest thing they could possibly have done.

Chadwick stroked his chin seriously. He said, "No, I am not a saint. I thought I might be a saint, but my software says no. I am rather upset about that."

Mondragon asked, "What the fuck do you mean?"

"Well," said Chadwick, "there are saints, you know. I had such a pessimistic view of mankind for so long that I never looked for them. I should have, it's a simple piece of symmetry. Just as there are psychic vampires, people who cause endless grief and misery to anyone around them, there are saints as well. People who cause happiness and long-life to those who surround them. I didn't look until nineteen seventy-five. It just hit me one day. Back when I looked for psychic vampires I had never thought of looking for clusters of happiness. There are almost as many of them, to my surprise."

Willis was surprised as well. "Well, what did you do with that fact?"

Chadwick said, "I couldn't think of anything to do. I thought about maybe rewarding them in some anonymous way like St. Nicholas tossing bags of gold into the houses of the virtuous poor, but that wouldn't seem to help. I mean, if I could figure out how to train people to go one way rather than the other, I would do so. All I know is that they are the same sorts of people. They have a place in the world that seems pretty secure. They live in the same house for years, or have the same job. They cluster together. If there is a psychic vampire around, there is a saint around. In a small town they are usually paired. In fact, if a small town has just one or the other, the town will live or die. A single psychic vampire in a population of less than a thousand spells doom for the community. Likewise, a single saint can cause the most godforsaken economically depressed area to undergo complete rejuvenation."

"But if this is as important as your other work, why haven't you at least leaked this to the world?" asked Willis.

"Well, there are many reasons I won't ever leak my work to the world. If I go along with the proposition that Mr. Mondragon offers me—which is that I let him catch me after I have destroyed my notes—there will be so much known in the world. It might help the world to know about positive and negative people, but I doubt it. Just think about. What if any kind of political group even knew there were negative people? It wouldn't take much to characterize their enemies as negatives, would it? What if some Democrat could find all the psychic vampires in America and proved through either statistics or lying that they were mainly Republicans? First there would be a political rebellion, itself a dangerous thing—but, much more to the point, there would be a social rebellion. People could then blame their ills—real or imagined—on others. 'I would have done better but my father-in-law was a psychic vampire.' All sorts of horrors will be out of the bag if I am run to the ground. If I must pay for my crimes it had best be by a gunshot in the back."

Mondragon said, "I can take care of that anytime you want."

Chadwick smiled, "Well, right now won't work out very well, will it? Currently you are probably not a suspect in my escape, which will be seen—I hope—as the actions of some group of followers or fans or perhaps some secret society. It would be better by far if the secret society myth is out there."

"Why?" asked Willis.

"You know, Mr. Spencer, I must say that you haven't given very much thought to the nature of your pranks in the bigger picture of things. The world is not a tightly woven together tapestry. It has holes and loose places and the fabric is just plain rotten. Think this through. One old guy is able to kill hundreds of people, and the FBI isn't even sure if I exist. That lets people know how loose the world is. What if thousands of people tried doing what I'm doing. What do you think would happen?"

Willis said, "There would be chaos."

Chadwick said. "No. Bad student! No biscuit! Think it through in stages. Try again."

Willis said, "Well, first there would be a big increase in the buying of nontraceable handguns, because let's say a thousand people tried to do your work."

Mondragon said, "Will you stop calling it work—it's god-damned murder. That's where all the people on this case have slipped the tracks: they start treating his trail of carnage as though it were taking out the trash."

Willis said, "You called it taking out the trash yourself on the trip to Amarillo."

"Well, then I guess I'm going crazy. I must have been crazy to allow you to talk me into trying this stunt."

"It didn't take much talking. Just a few Nonfiction Martinis."

"Screw you."

Willis returned to his analysis. "Let's say a thousand people buying nontraceable weapons. That would be a huge boost to organized crime."

Chadwick said, "OK, good. Then what?"

Willis said, "Most people are going to screw up their first couple of attempts. So there will be some unnecessary carnage."

Chadwick. "OK, I see that, but not as a big part of the picture. Did you ever screw up any of your pranks?"

"Oh, god. Badly. Still tears me up. Did you ever screw up any killings?"

"Sure. Sometimes the target lived. A couple of times innocents became involved. I've always felt partially responsible for the people that nice Ms. Wilson blew away. But go on."

"Well, the biggest danger would be personal judgment issues. They wouldn't let the Program decide. Everybody hates someone. Everybody acts as a psychic vampire sometimes. Maybe you just had a bad day and you bawl some waitress. You forget about it, but she obsesses on it, quits her job, and winds up in the street. So, if people accustom themselves to the idea they can just kill off anyone who looks like scum to them, people will be dropping like flies."

Chadwick said, "Good so far, now do you want to take that a step further?"

"Well, the murder rise would be connected with people actually revealing why they did stuff. You would have more and more people claiming in court that they had done a good deed, and therefore the idea would spread like wildfire."

Chadwick said, "Very good. You can work out other details later like an increase in people buying guns for personal defense, more accidental slayings and so forth. All of that will happen if and when Mr. Mondragon turns me in. That was why I was surprised when you brought him into this, I had guessed you were smarter."

Willis said, "My only interest is Virginia. Why did you kidnap her in the first place?"

"I didn't kidnap her. I just lured her on by appealing to her curiosity," said Chadwick. "And making her think you were in danger."

"But why did you want to get her involved in a killing?" asked Willis. "If your Program is as good as you say it is, you must have known that she wouldn't go for that."

"The Program isn't infallible. What it told me is that if I were able to get her to compromise her moral code, she should be receptive to the danger of what I do and give it up. I had no worry. She would go back to you and beg you to erase your copy of the Program and you would. The two of you would use your great powers of creativity to come up with some other fun activity, and I could continue in my mission for a while."

"You don't think simply telling her would be enough?"

"No. My guess is that you and she would keep your copy of the Program. Eventually you would try it out. Maybe it would be one of its many benign uses. I know that the two of you invest in small businesses a good deal. So you do a check—there are five people in this little software house, I wonder if any of them are psychic vampires? That would be reasonable. Nothing too bad there. Then when one of them turns up, you get to thinking 'It wouldn't be too bad if I just did it the one time would it?' and before long you would be out pranking again and ideas that should die with me would live on until someday some vast authority would get them."

"But you can't be sure of any of that," said Willis.

"Yes, I can. You haven't been listening to me all morning. Everything I said about how dangerous what I do is isn't something that I think applies only to lesser creatures than myself."

Willis said, "I don't get it—what do you mean?"

Mondragon spoke up, "He's telling you that he knows what he does is wrong."

"Badly put, but correct," said Chadwick. "It took me years to see the big picture. I know that if my work falls into the wrong hands—and that any hands are wrong—it would be one of the worst things that could happen to the world. All I have to do is erase my files—or at least until I found out there was an old copy of the first version of the Program lying around—I could use my wizardry to live as some comfortable old man with a big pension—I could even get Stone Mount Insurance to give it to me—I could read, watch TV, and live a normal life—thrilled by the good I had let loose in the world. But I don't."

"Why?" said Willis.

"Because I like it. I like to kill people. If I could walk away from it I would have stopped ten years ago. That was when I was very aware of shortness of breath when I climb steps. That was when I knew that I was getting too old. Every month I tell myself that it will be the last. Then I find just one more person, and I tell myself how much better the world would be with them gone. Just one more hit. I am a murder junkie."

26 The Good Breast

It was early for Virginia, about seven o'clock, and the sun had not yet risen on the morning of the Day of the Dead. Salazar had cleaned her up and set her in the van next to him with her hands cuffed behind her. He smelled bad, and he talked far too quickly. He was driving into the city of New York. She knew he could have driven last night, but that must have not fit his employer's schedule. He kept rehearsing her on the point that he had treated her well. He had seen to her needs. He had not handled her in a cavalier fashion. He used that word, *cavalier* at least three times. Probably one of his employer's words. It had been decades since she had been in New York. Her parents had taken her when she was ten, because of some business convention that Daddy attended. Usually it had been in Chicago and the family hadn't gone, but this time it had been in New York. It hadn't been a good trip, because of her parents fighting, and then her Daddy being alone with her. She had mixed that in her mind with things like the Statue of Liberty and the subways. She dreamed of the subways often, the IRT where the lights would go out and there was always a noise of rushing.

"Can you tell me who your employer is?" she asked.

"I could. I mean, I know who she is, but she doesn't think I do, and I don't want her to know that I have any power over her."

"That sounds like magical thinking: Know her name and you will have power over her."

"In the age of the Internet, that kind of thinking is pretty damn valid," said Salazar. "All I had to do was get the name of the owner of a blue car heading away from Doublesign on the night of the Fourth and I got you."

"And then what? She gets me because she knows your name, I don't get it. You haven't got anything."

"I got everything from her, everything."

"Then why are you so scared? You make this woman sound like she always has your best interests at heart, but you tremble when you speak of her. You've got to be a pretty brave guy, so why are you scared? Did she do something bad to you?"

"Everything she has done to me has been good. You don't understand the power of the good tit. She could take it away. Without her I am nothing, so I am in fear of her all the time. Her gifts have frightened me."

"Tell me about her."

"I've already said more than I am supposed to."

"If you don't tell me more, I will tell that you were very mean to me, torturing me with stories of how wicked she is."

"No, you can't do that, she will take it out on me!"

"Then talk."

"Look, I'm the one with the gun. You don't tell me what to do."

"You're not going to shoot me now—I know that you have to call her every few hours. You stop the van and walk away. You are using your cell phone telling her how much you have softened me up. You know she is not going to buy my making my big escape now. She would figure you out. So, tell me how good she is to you. That's the impression you want me to communicate to her isn't it? Think about it, you don't want me telling her how much you fear her. Think how mean she could be to you then."

"I'll tell you the rest of my story. That was more than I was supposed to tell, but it will seem excusable because it's hard to know when to stop a story. I was in the hospital, and the nurse asked me if I wanted to call my aunt and tell her myself if I was better. I said I would call her tomorrow, but asked for the phone number. I knew it was New York from the area code. I snuck out of the hospital and snagged a cab to my apartment. The Bureau had been there. They had looked through my stuff, taken my address book, and so forth. They hadn't tried to cover up their tracks in any way. They wanted me to know. I gave it about a fifty percent chance the apartment was under surveillance. But I didn't care, I was just going to pack up some stuff and go. I hadn't committed any crime. Sure, I left the Bureau funny, but so what? The worst they could do was question me, and they couldn't realistically detain me to do that. I had left my service pistol and badge. I realized I had no idea if the car was still in the Ramada parking lot. It was likely the Bureau had impounded it, that way they could be sure and have a nice chat with me when I went to get it. I packed a bag, took a cab to Bush International, and I was on my way to the city that never sleeps." He gestured at the city around him.

"When I got here, I knew I would have a very short time to make use of my Bureau connections. I called up a service in the NYPD, gave them my badge number, and asked if they could give me an address to go with the number. My badge number still worked, and they sent me to a small office in the Flatiron Building. I took an awful ride in the world's slowest elevator to Zembla Real Estate. It was late '99 and we were all a little spooked by elevators, which were supposed to stop working on the millennium. Knocked on the door. Tried the door and walked in. It was a small office suite. There was no one in reception, although the desk had the usual knickknacks you might find. I went to the inner offices. Two were bare except for desk and chairs. The larger office had prints of Paris on the walls and a very nice overstuffed chair. There was an envelope on the desk addressed to Abel Salazar. I still have it. 'Dear Mr. Salazar, I hope that you are feeling better. I think that I can offer some interesting employment as a special investigator, concentrating your efforts on the capture and delivery of Mr. Roy Chadwick, the so-called SKiller. I realize that your pursuit of Mr. Chadwick has no doubt left you somewhat drained, and that perhaps you should take a few months off to undergo psychological counseling, which I will provide at my expense. Please do not accept or reject this offer now, as you need a strong dose of healing before you can undertake an operation of such magnitude. If you wish to decline my offer of employment, do at least consider my offer of counseling. If you choose to reject both, I hope you will at least take the cash in the top drawer of this desk, to recompense you for your trip and other expenses. I had to see if you could find this envelope to know if you had the wherewithal to act in this matter; although I clearly suspected you had because of your former employment.' "

"How much cash in the drawer?"

"Ten thousand dollars. I pocketed it and went back to my hotel. I thought for a long time. She seemed so different from the Bureau. I had nowhere to turn, and here was money from somebody who had already picked up my hospital bill. She seemed to understand what I had gone through, and I felt that she cared. I really needed someone to care. I needed to explain about the blackness—about the sense of being another's creation, about what I wanted to do."

"So you called."

"So I called. She gave me the name of a private clinic. 'They will be waiting for you.' I was supposed to get three months of treatment before seeing her. That was her only condition. I could leave the clinic anytime I wanted. I didn't have to finish their therapy, I didn't have to see her, unless I went through the full three months I wouldn't rebel. Hell, I thought it would do me good."

"Did it?"

"It was very restful. It was in the woods in New Jersey near Princeton. I ate, I exercised, and I talked about my life. There were no other patients while I was there. After the first couple of weeks, we started on a program of psychodrama. It was way past time for me to learn to push people around the way I had been pushed around. They put on little plays. Gave me drugs. I got to be a South American dictator, a world chess champion, a pimp, a sadist, a necrophile."

"That's not really a move toward mental health. You had to know they were screwing you up. Why didn't you run away?"

"I thought about running away all the time. Real people don't have some unseen female voice paying for their fantasies to be acted out. They encouraged me to do really bad and mean things, telling me that it was just fantasy, no one was really being hurt. I did some. I liked it. Anyway my three months were over in a heartbeat. Time goes fast when you're living in Paradise. Then I met her. Well, sort of. She came to the clinic. We met in a darkened room. I couldn't see her face and I was told not to leave my chair, or that I would be shot. It was the first time I had ever heard anything like a threat, but they reassuringly told me that it was for simple security. She outlined what she would do for me. I would never want for money. I could visit the clinic anytime I needed to act out any of my fantasies. I could engage in any of my fantasy practices while working for her—as long as she didn't hear about them and they didn't interrupt my job of capturing Chadwick. Money would be no object. It was, she told me, her destiny to capture Chadwick and that I should be honored to be part of such a great thing."

"What did you have to do in exchange?"

"Number one, I had to vanish from the face of the earth. No taxes, no life partners, no mail. I would have to live underground because Chadwick was so good at ferreting out any place you leave a data fingerprint on the worldwide grid. Number two, I had to pursue no other investigating, business, et cetera, until I caught him. I could mess around under aliases on the Internet, I could make limited trips for my amusement, but at all times I was at her call. Number three, when I caught and delivered Chadwick, I had to allow her people to thoroughly search everything I had so that not even a breath of a record would remain. The clinic would give me some drugs that remove my memories and she would create a believable new life for me. A life without a bad past and a frustrating adolescence. I would think of myself a rich chess eccentric, and there would be papers to back it up."

"So you took it."

"You don't get to hit the 'reset' button very often in life. She took care of everything from having my groceries bought to having things I wanted brought to my lair. She could take it away today and I would be nothing—a poor, crazy Mexican on the FBI 'presumed dangerous' list. I know you've been working on me to make me like you. Hell, liking you is easy, but you've got to believe that I would a million times rather kill you than go back to the real world. I couldn't even recognize it anymore."

"You've never met her, have you?"

"Not where I could see her. I am hoping to today."

He pulled the van into a parking garage. He pulled some chloroform from the glove compartment of the van.

"Let me tell you the drill from here on out."

27 When All Else Fails, Television

Chadwick was snoring in the back of the car as Willis and Mondragon pulled into the driveway of Willis's home. Mondragon sneered at the dragon gate, and even more at the dragon door sparkling in the afternoon light.

"You rich people, you just think you can do anything. I gave up my damn life for your scheme. What's the worst that will happen to you?"

"The loss of my wife," said Willis.

"I don't believe him. He has no enemies that are tracking him down, he doesn't leave anybody. I know because I've looked his career over for years. He's taking advantage of the fact that your wife split."

"Why do you keep saying that? Just to fucking hurt me? What?"

The car stopped and they stood on the driveway for a moment looking at the antenna farm.

Mondragon said, "Look, she saw where all this leads. She saw that this guy isn't some superhuman hero, that's he's an old nutcase, and she knew she had to restart her life. You could imagine that, couldn't you? She had too bizarre a life and just took the moment to escape to reality."

"I can tell you one thing. Virginia isn't big on escaping into what you would call reality."

"You don't know, man. I have worked a lot of religious cult cases. You can have people that have knocked over 7-Elevens for ten years to get money to buy a landing pad for the Space Brothers, and then one day they just say, 'to hell with this,' and then they walk away. They get regular jobs and live in houses without posters of UFOs, and they forget. You run them down after a few years, you've got your case on them, and they don't even know what you're talking about. They're embarrassed like somebody hearing that they behaved badly during a drunk. That's where your wife is. She suddenly realized how damn silly it is to waste your life doing your little pranks. So she split."

"I don't believe you for an instant. Let's wake him up." Willis gestured at Chadwick.

"What we should do is kill him. Kill him and bury him and go back to our lives, before all of this swallows us, the way it did him."

"I don't believe you mean that, either."

"No, but I *want* to believe it," Mondragon said softly. The idea of Bureau Legend had almost no thrill now.

They shook Chadwick gently. His blue eyes opened, unsure of where he was at first, and then sad when he remembered.

The three of them went in the house. There was some hope in Willis that he would find her, some belief that somehow the phone calls and e-mails had just misfired, or that perhaps she was angry or sad or afraid or had some reason not to contact him. So he yelled her name a great deal and rushed through the house while the other two men looked concerned for him. Mondragon ordered a pizza and got Willis to tell the dispatcher where to deliver it.

The meal was quiet. Mondragon checked his messages. He had been afraid to—there were the calls he expected about where was he and did he know anything about the escape of Chadwick.

Chadwick said, "You've got to call them back really mad that they let me slip away and ask to be put back on the case."

"They'll suspect that I had something to do with it," said Mondragon.

"No, he's right," said Willis. "It would be crazy for you to be involved—we've been over that idea pretty extensively in the car here, don't you think? If you are going to catch him, you need to be looking for him."

"It's a wonderful idea. You can be hot on my trail, because you know where I am going to leave my next set of clues. Heck, we'll plant them together."

The pizza arrived.

Mondragon called the Bureau. His speech to his supervisor was short. Willis and Chadwick watched and ate stuffed crust.

"So, they lost him. He was only caught by accident. Stupid bastards, you know if they had one of us in charge, there wouldn't be this problem. . . .

"Because I knew she was going to Amarillo. I think I've mapped out his MO. . . . No. It's mine, goddamn it. I know why you assigned me this case, because you think I'm stupid. . . .

"Stop it? Because I was off the case. I was just checking my theories. . . .

"Yes. I figured his team might be able to help him escape. He's got a team, you know, and money. He has to have someone check out the sites before he gets there. . . .

"No I'm not saying more because I want to be back on the fucking case . . .

"He was caught because his trainee freaked out. Yes, of course, he has trainees. The woman freaked. We should be trying to find her . . .

"It's about goddamn time. Yes, tomorrow. I'll fly through Houston and pick up my service revolver, thank you. No, but you should watch your shop, especially John, the documents guy."

When Mondragon hung up, Willis and Chadwick applauded.

Mondragon said, "You were right. They couldn't think I had anything to do with it. That's not normal thinking. I had to be in Amarillo because I am some kind of genius, figuring out his moves first. Oh, they think I'm crazy, too—but that's not really a drawback for this case, is it?"

Chadwick said, "I loved the part where you gave me a staff."

Soon after dinner, Chadwick slept again.

Mondragon and Willis watched TV.

Mondragon said, "Why is he like this? You and I both know that he has iced more people than anybody in America and he's having the fucking time of his life. What's the deal?"

Willis explained, "He hasn't had any normal fun for many years. It's like he has worked on a really tough job. He's put in twenty-four seven for years, now this is fun. He gets driven around, he gets pizza. He gets to play at shit. This is his great vacation."

"You know that I am going to turn him in as soon as your wife is in your hands. I don't believe that shit of the world ending because they think about this guy. That has got to be the clearest case of delusions of grandeur I have ever seen."

"Well, you're wrong about that. If there was ever a case not to be hidden away, this is it. But I won't stop you, that was the deal we made. But you got to think long and hard about this—this is every person's fantasy. The next time some clerk treats you like dung, you'll think about Mr. Chadwick's solution, and maybe you won't ever kill someone, but you will do little mean things: a petty evil here, a mean-spirited prank there. That's how it will start."

"I can't believe that you're lecturing me on this. You're the worst. You fell for it."

"Who better than me? I know how it grabbed me."

"Why should I trust you at all? You're infected, that's all there is."

"I am worried about that."

"That hasn't kept you from being way too palsy with our friend in there. He was alone with you for—what?—five minutes, and talked you into this nonsense felony business that we are in right now. Tell me—did you or your wife come up with the idea for the pranks?"

"I don't see the relevance."

But of course Willis did. It had taken Virginia two seconds to capture his attention. All she had done was mouth the words, *help me*, and he was devoted to her.

Mondragon continued, "In Chadwick's hands you're putty, and your wife's hands. We'll pursue this and one of them will talk you into something more stupid and we'll be trapped in greater and greater problems."

"You didn't put up any resistance when I talked you into helping me spring Chadwick."

"Touché. But I at least know my goal. I know what I want. Your idea seemed to match it."

"My ideas will get us out of this, too—you just watch."

"Your ideas aren't worth shit."

Mondragon moved toward him, and Willis raised his hands. Mondragon took a swing, connected with Willis's right shoulder, while Willis swung his right hand up at Mondragon's chest. It was a glancing blow and didn't stop Mondragon, who realized a flurry of punches on Willis's head and shoulders. Willis fell back, grabbed something that later proved to be a candlestick, and whipped Mondragon's collar bone. Mondragon kicked at Willis's leg, and Willis teetered forward. A quick backhanded slap from Mondragon, and Willis was down.

"Your fucking ideas can't even keep you standing," said Mondragon.

Willis searched for a more clever response than the "Oh, yeah?" which came to mind and unfortunately escaped his lips.

Willis broke into laughter at his own lame response, and Mondragon laughed a bit, too.

"What we need to do is cut our losses," said Mondragon. "There will be forgiveness for you, since your wife is missing, and for me, perhaps some forgiveness because this is a case that makes people crazy."

"No. That's not what we need. What we need is advertising, and I'll tell you how to do it."

"What?"

"We've got a valuable commodity in Mr. Chadwick. We can sell him."

"Then I don't get to turn him in."

"Oh, come now. You guys do drug stings all the time. You can catch everybody. That will be your part."

Mondragon smiled a little, which Willis took as approval, but later in the night wondered if that may have been the subtle sign of going crazy.

28 Waking Up

The sheets were clean and smelled good. Virginia was in a flannel gown, with little yellow flowers on it. She could smell coffee being brewed. She sat up in her comfortable bed. Somewhere so far away beyond the thick wooded doors she could hear people talking, but the voices were too muffled for her to hear anything they said clearly. She had been having bad dreams. The doctor had told her that she had had a lot of bad dreams lately.

The door swung open and a nurse was there with a tray for breakfast. There were eggs Benedict and fruit and coffee with cream and toast and three jam pots. Surely this wasn't really healthy eating. The nurse was a big woman, given to fat, her blue eyes almost lost in the fat of her face. She wouldn't be the one to know about healthy eating. Well, she might have heard about the theory. Even her voice was too sugary.

"Good morning, Mrs. Night. Did you sleep well?"

"I am not Mrs. Night. Where the hell am I?" asked Virginia.

"Doctor!" the nurse cried out, "She's that way again."

"I'll be right there, Agnes," came a female voice. The doctor walked quickly into the room, her eyes fixed on Virginia.

She was tiny and old, but very full of energy and determination. She unsuccessfully hid her worry.

"Now, Mrs. Night, do you recall why you are here?" asked the doctor.

"First off, I am not Mrs. Night. I haven't been Mrs. Night for six years."

"But you did remember having been Mrs. Night this morning."

"Don't try a prank on me. I won't fall for this shit."

The doctor said, "No one's here to fool you, Mrs. Night. Here, I'll just call you Virginia and you can call me Anne. Agnes, give Virginia her breakfast. I'll talk to her later when she wants to talk. Talking is better when you have a full stomach. I am going to call Mr. Night and tell him not to come today."

"Oh, no," said Virginia. "Tell him to come. Tell him I want to see him, that I'm almost all better."

She thought that would put an end to their pranks, because they couldn't produce Tony.

The doctor beamed. "I'm so glad to hear that. You know how much he treasures his afternoon visits."

Agnes laid the breakfast tray at a little desk, and Virginia ate. It bothered her how familiar all of this seemed on some level. It was like she had been here before, but she knew that she had driven to see. She had driven to see. She had been driven to see? Someone drove her to see his boss. That had been yesterday, in New York. She was going to meet the chess player's boss. That was it.

She was Mrs. Willis Spencer. She and her husband got married in Austin. Momma came and Willis's momma came, and it was near a lake, and there were ducks. She had been Mrs. Night, but that was a long time ago. She and Willis liked to trick people, when people were bad. Maybe she had been bad and that's why they were tricking her. They had done something to her head, that was why she couldn't think good. There was someone else who robbed old ladies with her. No, that wasn't right. She had never robbed anyone. But someone had taken her in her Daddy's Caddy. Her daddy's Caddy. Someone had taken her in her daddy's Caddy to show her a helium balloon? No, that made no sense at all. Things were clear when she first woke up. Maybe she was sick. They were wrong about certain things. She hadn't been Mrs. Night for a long time. There had been some mistake, that was it. She would talk to the doctor and find out what was going on, and then she would feel better.

The breakfast was yummy.

After breakfast she asked for the doctor, but the doctor was busy with other clients and didn't see her for an hour. When the doctor came in, she was holding a small voice-activated recorder. She said "November fifteenth, Mrs. Virginia Night. Some evidence of continued confusion." She looked up at Virginia and asked, "Well, my first question is, do you know who you are?"

"I know who I am. I am Mrs. Virginia Spencer. I live at five-two-oh-six San Martin Drive in Austin, Texas. There seems to be some mistake here, and you have me listed under my previous marriage with Anthony Night."

The doctor's face fell. She moved to sit with Virginia. Virginia saw that the doctor had a small silver box on her waist.

"No, dear," said the doctor, "you are still Mrs. Night. You live in Dallas, although you once lived in Austin at the very address you just gave. Some of your real past is bleeding back in. Do you know what you do for a living?"

"My husband is independently wealthy and I spend my time doing volunteer work around Austin."

"That was true until you moved to Dallas. You really hated Dallas. You missed the art scene and the music, so you took up writing. Do you have any idea what you wrote?"

"I don't believe you. I have never written anything. Why am I here?"

"After your auto accident, your husband took you to the best surgeons, the best plastic surgeons, the best physical therapists he could find. He took you to many psychiatrists, as well. Most of them didn't help you very much. You are getting better here, and we aren't going to rush you. Now, before I tell you any more, is there anything you remember about coming here?"

Virginia didn't want to say anything, so she shook her head, no.

"OK, dear. You are at the Shelby Hearon Clinic for Past Modification in Princeton, New Jersey. I am Dr. Anne Jones. And I am going to make sure that you remember who you were and how you got here. Do you remember what you were working on?"

"A book?"

"Yes, that's good. A book about a serial killer. Can you remember the name of the killer?"

"Roy Helium. No, that's not right. Ray Chadwick. But he's not in a book, he's real."

"That's where your problem seems to come from. He's a character in your book. The book was called *Roy Chadwick's Private War*—does that help?"

"What was his war?"

"He was trying to get rid of mean people."

"No. I'm afraid I'm drawing a blank."

"Don't worry about it, dear. I'll let you look at the manuscript if you like. Yesterday you were able to write on it. Memory coming back to you is like sun through moving clouds. It comes and goes, but eventually there will be a sunny day."

"What can I do here? Are there limitations to where I can go on the grounds, or about me using the phone?"

"Of course not, dear. The grounds are covered in snow today, but you can call anybody you like. You just have to have Agnes place the call, so we can be sure you are calling a real person."

"Of course. Those fictional people waste all of your time."

"I know that sounds harsh, but here we have to insist on reality. You've got to interact with what's real and make your fictions your fictions. We do encourage you to write down things, anything you imagined about Chadwick, for example. It is not unknown for a writer to believe to a certain extent in the validity of her characters. But it will give me the key to your blockage if I know what your psyche hides behind the figure of Chadwick, so anything you write—anything about his motives and methods—are a big help."

"What about my husband? Is he just a fiction, too?"

"Mr. Night is not a fiction. In fact, he is one of the sweetest men I've met. Oh, you mean Mr. Spencer. Well, he isn't a fiction either. He found you when you were thrown from your car and drove you into Austin. You seemed to have created an entire life with him on the spot. He does ask Mr. Night about you every few days."

Virginia knew she was lying. She had to be. Virginia remembered her wedding with Willis. It had taken her months to plan it; it was one of the most beautiful weddings anyone ever had. They had rented the park by Bull Creek, and it was in the spring, so everything was blooming and the two mommas standing there with tears running down their faces, and everything was beautiful beyond belief. It was real, real, real. It had to be, because she remembered thinking that it was better than she had imagined it could be. But something had happened. That much was clear. Chadwick seemed real, but the more she remembered, the less plausible he sounded. Maybe they had something right. She would have to be very cautious.

"Tell me about my accident," said Virginia.

"You had enrolled in a night class called the Novel-In-Progress. You told Mr. Night that the classes in Austin were better because there were so many writers there. So you drove to Austin every Monday night, and then spent the night in a bed and breakfast. The night of your accident, it was your turn to take a sample chapter in for the group to critique. You were a little late, it was raining, and you skidded off the road, hit some kind of steel pole and wrapped your car around it. When Mr. Spencer came upon the scene, you had wandered away from the car. You were covered in blood and somewhat delusional. You got in his car and he drove you into town and dropped you off at the first hospital he came to. You didn't have any papers with you, and for the first couple of days, he came and visited you every day. He and Mr. Night have become great friends, by the way."

"And Mr. Night is coming to see me today?"

"He prefers if you call him, 'Tony,' and, yes, he will be here after lunch. Let's see if you can remember even a little more for him."

"OK, how do we do this?"

"We're going to try a few questions. Do you recall Chadwick's attitude toward women?"

"If he's fictional, what does his attitude matter?"

"He's your creation, so his attitudes must reflect yours."

"Well, I have a great attitude toward women."

"No, I don't mean the attitudes of your characters are your attitudes. I mean that their attitudes show something about you. A good writer can always write about someone with a completely opposite attitude than her own."

"Well, I'm sure that if I was going to write an entire book about somebody I wouldn't focus on a man with a bad attitude."

"You're not thinking, you're just being difficult. Mr. Night is paying a lot of money to have you here."

"All right, Chadwick had a bad attitude toward women, just like Mr. Night."

"How can you say that about a man who lives to see you healthy and happy?"

"We both know that Anthony Night is drooling away in a

asylum near Springfield, Missouri. What we both don't know is why you are doing this to me."

The doctor looked angry and reached for the silver box on her waist. Then she caught herself and spoke with professional concern. "Mrs. Night, I can tell that you must have some deep problems with Anthony. These may have fueled all sorts of fantasies, and you can get some regular counselors to help you there. I don't even care if you divorce him, but I am not wasting any more of my time today. There are people in this clinic who are receptive to help right now, and I am going to go off and be among them."

The doctor left the room, and before Virginia could go explore the grounds, lunch had arrived—pork chops smothered in apricots, asparagus, rice pilaf, hot rolls, iced tea and chocolate cake for dessert. Virginia, who always worried about her figure, hadn't eaten like this in years.

She could remember her mother's dinners being like this. See, she had her memory!

After lunch, the nurse brought two yellow and green capsules, and Virginia was told to take them. She refused, and Agnes looked sad and worried and said she would report this to the doctor. Virginia dived into her bed.

Virginia was working on escape plans when someone came into the room. She figured it was the doctor, and she wasn't going to give her the satisfaction of a scene. She looked up slowly from her bed and then let out a little shriek.

Mr. Anthony Night, impeccably dressed in a black business suit, stood there with a bouquet of red roses.

Spiders Are Better than Word of Mouth

"The only way your idea will work is if it is hidden just right," said Chadwick.

Willis's office was cramped and cluttered, totally unlike the spacious order of the rest of the Spencer home. Willis was at his keyboard uploading files to a Web page called SKiller.com. Willis seemed confident and driven. Mondragon was amusing himself with the poetry books in the library.

Willis said, "You don't have to tell me how to trick hackers. I have never fully left that world. You might even say that I got into college on a hacking scholarship."

That was true. Willis hadn't quite the poverty or quite the GPA to get into school. His applications for financial aid were turned down, based on a difference of a very few dollars, but an assault on a certain database on campus had fixed that problem and his parents had been able to care for his sick sister while Willis went through school. He was a backdoor boy—and, like most of his kind, never quite came to believe that the front door even worked. His backdoor life was an electronic prelude to his pranks, a sign of the yet-to-be.

Mondragon walked in.

Willis said, "You're right on time. You want to check the page out?"

Mondragon sat down and worked his way through the menu. The first page actually had a picture of Chadwick from his college yearbook and the question in big bold flashing red:

HAS THIS MAN KILLED
HUNDREDS OF NOT-SO-INNOCENT PEOPLE?

There were pages on his career, listing his math papers, his involvement with the insurance industry, and his work on DARPA-net. There was a glowing tribute to his father John Chadwick (Chadwick himself had written this—it was his condition for the scheme), there were profiles of some of the FBI agents who had been on the case, including Abel Salazar and William Mondragon. There were links to every page in the WWW that mentioned any of the SKillings as well as links to most conspiracy pages with questions such as

WHO DOES THIS MAN WORK FOR??

There was even a novel that someone had published serially on the Internet years ago about a deranged serial killer who tracked down and killed people who owned businesses with silly names like Mr. Lube Quick or Chicken Lips Boutique. (The novel had been written by D. B. Bowen, and featured a man whose wife had been killed by a falling sign of a giant chicken in a kilt, the corporate logo of McFried Budget Birds).

"OK, how does this put us in touch with them?" asked Mondragon.

Willis took them back to the home page.

"Here," he said, pointing at a mole on the left cheek of Chadwick.

Mondragon glanced at the flesh-and-blood Chadwick, who

had no mole. So he clicked on the mole. An almost blank page came up with a few non-English characters.

"It's a zipped encrypted file," said Willis. "We assume that they are smart enough to read it, which an amateur couldn't do, and that they will respond."

"What does it say?"

Willis called up the unzipped unencrypted file.

We have captured the Shitkiller from the Lousiana State Troopers. We want to trade him for Mrs. Virginia Spencer, the Woman smart enough to capture him in the first place. For an unharmed Mrs. Spencer, you, too, can own America's Most Wanted Serial Killer. Respond to this page with a JPG of Mrs. Spencer and we can negotiate in earnest.

"Why do you think they will see this?" asked Mondragon.

"Well, for one thing, I am going tell four hundred search engines to list this site, and I'm going on all of the alt.murder boards and plugging the hell out of it. We know these people must be net-savvy—that has been part of being a good investigator ever since Operation Sun Devil. They'll see this within the day and respond."

"You are making two big assumptions here. One, you assume that your wife is being held against her will by these people—who I must point out we have only heard about from an old crazy man. And two, that they really want him alive."

Chadwick said, "Of course they want me alive. They have some idea about my Program, and they want it. Nobody avenges the deaths of the people that I have killed."

Mondragon said, "You've told us that you are not infallible. Not only could some of your victims have friends or family that you don't know about—they may even have families that love them deeply. Your statistics couldn't be sure all of the time. If these people exist, they want you. They want your skinny white ass bad."

Willis said, "It doesn't matter what their motives are. It matters if they want to trade Virginia for him."

Willis actually thought their motives did matter. They might have killed Virginia because they were mad that she caught the guy—well, had him caught. Or maybe they just collected SKiller memorabilia. The WWW had unleashed strange passions. He had seen people snap up Manson memorabilia on the auction services. There were people who stalked FBI agents through the Web, people who found everyone of their perversions not only satisfied through the Web—but actually egged on. You like to see people have sex with horses? Well, my site is better because it has a zebra! The Web was perfect negative space that could be used to conjure anything foul. It was like darkness caught in a net. It taught you to be mean. Willis smiled despite himself when he remembered the shit he caused that professor who fucked up his transcripts. "Hopalong Ferret Face" found all of his files encrypted, all of his smutty notes to the department secretary in everybody's mailbox, all of his words-of-power called PIN numbers posted in a hundred places. It had destroyed the guy on campus. He was too old to quit, to go elsewhere, and so he spent the last few years before retirement being a laughingstock. Willis hadn't been mean growing up. He didn't come from an abusive family—he just had the opportunity to do mean things to mean people and get away with it. He knew that was what made Chadwick a true evil. As soon as Virginia was found, he was going to kill the Web page he had just created, and hope that the meme wasn't spread too far. It seemed to be the ruling idea though—everything that came in contact with Chadwick put out his evil message—a message that Chadwick himself thought was evil. It was like the eldritch tomes in the Lovecraft books he had read as a teen—once you have read the evil runes you are in their thrall.

"You're spacing out again," said Mondragon. "You are beginning to worry me even more."

"Sorry," said Willis automatically, a habit that Virginia despised. He immediately felt guilty for saying *sorry* and then felt stupid for feeling guilty. God, he needed to get away from the house, or by the time they found Virginia he would be a basket case.

"You know, we should go for a beer," said Willis. "Let me set up my counter and my stats machine, and we'll go."

"Are you out of your fucking mind?" asked Mondragon. "We can't go anywhere with him. He'll run at the first opportunity. As far as I know, this is just a stupid scheme that you two have cooked up in the hours I let you work on this Web page."

"No. Look we're getting crazy and we are already at each other's throats. Another two or three days of ordering in food and just sitting here will drive us over the deep end. You're back on the case. As soon as we hear something, we need to go pick up your service revolver and call in the SWAT teams or whatever—do you feel like you're up to that kind of activity."

"OK. We'll go. But he stays."

"No. You would have a cow a thousand times over trying to figure out if he had escaped. Mr. Chadwick will come with us. We'll get some good cooking, drink a few local beers, and I'll drive you by the capitol building. It will be fun."

Fun was a bit of an overstatement, but they did feel more sane and grounded when they got back.

There was e-mail waiting for them.

It was a short file:

i think we have much to talk about

It had an attached jpg of Anthony Night in a black suit hugging a smiling Virginia Spencer, who was wearing a blue nightgown.

30 Reunion and Revelations

When she saw Tony, she felt she had lost some great cosmic game. They couldn't have faked him—she knew her husband. She had always felt the game would end someday with him showing up. That was why she had wanted to kill him.

Or maybe that had just been a fantasy.

He stood in the doorway, nervous and unsure, and asked, "Do you know who I am?"

"Tony." Her voice cracked as she said it.

His face lit up and he ran to the bed. "You know! You know! You remembered!" he cried.

He threw the bouquet on the bed and thrust his arms around her. She was scared. He pulled her to him and started kissing her. "Dr. Jones! Dr. Jones! She remembers!"

Someone was running down the hall. Both Virginia and Tony were crying. Dr. Jones ran into the room.

"Be careful, Mr. Night. Recall what I said. Her old memories will come to displace the trauma-fantasy slowly. She won't have remembered everything. Let her go, you're scaring her."

Tony looked at Dr. Jones with anger, and she made a slight gesture to the silver box on her waist, and he immediately grew calm.

"Oh, my god, hon. Am I scaring you? You don't know who I am?" asked Anthony Night.

"You're Tony Night."

"I am your husband. I brought you here—do you remember?"

"I am not sure," said Virginia.

The doctor said, "Nurse Agnes told me that you didn't take your pills. Now you are going to need to take them or your new memories will fade away."

Anthony saw the pills on her bed stand and picked them up, and then poured some water from the pitcher into her glass.

"Here, hon. Take these."

"I am not sure that I want to," said Virginia.

"But hon, you're getting better. I want my Jinny back. Please."

His tone was heartbreaking. Could any of this be true? She took the pills (partially out of fear of him, of what he could do) and swallowed them. His expression was happy and excited.

"There, Dr. Jones," he said. "She wants to get better. You were right and all those doctors were wrong. They said such mean things about her."

Dr. Jones said, "I'll leave you together. But be careful, Mr. Night, don't hug her or make her feel trapped by your body, there are still too many panic reactions from her childhood abuse."

"I'll be careful, Doctor, I'll treat her like fine china," said Anthony.

Virginia didn't want the doctor to leave the room.

"See," said Anthony, "It was just like when I first found you. I told you that someday you would you know how much I loved you. I am so glad you are starting to remember. Have you been writing?"

"Writing?"

"Writing about this character Chadwick. Dr. Jones says you have to finish your novel, that you need to expel him from your mind, while taking the memory enhancers, which will help you get back on track. I can tell it's working—this is the first time you've recognized me. Every other time you thought you were married to that man who rescued you, Mr. Spencer."

"How long have I been in here, Tony?"

"You've been here since the beginning of October. Your accident was on the ninth of July. That's why there is so much about fireworks in your book. I've read parts of it. You have me in it as a kind of monster. I know that was because I treated you so badly for so many years. I thank god every day that I took counseling like you suggested, and I hope that I am repaying you in kind by getting you here. Think of it, we get the bad parts of our past nullified and we can have the happy marriage we dreamed of."

"I am feeling a little tired, Tony. I guess it's the medicine beginning to work. I think I need to sleep."

This was only partially subterfuge. She did feel weird, not unlike some of her drug experimentation in college. She needed to get away, because she kept finding herself believing this man. She might believe him if he told her that the moon was made of green processed cheese food.

"All right, hon. I don't want to overtire you, especially on a day when we've got our first good news for months." He leaned over and kissed her forehead affectionately. It was disgusting. That was the way Willis kissed her. Tony had never kissed gently. He was a "get the tongue in the mouth as far as it will go" type. He stood, and she was alone on the bed, which now felt polluted by his presence. He smiled and she closed her eyes. He didn't leave and she was scared by the noises, but he was only finding a vase for the roses. Just as he was walking out the door, she risked a peek. He saw it.

"Hon, I know you're really tired, but there is something I

want from you. Could I get your picture? It would give me something to look at at night?"

Nurse Agnes was summoned to make up Virginia. Virginia felt sleepier and much more blissful by the moment. She laughed at Agnes's jokes and had fun picking out a nightgown from the closet. Something deep in her mind told her that there was something wrong with there only being nightgowns to choose from, that she should have other clothes. Oh well, they were probably elsewhere. When Tony came in, he looked all handsome, like he had on their wedding. No family had come to that wedding, Tony had forbidden it. "It's just for us," he had said. She could remember all the happy times she had with Tony very clearly now. She hugged him. It wasn't his fault that he was fucked up. He was a sweet guy, and she could make him better. Oh, she was sleepy. She almost tripped on the way down the hall. Tony caught her as she fell laughing. There was a bright flash and everyone was applauding and she felt so good, and then Tony and Mr. Salazar were carrying her back to her bed, which was the softest bed in the world—it completely supported her back, and it felt so good that she didn't even notice the lights being turned out in her room.

When she awoke she was hungry and not exactly sure of where she was. She sort of remembered being in a clinic, but otherwise she remembered her wedding with Tony. Where was Tony? A husband should be with his bride on their wedding night. Maybe he was getting food for them at room service. She stood up, fell, stood again. Too much champagne afterward. That was it. She would go find Tony. She looked in the closet for a robe that would cover the see-through nightgown. There. She tiptoed out to the hall. She would sneak up on him and go "Boo!" He would like that, he loved games. She opened the door oh-so-quietly, like a little mouse, and stepped into the hall. This was a small hotel and smelled kind of funny. Well, that probably wasn't Tony's fault. She went down the hall, keeping close to one wall, and she heard voices. Tony was talking to that orderly, Mr. Salazar. She got closer to the room they were in. The door was mostly shut, so she was going to fling it open and scare them. But just before she did, she heard Tony talking about her.

Tony said, "I love her more than anything. I won't let her go."

Salazar said, "You won't have to, that's the deal. We just need you to help finish the profile on Chadwick."

Tony said, "I don't have anywhere to go after this."

"Of course, you do. Dr. Jones will give you a complete bill of health."

"What about Jinny?"

"She'll be totally cured. The doctor is great at past modification," said Salazar.

"Who will she be?" asked Tony.

"She will be someone who loves you. Always has loved you, always will love you."

"She has always loved me."

"Look, take some Xanax—you'll feel better."

"I don't have to take shit from a greaser."

"If you don't take shit from us, we'll put you back in the shithole. I'll put you in the bug-house. The bug-house, Anthony."

Salazar's voice had gone up high and taunting on the last few words.

Virginia ran down the hall. She lay back in her bed, afraid to breathe. Afraid to make a sound.

31 The Files of Roy Chadwick

The three men wandered into the house, which now smelled stale and was littered with fast food wrappers. Willis checked the Web pages constantly. The kidnappers had not responded to the proposed swap. Mondragon had called his supervisor at the Houston office and his boss's boss at Quantico. He left word that things were drawing to a close. Chadwick snoozed, read snippets from books, and watched trash TV. Willis found him watching *The Jerry Springer Show*.

"Looking for more victims?" asked Willis.

"The tattooed women of the lesbian three-way world are not likely to be psychic vampires. They may be quite a shock to their lovers, but they don't cause wide-scale death," said Chadwick.

"How can you watch this shit?" asked Willis.

William Mondragon walked in. "It's my favorite show. After *The X Files*, of course."

"OK, how can either of you watch this shit?"

Mondragon said, "It's about the depths of humanity. Humanity isn't that interesting except at its extremes."

Chadwick added, "For once, we agree. I have no love of

mankind except as an abstract ideal. But the sinners and the saints interest me."

Mondragon said, "Yeah, but I don't appoint myself to kill the sinners."

"You killed one bank robber who was seeking to escape arrest," said Chadwick.

"How the fuck do you know all that stuff?" asked Mondragon. "I don't mean that you hacked into our system. I mean, how do you remember it all? There has got to be something wrong with you. Do you have a chip in your head or something?"

"My memories are all I have. When I decided to become a serial killer, I knew I would have to lead a pretty simple life. It was easy for me. I had only been really close to a couple of people my whole life. My dad and my fiancée. So I chose the life of the mind—you try it twenty-four seven for several days and see where it gets you."

"Is that what makes you so detached? Don't you understand that we are about ready to turn you over to your enemies, who may or may not get a chance to off you while the FBI closes in? You make me so mad that you are so calm," said Mondragon.

"On the contrary," said Chadwick, "I am not calm. I am seething with ideas. There is nothing like an impending death to focus a man."

"Are you planning on escaping from us?" asked Willis.

"I will be at the place you arrange to make the transfer, I promise. I have had much to regret in the last few days, and I won't compromise Miss Virginia's safety."

"Then, what plans could you have?" asked Mondragon.

"The same plans of any old man, plans concerning my legacy and history. I want a chance to forgive my enemies, make my wrongs right, see to my heirs and assigns. Leaving the world is as busy a job as being in it."

Mondragon looked disgusted. "You know we're not scared

of you anymore, and we're not impressed, so the dramatic statements don't have that impact they once had. You are out of options now. If we don't hear back from the people that have Mrs. Spencer soon, I'm taking you in. You used to be our most interesting UNSUB, but now you're a pathetic old man."

"UNSUB?" asked Willis.

"Unknown Suspect," Mondragon and Chadwick answered simultaneously. Mondragon continued alone, "That's when they really interest us. When we just sense there's somebody out there, some pattern to a series of crimes—if only we can piece it together. Then we stay up night and day looking for them. I had a great admiration for you, when I didn't know you."

"On the contrary," said Chadwick. "You have a great admiration for me now. Everyone in the Bureau does. I don't match the profile of a bed-wetting, fire-starting, mean-to-animals twentysomething with a bad attitude and a dishonorable discharge. I gave you something to aim for. Once I started making them crazy, they stopped sending their best profilers from the depths of the Quantico building—I was the frosted lightbulb. For years at General Electric the engineers would tell the newest member of the team that if they could only frost a lightbulb on the *inside* the bulb would be a tons more efficient and cheaper to make. It was a big joke; they knew it couldn't be done. Then one new engineer stayed up all night and did it. This made G.E. the leader in household bulbs. You will be seen as the guy who caught me. Instead of making potshots at me now, you should be figuring out what to do with your fame."

"Yeah, right. There is no way I'll be able to explain any of this," said Mondragon.

"That's precisely why you should be working on a good story now. I'll agree to whatever you want to say. I don't have very long left in the world. All I want is to die with no copies of my Program left. How many copies do you have, Willis?"

Willis, who was about to leave the room to check his e-mail again, said, "I've got three or four copies. They're all here in the house, though, I don't even have a copy in our safety deposit box. I had begun to think about some of the social implications a while back. Look, I can't stand you bickering. I've got to go, I've got to see her. I don't care about any of this anymore."

He walked out of the room, carrying hundreds of pounds.

Mondragon said, "Poor guy. Do you think, really, that any of this will work?"

Chadwick said, "See? You do respect me, you want my opinion."

"Be real, man."

"I don't know. I have played only sure bets for decades. I have no idea who has her or what they really want of me. I liked her a lot. You know, I was going to be married once, and she reminded me of my fiancée. I have a sort of love for them, like they are my kids. I am going to act like some kind of genius around him, so that he has faith and hope. I am clueless."

"Has all your life just been identifying these little nasty people and killing them?"

"No. I do study odd people. I have quite a file on people that I can't predict. I used them to try and make the Program better, but some people, frankly, have so much free will that they're off the scope. You should see my file on weird crimes."

"Yeah, I think I would like that," said Mondragon.

Willis was yelling, so they ran.

He was reading it off the screen.

"They say that they have her and they are willing to trade in ten days. They say that there won't be a trade if she decides not to go along with it, but that we have to bring him either way. They say she is very sick and that they are helping her. My god, what does that mean?"

32 Passive Compliance

Oh, Dr. Jones, I think I am almost all better," said Virginia. She had thought of saying "all better," but decided not to risk it.

"That's very good, Mrs. Night. Why do you think you have improved so much?" asked Dr. Jones.

It was breakfast, and Virginia had managed to hide her pill inside a used teabag. She was well groomed and smiling. Today's objective was to get street clothes. Dr. Jones seemed happier than she had been before. It scared Virginia to see the old lady smile—it wasn't like the fake smile she put on for her patients. This was a real smile, an "I know something" smile, and Virginia, who likewise knew something, didn't like it.

"I can remember a good deal of my marriage to Anthony, and I think seeing him has been a real help."

"There's nothing like love to motivate someone," said Dr. Jones.

"Who do you love, Dr. Jones?"

"Well, you patients, of course, and I love my work and I love my clinic. It took many hard years to build this place. I began with almost nothing, a little cash from a pawnshop and my theories. But I made my dreams real here. Every day in every way I came closer to the fulfillment of my desire."

"What desire would that be Dr. Jones?" asked Virginia. Virginia really didn't like the old lady's tone, she liked it better when the old prune was lying to her, but this was the time for data-gathering, not "liking" things.

"The desire to see you all well, of course. I want everyone to remember what they need to remember. When that happens, my work will be done. Now I see that you wrote a good deal during the night on your novel."

"Yes, I think I'm three-quarters done with Roy Chadwick. He's beginning to bore me. I find real people much more interesting. Maybe I could write a book about you and your clinic, Dr. Jones?"

"What a sweetie! What more have you added about Chadwick?"

"Oh, I talk about his declining health, his need to walk with a cane, the probability that he will die on one of his adventures."

"Is his health bad? I hadn't thought of that. I had always pictured him as a young man," said Dr. Jones.

"Well, I guess we picture *fictional* characters based on real-life people, but in my novel Chadwick is supposed to be this sort of super senior citizen, a figure that has fought what he thinks of as evil, by using the forces of the world that scare most of us like the vast amounts of information in the world, and the ability to spot patterns that no one else can see yet. I want him to come across as somewhat sagelike yet all-in-all a man in his seventies who is subject to the very actuarial tables that inspired him in the first place."

"Yes. I guess he has to be old. Do you think he'll live much longer?"

"Well he's a fictional character, I could kill him off today."

"No don't do that!" said Dr. Jones. "It would be bad for your therapy. You must make him come to a just end."

"Why is the ending of my book important? I thought the

idea was to write this stuff out of me so that it didn't confuse my memories anymore."

"Well, if you don't come to a solid ending, you won't be able to get him out of your head. A false ending and he'll be there fouling up the wells of your memory, so to speak."

"But finishing the book is just a small part of my therapy, right? I mean the most important things would be my remembering my marriage with Anthony."

"Of course, dear."

"I think it would help me if I had some clothes and jewelry and so forth from my regular life, to help spur my memory. Do you think you could have Anthony bring some of these things for me?"

"That's a good idea. I'll call him and tell him."

"Couldn't I call?"

"I'm afraid the only phone you can phone out of the clinic is in my office."

"Well, I could go down there and use it."

"I'm afraid not. You see, it's my policy not to let our clients use the phone by themselves. I know that you're OK, of course, but if I let one client use the phone they will all want to, and that would be chaos."

"I understand rules are rules," said Virginia, and she suddenly realized how much Dr. Jones reminded her of the widow MacPhearson. Time for a different tactic.

"I feel really cooped up in here. I think I could write better if I could take my laptop out on the grounds."

"You are free to wander the estate, you know that."

"I just thought it might be better to have someone with me the first time I was out."

"That's a great idea," said Dr. Jones, "I'll get Nurse Agnes to go with you."

"No. She has to see other patients, and I wouldn't want to take up her time. Besides, I would feel safer with a man."

"We have an orderly named Fischer—he could take you. But remember, you need to write down all your thoughts on Chadwick. The sooner you do, the sooner you'll be well and free to be with Mr. Night. I'll have Agnes bring you a coat. That nightie won't be enough."

It took two hours before they let her go outside. She was beginning to think that they weren't going to let her go at all, but eventually the coat showed up. There had been pills at lunch, too. It seemed they were stepping up her medication schedule. She wrote furiously in her book. It was all nonsense, of course. She didn't know why they wanted Chadwick— maybe he had escaped the police in Amarillo, or maybe they weren't on the side of law enforcement—but whoever the hell they were, they weren't her friends. She played with things she knew. For example, she wrote that Chadwick hated his father, rather than idolized him, and that he had loved many women (from afar) after his failed attempt at marriage, and that his big regret was not having a wife and kids and a picket fence and a dog. She didn't want to make up anything that might be factually different from the things Chadwick had told her, because they probably knew a good deal about him and could spot the phony stuff.

Her head was getting clearer every hour. She didn't know what the drugs were exactly, but they seemed to create a kind of dreamlike consciousness characterized by accepting memory. In a dream you can remember the weirdest things, which seem true for a while. For example, you just suddenly remember in a dream that you have always worked in a Dairy Queen atop the Great Wall of China and that you give free cones away to people with tattoos. There is something going on that keeps your mind from rejecting the absurd premise. It just seems that it has always been so. Once there's a background, then the rest of your mind is quite happy to go with the flow. She had been *glad* to see Anthony. She felt that she belonged to him, even when half aware of her real life. If it hadn't been for the shock of hearing him and Fischer talking, she would have begun to believe in the bright shiny memories she seemed to have. The weird thing was that there weren't exactly any implanted memories—just the strong feeling that there should be good memories in these places in her head.

When Agnes brought the coat, Virginia went to step two. She really wanted to see Fischer. Any escort who could tell her about the clinic would do, but (to the extent that she remembered her trip here) he seemed not to be totally in love with Dr. Jones, but just thought of her as all-powerful. Maybe she could use that to her advantage somehow. You don't have to be too worried about what you let slip about an all-powerful being—they're still all-powerful even if you know their worst secret. She had to be careful and make him think that she was still deeply under the spell, of course.

It was cold outside and overcast. The snow had been melting for days, leaving wet yellow grass and piles of brown nasty leaves that had once dropped, bright red, from maples. The paths were graveled concrete that ran to maroon wooden picnic benches that could be easily watched from the clinic. Fischer was in a shiny quilted coat that reminded Virginia of the coats that kids wore to school on the few days it was cold enough to wear a coat in Austin. She had a deep sense of wanting to be away from this dreadful place as they stepped outside.

"All you all right?" asked Fischer.

"I'm just cold. I guess I haven't been cold in a long time," said Virginia.

"Isn't it cold where you come from?" asked Fischer.

"Sure, it gets plenty cold in Dallas, but not like here. Where is here, by the way?"

"Jersey," said Fischer.

"You like it here?" asked Virginia.

"Well, I like the clinic and Dr. Jones, but I prefer southern climes. So you're from Dallas?"

"Yes. I live there with my husband. You may have seen him, he comes to the clinic pretty frequently."

"I believe we've met. His name is Bill something-or-other."

"No. Anthony. Mr. Anthony Night."

"Oh, yes, that's right. Dr. Jones said you wanted to sit outside and type for a bit—why don't we head for that table? The trees behind it shelter it some from the wind."

"That would be nice. You know, you don't have to sit with me after I get started writing. I just wanted some company that wasn't Nurse Agnes."

"Tired of 'Good morning, how are we today?'" asked Fischer with pretty good mimicry.

"Oh, god, yes. Were you a patient here, if I might ask?"

"What makes you ask?"

"Well, you say you love the clinic, you can do a pretty good imitation of Nurse Agnes. It doesn't sound to me like it's just a job for you."

"No. It's not just a job. Dr. Jones helped me out."

"Did she help you remember things?"

"Yes. Memory is her specialty."

"What if she made you remember wrong things?"

"What do you mean wrong?"

"Well, not real—or incorrect, somehow."

"If you remember something, then it's real."

"No, you could remember something that's not real, just more fun."

"That would be better then, wouldn't it?"

"I think that would make me crazy," said Virginia. "You've got to have something real to stand on, because that's where you're standing if you realize it or not."

"No. That's wrong. You've got to have something you believe in to remember. Think of a guy who's a total failure. Every morning he wakes up in his grubby apartment, where he shares a bath with the guy on the other side of his wall. He remembers that he is a failure and he goes out that day to fail at his burger-flipping job. What if you could make him remember that he was the next Rembrandt, so that he starts painting—full of confidence. Then every morning he gets up early, works on his canvases, and soon he has enough paintings for a show. That would be better."

"Maybe, until the show came and he had no talent."

"But what if he had talent?"

"If he had talent, would he have been there in the first place? His fate might have been to work in the burger joint, at least until he found something he was good at like electronics and pursue that. False memories would really hurt him in the end. Think of the poor slob surrounded by bad paintings."

"Surrounded by bad paintings. Yeah," said Fischer slowly. "I guess it wouldn't matter if he knew they were bad, they would just be bad, wouldn't they? People would just toss them on the fire, and nobody would remember him. That would be just like what he was."

"Well, that's just my opinion. I'm ready to start typing now. Thanks for walking me out here. I hope we can talk more."

"I would like that," said Fischer.

33 The City That Never Sleeps

"Why Central Park?" asked Willis.

The three men were leaving Bergstrom International Airport from Austin. They looked haggard and haunted. Chadwick leaned on his cane, which had let them board the jet early. Mondragon looked grim. It had been days, maybe weeks, since any of them had slept. Willis was the worst. He had a great imagination, and he could think of any number of terrible scenarios that could have happened to Virginia. He had never realized that his playing at pranks for years made him such a great self-torturer. His first programming teacher had said once that he was a "laid-back sadist," and at the time, he thought that was very funny. He used to mention it with a certain pride to anyone who would listen. Big joke. He would give anything for true unconsciousness; his sleep was even more haunted than his waking hours. If Hamlet's theory of endless dreams of horror as hell were so, Willis had been a dweller in that underworld for quite some time. Surely any guilt that he had had should be burned away. The problem with life lessons is that they go on too long.

They were sitting over the wing, statistically the safest

place to be in a plane. Chadwick had insisted. He got the window seat.

Mondragon said, "Central Park is a great place for a prisoner exchange. They can see we have come alone, we can see that they have come alone. There won't be any gunfire because of the crowds."

Willis asked, "Why are they making us wait? Why don't they just give her to us now?"

"The longer you wait," said Chadwick, "The more powerful they become. You worry more and more. We all worry."

"Besides," said Mondragon, "They may not be in New York. You could only trace their source node to Pennsylvania. They could be anywhere, and are taking time to deliver her."

"Did you find out about Night?" asked Chadwick.

"He was released on medical leave. His family indicated that they wanted to try a new therapy on him. The Bureau was only able to discover that the new clinic he went to was in the East, maybe New Jersey or Connecticut. His dad was very closemouthed with the agent, and there was no legal pressure we could put on him. The dad let slip that they didn't have to pay for the 'poor crazy SOB' anymore," said Mondragon.

"Therapy?" asked Chadwick.

"You know something," said Willis.

"No, I was just thinking aloud," said Chadwick. He soon feigned sleep as he did when he didn't want to answer questions. Movie, dinner, drinks, and after two eternities they were sharing a cab into mid-Manhattan.

The brownstone had an impressive location. It was an easy walk to the Metropolitan Museum, Fifth Ave, Central Park. Neighbors on either side had faces that you might recognize from People magazine or the evening news. The inside of the brownstone was shocking in its mustiness and dirt. It is hard work keeping a five-story building clean, and evidently not work that Chadwick had been interested in. His bedroom was a small servant's room on the first floor. It had old people's furnishings as advertised on TV—a Craftmatic bed, a special handrail for the bath tub, a hot plate. The rest of the brownstone had dusty mod furniture that had been really "kicky" in the seventies. There was gas in the kitchen, and the refrigerator still worked (by some miracle), so Willis was dispatched to the nearest market to get supplies. The bedrooms had cheap bookcases that Chadwick had assembled over the years. They were stuffed with books on every conceivable subject. There were all the popular classics of the sixties and fifties and even scores of Reader's Digest Condensed Books mixed with an incredible array of math books. There were books on catastrophe theory, chaos theory, topology, finite mathematics, grid theory, mapping, number theory—and even disciplines that Willis could not identify. There were easily two hundred dissertations on the shelves in English, French, Russian, and German. There were notebooks written in various hands, some of which bore marginal notes written in characters that seemed to be of Chadwick's own devising. There were privately published journals by people like Taylor Kramer Mason and Kristen Munchower. Willis came to realize that he had been fooling himself. He had thought that he was about as smart as Chadwick, since he was able to use the early version of Chadwick's program. That was similar to thinking you were as smart as Einstein because you could read $E = MC^2$. He couldn't even read Chadwick's source documents. Willis had spent his whole life being smarter than anyone around him, he had never seen anyone as smart in comparison to him as he had been to the dumb jocks he used to tutor in high school.

The intelligence suddenly seemed a huge waste. This was a guy who could have advanced human knowledge. He was a true genius, and he had spent his life in a rather silly quest to eliminate some unpleasant people. He could have gone anywhere, done anything—clearly his economic models got him any kind of wealth he needed. Yet he lived his life in a tiny room of a brownstone—one that most New Yorkers would kill to own. His furnishings were covered in dust, and the house smelled like a used bookstore. He was like Salazar and his chess. He could have had a life and just played at it. If Willis ever got Virginia back—no, *when* he got her back—they would do more than just have an endless honeymoon. They would change the world in real ways while they played. This whole building was a monument to human folly.

Willis and Mondragon took bedrooms on the second floor. The beds had been made decades ago and the two men had to push piles of books off them. Chadwick seemed quiet and sedate and slept a lot. Willis wondered what would happen to the house and the books and so forth, once Chadwick was behind bars.

While Chadwick slept, the two men discovered that there were two locked doors. One was in the basement near the oil heater, the other on the third floor. His equipment must be in one of the rooms. Chadwick probably meant to destroy it, before he went to Central Park for the exchange in four days. That was a good thing, Willis knew, but he wanted to see it. He wondered if it were some customized supercomputer—like the sort of thing the Chudnovsky brothers built to find the first two billion digits of pi.

As the three men had their doughnuts and coffee the next morning, Willis said, "We found your locked rooms, and we want to see them."

Chadwick said, "I can predict with one hundred percent surety that you don't want to see them. You won't like the results. In fact, you'll be quoting me about that this time to-morrow."

"Just don't play at this anymore. We're going to see your secret," said Mondragon.

"Oh, of course, you will. I knew that was coming. I just calculated the effects. We can go now if you like. I guess your big interest is equipment," said Chadwick.

"Yes, our big interest is equipment," said Willis.

"Let's go look after the chocolate glazed," said Chadwick slowly enjoying his last doughnut and the sense of power. His step was very lively up the stairs. He seemed to have thrown off the tiredness that he had shown since Willis had first seen him in prison oranges in Amarillo. Maybe he was just a show-off at heart.

"This is not what you're expecting—I hope you don't think I'm a foolish old man," he said as he put the key in the door to third floor bedroom. He actually giggled as the door swung open.

34 A Bergman Moment

"Yes, Tony. I can hardly wait to go back home with you. Dr. Jones says I can leave in a few days," said Virginia. She had practiced the phrase in front of the mirror about a hundred times, Night looked like he bought it. He had a stupid happy smile all the time now, but sometimes she could see the old cold snake underneath that happiness.

He had brought her street clothes. She had discovered from her fellow patients that the clinic was only a few miles outside of Princeton. She knew she had to work quickly. The dosage of the pills had been stepped up to three a day, and she couldn't manage to hide them all the time. She spent as much time as she could in the recreation room learning to mimic the endless smiles of her idiotically happy fellow patients. All were here to get new lives, to get memories to replace the real fucked-up tragedy of their lives. They paid good money for this. From time to time she caught herself wondering how Tony could afford it, then she remembered that was the drug talking. The best way to fight the drug was to overact. If she pushed beyond what the prompting of the one pill she usually had to wind up swallowing, she could defeat it. She figured she would have no mind at all if she were taking the three a day that Dr. Jones prescribed for her.

"I am so happy that you are getting better. It feels like you have been away from me for years. Every night I dream of things I could do with you," said Night.

She repressed a shudder.

"Yes, dear. Dr. Jones says I am her best patient, her masterpiece."

She had spent four hours filling out tests for Jones, trying to look as much like she was under the spell as possible. She even claimed not to know what Mr. Spencer looked like. Dr. Jones was clearly proud of her. It was important that Virginia be "cured." Virginia couldn't figure out why, but as Dr. Jones's happiness increased on an almost hourly basis, she knew that it was a bad thing.

"Dr. Jones said you remembered our house in Dallas."

"Well, of course, I remembered it."

Dr. Jones had shown her pictures. She had no idea if there even was a house in the objective universe that looked like the pictures, but just hearing Dr. Jones say "It is important that you remember this, Virginia," caused her to feel like she did remember it. The treatment must work at about one hundred percent efficiency if you really wanted to have it done. Shit, these people could remember landing on the moon. She *did* remember most of her talks with Salazar on the way to the clinic, and she felt she might be able to get him to help her by looking the other way for a moment. She didn't think she could get past the guards by herself.

"Yes, I'm looking forward to seeing it," said Night.

"What do you mean, honey? You've seen it hundreds of times," she said.

"I mean seeing it again," he said.

Poor dumb bastard, he was out of his league. They probably would have made him more convincing if they had had longer. But with the drug, it probably didn't take much.

Anthony Night kissed her and said, "I've got to go now, and I know you still have some work to do for Dr. Jones by finishing that novel of yours."

"The muse is really singing to me."

She had been typing anything she could think of in her book about Chadwick. Parts of old *Alfred Hitchcock Presents*, novels from that Texas fiction informal class that she and Willis had taken, parts of patients' life-stories, anything she could think of. She had set an arbitrary word count of seventy thousand words—she remembered asking a friend of hers in Austin, Nicholas Askel Denning-Roy how long a novel was. He had given the sixty-thousand-word minimum—of course, he had been working on his *War and Peace*–size epic for years. She was close now, fewer than seven thousand words to go. She had thought about erasing big sections, or claiming file loss or somesuch, to play the part of Penelope and the loom, but it was clear from Dr. Jones's excitement that things were coming to an end, anyway.

Anthony left. She knew from his previous departures that he didn't drive away. He was somewhere else in the complex getting his own therapy. She rang Nurse Agnes and asked if Mr. Fischer could accompany her on a walk outside.

He would be down in a few minutes, which gave her enough time to steal something from the recreation room.

All the snow had melted, and it was a nice sunny day. Fischer was all smiles, and Virginia talked about her progress with the therapy. He seemed relieved that she didn't start questioning him about the idea of false memory. They walked out to the bench. He was about to leave her to work on her novel when she said, "I've got a surprise for you."

"What?"

"I know you're really into chess, so I borrowed this board from the rec room." She pulled the folded cardboard chessboard from under her coat and began pulling the small plastic pieces from her pockets.

"I don't play chess with nonranked players," he said.

"Oh I'm ranked," she said. "Or at least, I was. I was in the chess club in high school. I played tournaments and everything."

"I couldn't. I've got work to do."

"Of course, you can play. It won't take long. I'm sure I've forgotten most of what I know."

"No. I don't think so."

"Surely you're not afraid of little ole me?" she said in her best Southern belle impression.

"Well, this will sound a little strange, but I haven't played a live opponent for many years. I do all of my play on the Internet."

"It can't be any different can it?"

"No, I guess not. Playing chess on the Internet was part of the therapy that Dr. Jones had me do. She said I needed space from people."

"But you're all better now, right? That's why you are an orderly."

She had been setting up the board while she spoke.

Fischer looked nervous. She had made him white, a natural advantage; she had chosen the red pieces for herself. He looked like he might run, then he got a confident smile and sat down.

"So, you haven't played in years?" he asked.

"Oh, no. Mr. Night doesn't play chess."

He did play. She had made the mistake of beating him at chess, so he had come to her dressed as Knight and made her his horse for three hours. . . . She had thrown the set in the fire later.

Fischer's opening was standard. You could find it in most "how to play chess" books, but by midgame, he had failed to dominate the center of the board. He didn't know he was playing sub-par until she tricked him into losing both of his rooks. Then he broke out in a sweat. He kept looking toward the clinic, not out of guilt for playing, she realized, but with a prayerful supplicating look. He wanted help, invoking a god that had fed him fake memories. He was a worse player than Willis, and Willis, frankly, sucked.

She began playing aggressively, first forcing him into sacrificing his queen and then driving his king into a pocket next to a useless knight. Checkmate.

He was crying.

She said, "I guess you haven't been playing very good people on the Internet. Or do you just take a pill if you lose?"

He wouldn't look up.

"No fake memories help you here, do they?" she asked. "What do you really do well? Do you get a chance to do it? She took you hostage a long time ago. She pays you, makes you feel that you are a little god. Then you identify with her. A little bit of the Stockholm syndrome."

He had begun to sob.

She risked it.

"I guess you're just a pawn."

He jumped up and knocked the board onto the wet yellow grass. She had expected that. He then slapped her and ran off. She waited a long time before she went inside. She didn't want Nurse Agnes to see the slap mark on her face. It was her biggest hope, so far.

35 The Cave of Aladdin

The first thing that struck Willis was the colors, the reds, yellows, blues, greens, and blacks; the second thing was the machine in the corner, and the third was a column topped by a antique oil lamp that looked exactly like every illustration he had ever seen of Aladdin's lamp. Unlike the rest of the brownstone, which was filled with dust and faded furniture—basically a symphony of grays—this was a riot of color. Both Mondragon and Willis had stepped backward when Chadwick opened the door—it was so overwhelming. But now Willis walked forward, willing himself to remember every single detail. Mondragon followed him, and then Chadwick, who closed the door behind them.

The walls and ceiling were covered in comic book covers. The windows had been boarded up on the inside and were likewise covered with covers.

RIGHT ON WITH THE **NOW** SUPER-HERO! *HELL RIDER*
NoMan *THE INVISIBLE T.H.U.N.D.E.R. AGENT!*

FANTOMAS La Amenaza Elega
The Amazing Adventures of HOLO-MAN

UltraMan

Skate Man

Solar Man

Ghost Rider

Darklon the Mystic

Captain Marvel

Captain Guts: America's Savior

Batman

The Owl

The Shadow

Judge Dredd

Captain Future

Captain 3D

J'onn J'onzz Manhunter From Mars

Jack O'Lantern

Ibis the Invincible

Green Lantern

El Diablo

ZOR Y Los Invencibles

FATMAN: The Human Flying Saucer

All these, and countless *Spiderman, Superman,* and *Green Hornet* covers. There were neat stacks of boxes full of these comics, labeled and indexed and wrapped in plastic wrap. The carpet of the room was a Spiderman design, and the one chair that sat in front of the machine likewise was upholstered with Spiderman fabric.

Chadwick was laughing like the best movie villain/mad scientist at this point, and Mondragon looked scared.

The smell of the room hit Willis about then. Frankincense—there was a tiny stream of sweet smoke coming from the lamp. Willis turned to speak with Chadwick, and saw that the door, which Chadwick had closed, had a costume hanging on the back. Red-white-and-blue cape, a matching spandex shirt (blue with the words THE ERASER in red and white sequins), a bright red gas mask, a pair of red vinyl boots, and a skullcap made to look like the eraser of a pencil.

Chadwick tried to adopt an heroic pose, "Yes I am *the Eraser!*" He then coughed miserably from the attempt.

"Oh, my god," said Mondragon. He reached for his shoulder holster which he realized he wasn't packing.

"Do you dress up like this when you plot your SKillings?" asked Willis.

"It's my little game. Dad used to forbid me to read anything but math books as I was growing up. Mom always sneaked me comic books. I knew that I had the brains to be a superhero, so I became one."

Willis needed to get the conversation away from this. "That's your computer?"

The machine in the corner didn't look like a computer. It had rows of dials and a small oscilloscope that occasionally showed a new type of sine wave. There was a big console full of glowing buttons. It would have looked at home in the Bat Cave.

Chadwick said, "It is a lot more sophisticated than it looks. I designed it so that I could be the only one to read the output. You want to watch? You think of some questions, while I change."

Mondragon said in a small voice, "He's a lot crazier than I thought."

Willis said, "Let him do his thing, this will be our only chance to see this."

The old man began stripping in front of them, not the most appetizing sight. Willis sat down in front of the machine.

"No, not yet! I must show you. Please indulge me. I have dreamed of showing this to someone since nineteen seventy-five. Please." Chadwick was sticking his thin shaky legs into blue Spandex tights. "Please step away from the machine."

"OK," Willis said. "What's the genie lamp for?"

"It's an incense burner. This is my shrine after all. Besides, it keeps the smell of the pulp from being overwhelming.

Willis stared at the machine. Occasionally the dials moved, or a tiny clicking sound could be heard. He saw there was an old-fashioned radio mike attached. Maybe the thing had voice interface. He could see no way this thing could give any useful information. There didn't seem to be any place for printouts, and there were no displays (unless the oscilloscope doubled as a video terminal). Of course, the real computers—the supercomputers that he guessed Chadwick had to have—could be in the sub-basement looking very normal and not interfering with his fantasy. God, could a grown man play at this month after month, year after year?

He turned his attention to the comics, so that he didn't have to watch Chadwick change. Mondragon had already picked up a *Spiderman*. Willis went through the *E* file—there it was right after *Elongated Man: The Eraser*. There were three issues from 1972, apparently the whole run. The drawing style was crude, underground comics rather than DC or Marvel. The first issue was color, the other two black and white. He read the origins issue.

Ray Nassivera, a mild-mannered insurance claims adjuster, was laboring on claims late on the eve of his marriage. An accident in a nearby nuclear plant sends a bolt of "ovidian energy" into Ray, merging him with his pencil eraser. When he comes to the next morning his head has been made into a giant eraser, and he has the ability to rub out (literally erase) miscreants. He is also gifted with the ability to foresee crimes before they happen so that he can rub out the criminal and make a more perfect world. Realizing the great burden such a rubbery state would place on his bride-to-be, Ray fakes his own death and takes up life as a crime fighter in a secret lair called the Pencil-Box, a brownstone in New York City.

Willis checks. No author is listed. There are no ads in the

back, no indications that Perfecta Press had any other comics. It had sold for a quarter.

"Sell many of these?" he asked.

Mondragon looked over, saw the title and did a double take.

Chadwick, now fully into the Eraser costume, which showed that he had certainly shrunk over the years, smiled. "I got a few comics shops in Manhattan and Long Island to carry it because I was such a good customer. It sold so badly that I was embarrassed. Ironically, the issue became really collectible a few years ago. I could make a mint if I could carry the cases full of them out of my basement. I bought this place because it looked like the brownstone the artist did for me. Kind of silly, I guess."

It is hard to know what to say to a seventy-year-old man in a superhero costume asking if he is silly. Willis shrugged.

"OK," said Chadwick, "I'll show you the machine. Help me move a couple of chairs in here."

Two chairs from a smaller unused bedroom were set up in front of the machine.

Chadwick once again closed the door behind him.

"It's part of the atmosphere. I wanted to feel like I have a secret lair. The output is revealed by the dials. I just read them quickly, I guide the search process by voice. What sort of question would you like to ask?"

Mondragon, "Can it tell us where Mrs. Spencer is being kept?"

"The machine and I can profile the killer, much like the profilers in the sub-sub basement at Quantico. Then with the profile it can search almost anywhere for someone that matches. I just cut off uninteresting leads. Let's start."

Chadwick set down. He wore the whole outfit from the eraser cap to the gas mask, which he had dangling under his chin. He touched a few of the buttons. "It takes a while to wake up. It is distributed over many computers, not just ones here." Two of the dials swung on, their needles pointing to a red region marked DANGER.

Chadwick said, "This may take some time. I'll put in more incense. In the meantime start describing your wife. Just talk into the machine. Anything that comes to mind."

Chadwick picked up a couple of blue cones that had been lying next to the control panel and opened the back of the lamp.

Willis spoke into the mike, "She's young and pretty and likes to laugh. She likes to see how much she can change things, so she's always buying some old piece of junk from an antique mall and making it into something beautiful. She likes to make things out of clay. She always makes her Halloween masks out of papier-mâché. She hates to sew, she doesn't cook, and she likes charades and role-playing. She wants to write about all of our pranks and see that it gets published safely after we're dead. She's afraid to have kids, because of the way her life went. She's a natural blonde, she's the most wonderful—"

Chadwick said, "That's enough for a start. Now let me show how it is done."

He leaned close to the microphone and said, "Omega." Then put on his gas mask. Willis suddenly realized that there was a lot of smoke in the room from the incense burner, and then the comics covers started something alive as the legion of superheroes all flew forth into the blue smoke and the chair he was on was tipping over very slowly and Mondragon was standing up, no he was falling down and the Eraser was towering over them a hundred feet tall and then the floor came up and then it was black.

Willis hurt bad, but something kept him from waking up for a long time. He was in a black dream of being late for a flight or an algebra test or the day of his wedding, and the alarm clock wasn't going off and there was someone heavy, oh she was very heavy on top of him and he couldn't move and it was awful he was going to miss the flight.

Then he was awake. There was cloth over his face and it was dark and he didn't know where he was. He pulled the cloth off of him—it was slick and smelled like a rest home—and then he saw he was staring at a ceiling covered in comic books posters dimly lit by banks of colored lights and there was someone snoring next to him. He tried to yell and made a terrible coughing, whimpering noise. All at once he knew he was hungry, thirsty, hungover, and really needed to go to the bathroom. He stood up. Mondragon was still out. The cloth on top of him had been the Eraser's cape. He stumbled out of the room to the bathroom, which toilet's water was almost evaporated, and whose bowl was black with dried algae. He took a piss. The saw there was note pinned to his shirt. Written in a shaky hand with blue ballpoint it read:

Dear Willis,

You're not the only one who can pull off a prank. I wish you great luck in what you need to do. I hope you'll come to understand my actions.

Roy E. Chadwick esq.

Roy E. Chadwick Esq.

Willis began yelling for Chadwick, but expected no response.

He went back to Aladdin's cave. He turned on the light and began shaking Mondragon. Mondragon started to punch him groggily and then woke up as soon as he figured out where he was.

"What time?" asked Mondragon.

"Nine o'clock. At night. There wasn't any light through the hall window."

"What day?"

36 Vain Attempts

That part of her escape plan included getting her hair done was something Virginia thought Willis could not understand. Her blond hair had grown somewhat in her captivity and basically looked like shit. Many strands fell out each time she pulled a comb through it, no doubt due to stress. She had put on a little weight because of the fattening cuisines of the clinic. All of the patients were chubby, but that didn't matter, since all of them (well, at least the women Virginia talked to) remembered themselves as being slim and good-looking. It was the first time she was ever around women who were totally confident in their body image. The clinic had a beautician who came in once a week from Princeton. When she told Dr. Jones that she needed a makeover so that she would look good for Tony, Jones had almost gushed with relief. Tony had been full of happiness at the idea. She recalled that very soon in their marriage she had stopped trying to look good for him, but instead tried to figure out how he wanted her to look and then fasted and primped into that mode driven by fear, or a real desire to please, depending on where she was in her abuse cycle.

The beautician did a great job, and Virginia took this as a

time to prattle on about how much she was looking forward to going home. The beautician told her that she loved to come to the clinic because everybody here seemed so happy—it wasn't like cutting hair in a rest home, which had been one of her jobs when she first started out. The beautician asked about Dallas, and Virginia had almost convinced her to move by the end of the session. She helped Virginia with makeup as well. The stuff that Dr. Jones, not exactly a woman brimming with fashion sense, had supplied her was crap.

There. She looked good in the mirror. She hoped she looked like the kind of woman that a man would stop and give a ride to.

She told Dr. Jones that she would be finishing her novel today and thanked her again for letting the orderly sit with her. Dr. Jones told her that Fischer was sick, and that she wouldn't see him today.

That would make things hard. She went out to her picnic table to type more nonsense into the laptop, but Fischer came out a few minutes later. He acted like he had a bad cold, but she realized that he had been crying. He came and sat by her for a minute or two, when she realized he wasn't about to say anything, she began with, "I didn't mean to be so rough on you, but I had to get through."

He said, "I feel like it's over now. I wasn't able to catch Roy Chadwick, and I'm not a chess champion. I'm just whatever her pills made me. It can be pissed away in a few days."

"If the treatment only lasts for days, how does she keep people under?" asked Virginia.

"Nobody wants out. The longer you think everything is hunky-dory, the more you desire *never* to think of the bad stuff. You start thinking about it and your heart gets all fast and your palms sweat, and your first instinct is to go take another pill."

"I want out. I want to go to my real husband. Why does she want to do this to me?"

"I don't know. She has never remade someone who didn't ask for it before. She's got some point she's trying to make with you. She doesn't tell anybody anything, you know, never has. I think she thinks she's above us all since she doesn't take the *kheft*."

"*Kheft?*"

"The drug. The memory-maker."

"I still want out."

"I know."

"Will you help me?"

He sat silent for a long while.

"Yes," he said. "There are guards at the gate with hypno-darts, not guns. There aren't many breakouts. The guards are there for break-ins. She controls people by means of the *kheft*. If she shuts off the supply they try to break in here. You've seen the sign."

"What sign?" she asked.

"Don't tell me you've been here all this time and don't know the name the patients have for the clinic. It's Eden."

"Until a couple of days ago, I thought it was a place for spies or prisoners. I never even guessed that normal people came here for normal problems."

"They come here to be told that their problems aren't normal. That they are the biggest problems in the world, and only Dr. Jones, the good momma, can make them go away."

"This place scares me, so how can I get out?"

"I am not going to stick my neck out, but here's what I will do. I'll go into Princeton tonight and I'll hire a couple of students to make a break-in attempt at eight o'clock. I'll tell them it's a test of our security system. At exactly eight, you wait over there." He pointed to a gazebo. "You can hear the guards leave, and the alarm. Just run through the door. You'll need to sneak out at six-thirty when the *Simpsons* rerun is on—everybody watches it. Then just be hidden till you leave. Go left on the little road away from the clinic, you'll hit the highway in half a mile. Just pretend to be a motorist in distress. Will your husband help you out?"

"If he's not crazy with grief. God knows where he is. Are you just going to stay here, stay with her?"

"It's all I have. Chadwick used all of my dreams to make me his pawn, then she let me get new dreams to make me her slave."

"Won't you wind up telling her that you let me escape?"

"Sure. She'll figure it out and make me tell, and then she'll put me in deeper and I won't ever remember losing to you in chess or having a bad life at all. It will make me less able to function, but I'll be a gardener. That's what my old man did— take care of the lawns of the rich people in Thalia. I guess it's not so bad, I'll probably think that I am the deposed dictator of a South American country. We played with that before. It just took too much *kheft*."

"You know that I will always be grateful."

"Well, I know it now and it helps."

He went back inside and she finished her novel. It was a total lie. She had made Chadwick into a simple man who longed for a regular family, that had avoided women out of a sense of unworthiness, and merely sought a good maternal experience. She made him regret each killing and vow to lead a better life. She gave him past things that he had overcome— smoking and alcoholism. She made hobbies for him—painting and orchid raising. She hinted that his paintings had been in various shows under a pseudonym, and she gave him a nervous tic when he talked. She didn't talk about his cane or the computer display she had seen with the weird cascading crystals. She established firmly that he lived in Dallas—in the big ball locally called the Dallas Phallus. After all, if Dr. Jones were going to give her a life in Dallas she could do the same to someone else. She concluded the novel with him deciding to renounce his life of crime and take up world traveling.

It took her three hours to crank out the last two thousand

words. They were misspelled, badly organized, full of passive sentences, and had way too many gerunds. But it was done. She figured that it would give Dr. Jones something to do while she was escaping.

She went back to her room and told Nurse Agnes that she was really hungry. Agnes pointed out that dinner was soon, but Virginia whined until Agnes brought a tray of cookies, which she stuffed in the pockets of her coat.

Ten minutes before dinner, she called for Dr. Jones.

"I finished it. *The Private War of Roy Chadwick*, I wrote down everything that was going to be in my novel. I can't print it out, and I was wondering if you could make a copy for me. I'll want to revise it before I try sending it to my publisher."

"That's wonderful. Now you know that it was all fiction."

"Yes. I remember the novel clearly now, and I'm so glad for the chance to write it all out."

Dr. Jones took the laptop away from her. "I can hardly wait to read it, but I do have one editorial suggestion. The name *Roy Chadwick* is sort of dull; if you send this out for publication change it to something more romantic like Sebastian McBride."

"All right. I have no investment in the name. Now that the book is done, when do you think I can go?"

"I call Mr. Night tonight—I would like to take you on a brief trip to New York first to show you off to a colleague, and then you're off to your long happy marriage in Dallas. We'll go to New York the day after tomorrow."

"I don't know how I'll ever be able to thank you."

"Just being what you are is my thanks."

Dr. Jones smiled and left the room, and Virginia scrambled to get everything she might need into her coat pockets. She laid the coat on the bed and ambled down to the dining room. She had thought of having Agnes bring her dinner, but decided that it would be good to be seen among the crowd before she slipped away.

She was so nervous that she almost choked on each mouthful of vegetable medley.

Back to the room very nonchalantly, and then she put her coat on and listened by the door. She heard the opening bars of the *Simpsons* theme song and walked out. Down the hall and out the door and to the gazebo. She pushed herself behind a column so that she couldn't be seen from either the guard shack or the clinic. If they hadn't noticed her, she would be all right—if they did, they were bound to come check soon.

This waiting was much worse than waiting for Chadwick had been in Doublesign. Her body turned against her almost immediately. She needed to go to the bathroom. The temperature in the afternoon had been chilly, but with night it became very cold. She had seen frost every morning for quite some time and wondered if she would get frostbite tonight. She wondered if Willis would be by the phone in Austin. He might be anywhere trying to track her down, or maybe he thought she had just run off. Maybe Dr. Jones has him somewhere making him into someone else. She wished she knew why Jones did this. What was the point? It took a lot of effort—what did the woman want? It was taking a long time. Surely eight o'clock had come and gone. Maybe Fischer/Salazar was just playing with her—getting revenge on her chess victory.

Then a muffled ringing from the guard shack. Could that small sound be the alarm? She heard people running out from the shack, but she couldn't look without revealing herself. Then she couldn't hear them and she ran.

The gate was closed, but the smaller gate next to the shack was unlocked. She let herself through, turned left on the little road, and ran into the night.

37 Holmes, You Are a Master of Disguise

They had slept for thirty-five hours. The meeting with the kidnappers was the day after tomorrow, and of course Chadwick was gone. Whatever the poison was, it left them with screaming headaches, and the trip to the hospital had done them no good. Willis discovered the key to the brownstone in his pants pocket and wanted to explore it again when they got back at three in the morning. Mondragon was on the phone getting the New York police to throw out a search net for Chadwick, and getting his Bureau friends to set up for the pickup in the park.

The first thing that Willis tore into was the machine in the comics room. As he had suspected, it was nothing but flashing lights and dials rigged to move around. There was a single button that Chadwick had tripped that activated a heat wire in the lamp. The microphone wasn't connected to anything. The whole room had been built just as a trap. It was all older equipment. Chadwick had built it long ago, probably when he first bought the brownstone.

He had to break into the door in the basement. The stairs beneath were narrow and steep, but at least they were lit with a naked bulb. He went down and away from the brownstone—halfway down he felt the rumble of a passing subway train.

When he finally entered the cold room with the Victorian furnishings and the Edwardian skeleton, he was ready for another
trap. The skeleton had an envelope pinned to it. It was addressed to Willis.

Dear Mr. Spencer,

My first and most important task is to make sure that no
copies exist of the Program. A series of code that can find any
human being and predict their action with 98% certainty is far
too strong a force to give to industry or government. I could
obviously never figure out what to *really* do with it. I am like
Dr. Faustus in Marlowe's play. Unlike Goethe's more famous
version, Marlowe's Faust had great power but couldn't think of
anything important to do with it—he amuses himself by tele-
porting to Rome to punch the Pope in the nose, or Istanbul to
pull the sultan's beard. I have had my fun. Unlike Faust I had
more than 24 years of it. There is some computer equipment
down here, but nothing on it—most of the Program is in my
head, everything else was just getting the data to display itself
correctly. That secret has to disappear.

Now you are rather in a pickle with your wife due to be
delivered to a path by the Central Park reservoir. The questions
are two. Who has her? And can you come up with a plan to get
her back safely without my aid? These are very tough questions. I have, however, discovered that you and the interesting
Mr. Mondragon have adequate skill in problem solving to know
that you will come up with a solution to the second question.

Please do tell Mr. Mondragon that he was the best of the
agents sent after me. He found me, zeroing in more quickly
than any of the others. If he just lies his way out of the current
pickle he's in, he will be one of the best agents the Bureau has
ever known. If he tells too much of the truth he will wind up in
a mental institution. I think both of you can figure that one out
without the Program.

I can also predict with 100% accuracy although you have a

low opinion of me now, you will have a lower one soon, but in the end a real soft spot for me. Since I know you're wondering—I never really dressed up in that costume. I just thought people would buy it if they ever came to my lair. I choose the *Eraser* from my favorite Robbe-Grillet novel, but I did create the comic books. I also tried to sell my life story as a TV script, the same year that *Charlie's Angels* came out. I guess if I had been three chesty babes it would have been better.

Best,

Roy E. Chadwick esq.

Roy E. Chadwick Esq.

Willis couldn't believe it. Chadwick didn't give a damn if Virginia lived or died. His giving his word to be at the exchange was a farce. He had really just wanted to bring them to New York so he could erase his Program and play a prank out of a comic book. This was what his genius was good for.

He knew that he had to have a plan in mind before he went upstairs. The exchange had to go through; he couldn't risk having Virginia hurt by these people. He looked at the skeleton and the boxes of comics.

He dropped into Chadwick's chair.

He poured himself a brandy. A train passed by and he saw the small window out into the tunnel system. He wondered what the train riders saw. He remembered Virginia explaining how pranks work to him, "In unusual or stressful situations people always see what they expect to see." It was how stage magicians could pull off such interesting shenanigans on their volunteers from the audience. The bright lights of the stage, the pressure of being watched and it was easy to make the rube think the rubber pigeon was a real one. Well, since they were expecting Chadwick, let them see Chadwick. Willis was only slightly taller than Chadwick. He could be wired for sound, or a tracker or something. One time he had played an old man during a prank. They had convinced a dishonest attorney that Willis was the guy's father back from hell and mad that his son was going to join him. It had been a great role for Willis, he had done the old man's voice for months afterward.

Willis would go off with the kidnappers, who were about to be mobbed by FBI agents all around the park anyway. Virginia would be safe. Mondragon would have some people he could catch, and Willis could explain everything about Chadwick. Now that Chadwick had simply left them, Willis felt a big desire to get back at the guy. This wasn't funny. His wife's life was on the line, who gave a fuck about his precious Program?

The skeleton had a silver-headed cane. Willis removed it so he could practice walking with it. There were some of Chadwick's clothes in his bedroom. He would go change and then ask Mondragon about FBI makeup artists.

38 An Injection of Clarity

Virginia ran for as long as she could, before she headed off the road to pee. She could hear the highway. It was really cold and she hoped the sight of a lone woman shivering in her coat would melt the heart of some motorist.

When she got to the freeway, she realized that she didn't know which way Princeton was. However, it was a divided highway and crossing it looked dangerous, so she felt the decision was made for her and walked with the traffic, sticking her thumb out to passing cars. She tried waving one down and was almost run over for her trouble, while the driver lay on his horn. They don't drive friendly like Texans, she decided. She kept a slow run going. There were many cars. One was bound to stop.

Half an hour later, she wasn't so sure. The traffic had died down considerably, but billboards advertising coffee and grinders were growing more common, and she was clearly heading for Princeton.

Finally a car stopped. It had stopped about a hundred feet in front of her. The driver was stepping out as she ran up.

"My god, are you all right?" the man asked. He was a young man in a dark suit.

"I need to get into town. My car broke down and I was afraid I might freeze."

"We'll get you into town." He was opening the back door for her. "My grandmother and I are on the way to our apartment."

He was helping her in as the grandmother looked around.

"We were worried about you, Virginia," said Dr. Jones. Something hit the back of her head, and she pitched forward.

Something smelled very bad and she had to draw her nose away. She was strapped down on an operating table. Dr. Jones was pulling a little bottle away from her nose.

"I guess your recovery wasn't as far along as we thought it would be," said Dr. Jones, "No matter. I can put you through intensive therapy in the two days I have left. I got what I really needed, anyway."

"Why are you doing this?" asked Virginia.

She could see there were other people in the room. The man who drove the Mercedes that had stopped for her, Anthony Night, and Salazar/Fischer. S/F wouldn't look at her. He was covered in sweat and just stared at the floor.

"You notice that Mr. Salazar isn't doing so well?" asked Dr. Jones. "I had to give him a shot of this." She touched the silver box on her waist. "It's the antidote to the *kheft*. I call it *alethiaum*. Small doses remove all of the *kheft*'s effects, large doses remove all the lies we tell ourselves. I can make most patients attempt suicide with a large enough dose. The drug is completely nontoxic—it is only real unrepressed memory that is toxic to most people. I take an injection every day, just so I won't fool myself. Did your hero tell you all the things that my drug enables him to do? Oh, he told you that it makes him remember his great skill as a chess champion, big deal. But that's a small thing."

Salazar suddenly looked up and lunged at her, the driver caught him and slammed him against the wall. Dr. Jones said the word *security* loudly, and two guards came in. They all began getting Salazar into a straitjacket.

"Put him on suicide watch. Don't give him any *kheft* for eight hours—I'll need him for the drop-off."

They pulled Salazar from the room.

"My drug enables him to engage in his necrophilia without guilt. You probably didn't know what kind of man you were picking for your hero, but you have a problem with that in general, don't you? Mr. Night was certainly a poor choice."

Anthony looked at her in raw anger, but she merely tapped her silver case, and he looked down at the floor.

"Tell me why you're doing this. I never hurt you."

"This is true, you never hurt me, but all those people you modified never hurt you—except for Night. See he's looking at you now. He has no idea of what you and Mr. Spencer pulled off. I made that memory go away. Did you ever think that none of the people that you modified with your pranks ever became happy, productive members of society? None of them. Some stopped being as awful, but what cures do you have?"

"I didn't fuck with their brains."

"Oh really? Putting them in darkened rooms and pretending to be the goddess Kali doesn't alter people's brains? The difference between you and me is that between art and science. I can make people into what they want to be. Some of the most important people in America have passed through Eden. Directors of huge corporations, important men in government. They may leave here thinking they are the King of America and keep a crown in their bedroom, but they still direct their corporations."

"So, why are you fucking with my brain? I'm not the director of a large corporation. I don't control the reins of government. I do volunteer work in Austin for the symphony, and I do a few pranks with my husband. You aren't shaping the world by shaping me."

"On the contrary, my dear, you are the one I'm most interested in shaping. I want to show you off."

"To who?"

"To Mr. Chadwick, of course. We have an ongoing argument as to method. Since he saw you as the devoted wife of Mr. Spencer, he will get to see you as the devoted wife of Mr. Night. You see, he has met you and Mr. Night, when he investigated you, and he has met Mr. Spencer. When you show up arm-in-arm with Mr. Night, Mr. Chadwick will see the correctness of my approach."

"You're lying," said Virginia. "I can hear it in your voice. There is something more."

"What a great counselor you would have made," said Dr. Jones. "In this stressful situation you still have your wits and ability. I actually have no doubt that you are every bit as gifted as I am. In other circumstances, you could have been my apprentice. I am, after all, on in years, and I need someone to carry on the great work, but I think it has to be someone untouched by *kheft*. I should have caught you years ago, before Night got his nasty clutches on you. You know, I think I'll make Night less nasty for you. I won't change him too much, because he has been such a dear in helping me."

"You didn't respond to me, what are you hiding?"

"My dear, you aren't in any position of power. Of course, I'm lying a little bit." Dr. Jones smiled, "This isn't the movies where the villain reveals to you her secret weakness so that at the crucial moment you can hit the switch. In fact, dear, I am not the villain at all. In less than twenty-four hours, you will think that I am your hero. You may even think I am god."

"I'll do and say anything you want me to, just let me go back to my husband."

"No, dear, that's the one thing I won't do. You have been too wicked for that. You hurt me too deeply."

"But you said I never—" began Virginia.

"Yes, dear, but I also told you I was lying to you. You

leave," she said to Night. "Get Agnes in here, we are going to have a Level Three session tonight."

The driver left. For a moment Virginia was alone with Dr. Jones, trying to think of some angle to save her mind. A plan occurred. Well, it was worth a shot, anyway.

Nurse Agnes came in and things soon became unpleasant.

39 Strolling Through the Park

Mondragon admired Willis's transformation.

"You are good at playing an old man. You sound like him."

"My dear Mr. Mondragon, I am him. I wear his pants. The shirt is a match, the slight limp is his, and I am the single most important man in the early twenty-first century. My Program can topple governments."

"Yeah. You don't have to do this for me, I'm quite sick of his voice."

"But you were the best of all the agents sent after me."

"Oh, please. Now remember not to turn on the tracking device until you are in their helicopter. They will scan you for devices when they pick you up. I have a wire on me, they'll be expecting that."

"What makes you think they'll have a helicopter."

"They can't be expecting to walk out of the park. It's too big, there are too many places for Agents or cops or whoever the hell's there to stop them. This guy is really and truly wanted by high-level people. As soon as I told the Bureau about the guy, I got attention from the top. I'm sure the CIA, the NSA, and god-know-who wants him. Since they can't have him, they want whoever wants him."

"They're not going to shoot down the helicopter, are they?"

"I don't think so," said Mondragon. "Now I've got the whole operation here in my ear." (He tapped his earpiece.) "You don't do anything without my approval."

"OK, let's do it."

It was a warm day for late fall. Willis walked slowly, careful not to let his anxiety affect his cane. He wondered how many of the people—jogging, playing with dogs and Frisbees, flying kites, riding in horse-drawn-carriages—were agents. They passed a homeless old bum as they approached the site. The guy smiled at Willis, and then took a long pull off his brown-sack wrapped bottle. Willis wondered if it was a bottle or a high-tech gadget. Come to think of it, he could appreciate it more if it was a bottle—if the codger was interested in sharing it.

Mondragon said, "This is the bench nearest the exchange site. You sit here. Our target is approaching. This way they can see you and I can see Mrs. Spencer."

Willis sat.

Mondragon walked ahead slowly.

Two people were walking around the chain-link fence that surrounded the reservoir. It was a stylishly dressed older woman and Anthony Night in a slightly out-of-date business suit. They walked up to Mondragon. He pointed back at Willis; Night pointed away. Willis could see Virginia and the man called Bobby Fischer. She was talking to him animatedly. Mondragon made several gestures indicating slowness with his hands. A consensus was reached. Mondragon turned and began walking back to Willis. When he was a few feet away, a look of horror filled his face. Willis thought for a moment that Mondragon was going to faint. He grabbed at the wire leading to his ear.

He didn't break stride. He said to Willis, "Just act like everything is normal. We're going to walk over there and exchange you for Mrs. Spencer. I just heard that the Bureau is pulling all support for this mission. The orders came from the Director himself. I am on my own. They won't support me in anything that is about to go down."

Willis rose and began his old man shuffle toward the exchange point. "My god—why?"

"I have no idea. We're probably fucking around with the big boys. I'll get your wife safe, and if possible you. We're going to have to play it by ear."

Willis and Mondragon made it to the site a little faster than Virginia and Salazar.

Dr. Jones greeted Willis, "So, Roy, I see you walk with three legs at this time of day."

"It is, indeed, the evening of my life, my dear," said Willis.

She stared at him. "I don't believe it. You have no idea who I am."

Salazar yelled, "Watch out."

The bum that Willis had passed earlier had walked to join them. The bum stood a little taller and smoothed his silver hair.

"No, Alesia, Mr. Spencer does not remember you, because it wasn't he who left you at the altar," said Roy Chadwick. "You seem surprised, Mr. Spencer. I told you that I would be here. I gave you my word, in fact. You didn't seem to recognize me on the way in, but then, you were doing a capital job of impersonating me."

"You're still the answer man, aren't you, Roy?" asked Dr. Jones.

"Oh, no, my dear. I have no answer to your being here. My Program said that you would find someone else and be happily married and dead by now."

"I am sorry to disappoint you on both counts," said Dr. Jones. "All I have done is work on the problem you gave me so many years ago. You told me that you couldn't marry me because you would always remember what that little man had said to you. You wrote in the little note, which you had delivered to the church that you were just too poisoned, so I developed a way to unpoison you. I began by marrying the best man in the field of memory-change, Shelby Hearon, but my techniques went far beyond his. I can make anybody remember anything. You met the lovely Virginia Night, didn't you?"

"Her name isn't Night," said Willis.

Night laughed at him. "She doesn't know who you are," said Night.

"I only know two things," said Virginia, "That I love Tony and that I'm supposed to sing a song. I beat you at chess, I beat you at chess, I beat you at chess."

"Shut up," said Salazar. "Make her shut up."

"It doesn't matter," said Dr. Jones, "That got past my conditioning. I'll fix you later."

Virginia kept singing the childish song.

Salazar said, "I'll hurt you. I'll hurt you bad."

He grabbed the silver box from Dr. Jones's waist and pulled a syringe out. Jones was yelling, "No!" Night was trying to stop him, Willis grabbed Night and threw him to the ground. Virginia bent down, saying, "Tony, are you OK?" and Salazar rammed the syringe in her arm giving her a shot. She passed out. Mondragon pulled his gun and fired toward the sky. Everyone stopped moving.

Chadwick said to Willis, "I totally envy you. Look how smart she was. She didn't take on the primary conditioning, but made herself remember something as childish as the 'I beat you' song. I predict that she'll wake up in possession of some, maybe all of her memories. What an amazing woman."

Dr. Jones said, "You could have had a woman just like that. I am just like that. Can't you see everything I made, all these years, just to impress you? You are an idiot. Together we could have the life they were trying to have."

Chadwick shook his head slowly, "You did all this for me? I never knew you had such fire in you. I never knew. All these years. We could have done everything."

"We can still do everything," Dr. Jones said.

"No, not with the information I have in my head," said Chadwick.

"I can change that," said Dr. Jones, "I have an alternative life for you. She wrote it for me. A life where you give up killing and take up world traveling."

"Can you make my knowledge go away?" he asked.

"I can make you forget anything," she said.

"Then let these people go," he said, "And I will be yours."

"Wait," said Mondragon, "I can't let you walk."

"You have to," said Dr. Jones. "I control enough people at the FBI, that's why your mission was scrubbed. You take in those two, Night and Salazar. They'll confess to everything in about six or seven hours. You won't be able to do anything about me, but you'll find out a great deal from him." She pointed at Salazar, who merely lay on the ground and whimpered.

Virginia opened her eyes.

"Willis?" she said, and he helped her up. "I hate the costume. Let's go home, honey."

40 A Final Bow

With a good deal of help from Virginia Spencer, William Mondragon did create a story that attributed most of the SKillings to Night and Salazar. This satisfied whatever conspiracy power Dr. Jones held over the FBI and brought a good deal of fame to William Mondragon.

When William finally went back to his office after being feted for the capture of the pair who had been the SKiller, he found a thick envelope on his desk. It was from New York City, and it had no return address. Inside were a thick sheaf of computer printouts and a letter from Roy Chadwick.

Dear Special Agent Mondragon,

I want you to know how much I have enjoyed your company these last few weeks. I realize these have been trying times for you, and I am sorry to have gassed you at my house—a rather poor attempt at hospitality. If my predictions are correct, you have caught a person or persons that you have sold to the FBI as being the real ShitKiller. This has brought you a good deal of fame in the Bureau and is probably eating you alive with guilt. I hope this package helps, these are the weird crimes that I have encountered during my long strange career with as much documentation as I can find. Use your new position wisely and you can have a lot of fun hunting down these cases—some of which will make mine seem as dull as Sunday school.

Best,

Roy E. Chadwick esq.

Roy E. Chadwick Esq.

After a week's rest in a New York City hospital, Willis and Virginia Spencer flew home. They took Willis's car out of long-term parking and drove to where their house used to be.

The neighbors ran out to tell them that the house had gone up in a fireball eight days before. A delivery truck had left a package on the stoop and then there was a blinding orange flash that night.

They were overwhelmed at the news. They drove to a hotel and ordered soup. After a few hours, Willis went and got their mail, while Virginia had started to call up her mom.

Chadwick had sent them a letter as well.

Dear Virginia and Willis,

As you no doubt know, I have destroyed your house, since Willis told me that the only copy of my Program was there. Now the world doesn't have that to worry about anymore. You will find a smaller Program in the diskettes with this letter. My father began his career doing stock market analysis, and a few years ago I took up the hobby. I developed a program that can predict stock market changes with 89% accuracy. With this Program and the ten hundred-dollar bills inside, you will be able to generate sufficient wealth not only to rebuild your home, but to do pretty much anything you wish with the rest of your lives.

I admire your choices. If I had been brave and chose love,

my life could have been what yours may yet be. I want Willis to know that he is a hundred times smarter than me, whatever he might think, because he chose love.

I would say that I am sorry that your lives took such a strange fate because you found my Program, but in the long run, it had to happen to someone. That's just the odds. I'm glad the fun part can happen to you now.

And you see, it is as I predicted. You hated me when I left you in my brownstone, hated me more when you found out I blew up your house, and for years afterward will love me when you find out that my stock market program works.

Since you know I have a good track record, you'll be suitably impressed that I am predicting that you will live happily ever afterward.

Best,

Roy E. Chadwick

Roy E. Chadwick Esq.

They each read the letter, held each other a while, and went to sleep, dreaming of what to do with the next phase of their lives.

The beginning of things always surrounds us, but only those with the strength enough to dream take joy in this fact. The rest of us merely find the light of dawn an annoying reminder of another workday.

About the Author

Don Webb is one of the rising stars of the mystery field. Locally known for his culinary expertise, he teaches writing and enjoys an endless honeymoon with artist, Guiniviere Webb. Don's short fiction has appeared in more than 250 venues worldwide.